THE GIRL FROM THE COAST

THE GIRL FROM THE COAST

A Novel

PRAMOEDYA ANANTA TOER

Translated by Willem Samuels

HYPERION

EAST

ISBN 0-7868-6820-1

Book design by Caroline Cunningham

FIRST EDITION

1 3 5 7 9 10 8 6 4 2

PART ONE

She was only fourteen at the time, a wisp of a thing. Her profile, the line of her nose, was nothing extraordinary, but she was attractive, nonetheless, with honey-colored skin and slightly slanted eyes. In her fishing village outside the regency seat of Rembang on the north coast of Java, she was the flower of the town.

The girl's life, her soul, was each day filled by the sound of the waves and the sight of the small fishing boats that set off at dawn and returned in the late-afternoon or early-evening hours to the river's estuary. There the boats set anchor, unloaded their catch, and waited until the next morning when buyers would come from the city for the day's auction.

She had left the nineteenth century behind and entered the twentieth. She was leaving childhood behind. Even so, the coastal wind that whistled through the tops of the casuarina trees that fronted the shoreline did little to hasten her growth; and despite the passing of days, she remained a person of slight stature, the wisp of a thing she had always been, the girl with the bright and gleaming eyes. But unaware to her—enveloped as she was by the unceasing sound of the waves, the whistling of the wind, and the coming and going of fishing boats—there was a man who had taken note of her and informed his employer in the city of this village girl's beauty. One day, the man returned to the village and paid a visit to the home of the girl's parents. No more than a few days later, the girl learned she had to leave her hearth and home behind. She had to say good-bye to country ways, to her hometown and its salt-sea smell. She had to put out of her mind the nets she repaired each week, the tattered sail that hung in her mother's kitchen, and even the odors of her native home.

She was taken to the city, where her body was wrapped in lengths of batik cloth and her torso cloaked in finely embroidered *kebaya* she had never before dreamed of owning. A gold necklace encircled her neck, its thin strand pulled downward toward the cleft of her small breasts by a golden, heart-shaped locket.

The day before, she had been married, in proxy manner, with a dagger representing her husband-to-be. At that moment, she had become aware that she was her father's daughter no longer, that she was not her mother's baby anymore. She was now the wife of a *keris,* a dagger standing in for a man she had never seen.

The bridal procession consisted of just two carriages carrying, besides the girl and her parents, two uncles, several relatives, and the village chief. Their provisions were equally spare: a few lengths of cloth, homemade cakes, and food the sea had provided since time eternal—seaweed and several kinds of fish.

As the convoy made its way from the fishing village toward Rembang, the girl's mother found herself constantly having to repair her daughter's makeup. Time and again she checked her daughter's face, only to find that the powder on her cheeks was scored by tracks of tears.

"You mustn't cry," she scolded her daughter. "You're now the wife of an important man."

The girl didn't understand. Neither did she know what lay ahead. All she knew was that she had just lost her entire world. Why couldn't she live where she wanted to, she asked herself with fear and apprehension, among the people she cared for and loved, in her seaside world of pounding waves?

"Don't cry," her mother repeated. "Starting today you'll be living in a big house, not in a ramshackle hut like ours. When you have to relieve yourself, you won't have to do it on the shore. And you won't be mending sails or nets, either. In the city, you'll be sewing with silken thread. So, please, don't cry anymore."

She was only fourteen years old, and the thought of objecting to having to relieve herself on the beach had never crossed her mind—except when there was a full moon, that is, which drew the snakes from their lairs to the moonlit sand. She was afraid of snakes.

"Stop your crying, child!" the girl's mother demanded. "You're the wife of a rich man now."

But the girl could not stanch her sobs, and finally, she began to wail. She had never ever thought of herself as being poor.

The sight of the shoreline that paralleled the road, dotted with clumps of seaweed and knots of scraggly brush, where sea lizards skittered across the sand and crabs warmed themselves in the sun, scarcely held her attention. She was hardly conscious of the rhythmic clopping of horses' hooves on the roadway, but when the carriage suddenly stopped, she raised her head momentarily.

She watched as her father stepped down from the lead carriage and walked back to the one in which she was seated.

"Are you going to shut up or not?" he asked.

Like a frightened snail, the girl's small body shrank further still. Her father was a fisher and a seaman, a hardworking man who did not put up with whining. She knew well the slap of his rough hand, but the hurt she was now feeling was different. Why did she have to suffer such pain? She buried her face in her mother's lap.

"Let her be," she heard her mother say. A short while later, she felt the carriage begin to roll again.

"Your father is right," her mother said to her. "There is no parent in the world who would willingly throw his child into the lion's den. You know that, don't you? All your father wants is for you to have a happy life. Look at me. Old as I am, I have never in all my life owned a piece of batik as fine as the one you're wearing."

"Then take it," the girl pleaded.

"Just look at the things you're wearing: that batik and *kebaya,* that necklace, those pretty earrings, and that gold dragon-head bracelet. Your father and I have had to work ourselves to the bones so that you could have such things . . ." Now it was the girl's mother who could not speak. She swallowed, trying to keep the tremor from her voice. "Oh my, I never dreamed my little girl would have such things." Suddenly, the tears she had been trying to hold back burst forth.

"Oh, Mama, don't you cry too," the girl uttered amid her own tears.

Her mother turned her head away from her daughter to stare out the carriage window at the sea that had sustained her through her mounting years. She could not tell her daughter that she was crying from the joy of seeing her escape life in the fishing village, of knowing that she would be a woman of high standing who would not have to toil or sweat or run about collecting the sun-racks of drying fish whenever it started to rain.

"Starting today . . ." she began to say but then found herself unable to continue this stream of thought and changed tack: "You're lucky to be the wife of a pious man. They say he's made the pilgrimage to Mecca twice already, so there's no telling how many times he's read the entire Koran. When a woman marries bad, life is going to be all the worse for her," she stressed. "But when she marries good, then it's good for her, too. What do you have to complain about him?"

"Him?" Who was this man she had been married to? the girl asked herself. She closed her eyes but could not picture him. Was he a better man than Tumpon, her brother who had been lost at sea in a storm? Was he a better man than Kantang, another brother who, when diving to free a net that had snagged on a coral reef, never surfaced again, and whose only visible remains were a liquid billow of red, and even that, the sea had sucked back in after a shark had torn his stomach in two? Would this man who was her husband give his life for his family as Kantang had?

"He's an important man," her mother continued, "religious advisor to the government, a powerful man the Regent relies on for advice. Even the Dutch Resident is said to visit his house. At least that's what everyone says."

Entering the city, the carriages turned onto a street lined with Chinese shops. The sights that day were similar to the ones she had seen two years ago when she and the other villagers had traveled en masse to the city to attend a night fair. She recalled the stuffed alligator that hung above the door to a shoe store. And the ceramics factory with its many samples of tiles with multicolored flowers. And all the big buildings of the city, with white columns so high and so huge she could not even put her arms around them.

As the carriages approached the city's central square, the girl's father began to adjust his clothing. He then cleared his throat and scratched at his neck. Her mother, seated closely at her side, looked anxious and afraid.

The carriages turned to the right, and the public school and grand mosque came into view. She still remembered them, too. Just across the square was the regency's central office building. Beside that was a Dutch primary school and, next door, a multistoried dwelling.

Her heart beat faster. Her father seemed to be having difficulty as he stepped down from his carriage and made his way toward hers. His face was pale and his voice was weak as he spoke to her: "Time to get out of the carriage." His eyes scanned the surroundings until coming to rest on a large gateway through which they had to pass. No one was there to greet them, not a single person. "Come, come, get a move on." He gestured for her to step down, though he himself did not move from the spot where he stood.

After all the members of the entourage had disembarked from the two carriages, they gathered together, in a tight cluster beside the road, confused as to what to do. The masonry walls were far too high for them to be able to peek inside. The mother of the girl took her husband's hand in her own. He whispered, as if automatically, "Come, come," but still he didn't move from his place.

In the end it was the girl's mother who first began to walk ahead. But when she turned around and saw that no one was following her, she stopped and stared at her husband with dismay. The girl's father grasped his daughter's hand, making it difficult to discern who was supporting whom. Finally, the bridal procession began to move slowly forward through the gateway, one step at a time.

In front of them was the high-roofed building visible from the outside; it appeared to be a receiving pavilion for the main house that sat beside it. The group hesitated to move forward until, from the walkway running between the two buildings, a manservant emerged. He came toward them, all the while looking at them appraisingly from their heads to their toes.

The tone of his voice was curt: "What do you want here?"

"Is your master here?" the girl's father asked in reply.

The man's eyes inspected the girl as he spoke: "The Bendoro is taking a nap."

A stillness filled the air. The sky overhead, darkened by the tops of banyan trees, and the sound of the waves in the distance cast an unsettling chill over the bridal party. The girl's mother opened her mouth to say something, but no sound escaped from her lips.

"We just arrived from the village," her husband then explained. "We are here to see your master, the Bendoro."

The manservant turned and went into the house through an open side door that was set in the lower part of the wall. The bridal party could see nothing but the massive whitewashed wall. To their right, the foundation of the main structure rose at least as high as the girl's waist. Beside it was the open-air receiving pavilion, a traditional *pendopo*-style structure, the roof of which was supported by three parallel rows of columns, six in each row. The girl knew without trying that her arms would not fit around them; she doubted that her father's would, either.

Over their heads, swiftly flying sparrows flew about among the restless swallows while crows, perched in the distant banyan trees, incessantly cackled their frightening caw.

An old woman then appeared at the doorway, beckoning to them with her hand. At once, the bridal procession began to move, making its way through the doorway. Following the old woman, the group passed beneath the huge windows of the main house, making its way to the back of the house. They crossed an inner courtyard that was planted with pomegranate trees. A hedge of sour-fruit lined the edge. At the back of the house, they climbed a set of stairs to the raised ground floor and entered a room that was at least four times larger than any house in the fishing village. In the very center of the room was a low marble-topped table. Passing that, they entered a room that was so very long it seemed to grow narrower at the opposite end.

Inside the room were a few chairs and, close to the wall, a sofa. The only light in the windowless room came from the sunlight that streamed through a number of clear roof tiles overhead. Unlike the more substantial buildings facing the street, the walls of this room were made of wood, not brick and mortar. Hanging from the walls were ornamental wooden placards carved with Arabic calligraphy—verses from the holy Koran, apparently. Near the doorway there hung a large looking glass with a thick wooden frame carved with Chinese motifs.

On the opposite end of the room was the doorway to yet another room, the doors to which were open wide. They could see inside the room a large bed with iron bedsteads, its posters topped with shining brass knobs. An open mosquito net dangled from ivory hooks that were attached to the ceiling overhead.

The party was left standing in the long room. No one spoke. Even the girl seemed to have forgotten her tears. No one had the nerve to move, let alone to leave the room. The only sign of life in the house was the occasional sound of people whispering outside.

Eventually, to their great relief, a maidservant came into the room; she was carrying a tray with cups of sweetened tea in her hands. A baby, in its sling, was on her back.

The villagers followed the servant's every move, both watching to see what she would do and wondering whose child she carried on her back.

She placed the tray on the table and then motioned to them. "Please, have something to drink," she said, and then bowed while stepping backward, away from them, toward the entrance to the room.

"Is the master still asleep?" the village headman inquired.

"He usually sleeps till five."

"I'm the headman of the village . . ." he interjected.

"But I wouldn't dare to wake him."

"Whose child is that?" the girl's mother asked with a soft and tremulous voice.

The maidservant repositioned the baby's sling so that the baby now hung at her side. The child looked to be about two years old. He had a prominent nose. His eyes were closed in sleep but his mouth was open, revealing an even row of small white teeth.

"It sure is quiet here," the headman commented, only to be silenced by the maidservant.

"Not so loud," she reprimanded, "you're not in the village now."

"Whose baby is that?" the mother whispered again, her voice strained with uncertainty.

"The Master's," she stated frankly.

The mother bit her lip and straightened her shoulder sash.

"Where's his ma?" the father asked.

"Not so loud," she reminded the group again. "And don't say 'ma.' An upper-class *priyayi* child doesn't have a 'ma.' He has a mother."

"Then where is his mother?" the father hissed.

"She's gone back to her village."

"So when is she coming back?"

"She's not coming back. The Bendoro divorced her."

"Why did he divorce her?" the girl's father now demanded. "And when?"

"How would I know? That's the Master's business," she said with a huff. "Besides, that was about two years ago."

"But the boy can't be more than two years old," the mother now interrupted.

"That's right," the servant remarked. "Never even seen his mother."

"Why not? Did she die?" the mother asked.

"No, I just told you, she went back to her village. She's not been here since then."

The girl's mother took a deep breath, then exhaled loudly.

"Please, not so loud," the servant said again. "The only people whose voices are supposed to be heard in this house are those of important visitors who have come to see the Master, and the Bendoro himself, to be sure."

"But, but . . ." the village headman stuttered.

The servant immediately silenced him—"Be quiet!"—then turned and slipped away.

The girl's mother stared at her daughter. She then raised her daughter's chin with her hand and looked into her eyes. The girl spread her arms to embrace her mother, but her mother pressed her hand against her, forcing her to stay in place. With the other hand she smoothed the wrinkles from her daughter's clothing and repaired her makeup. She looked at her husband, who in turn looked at the village chief.

The girl stared silently at her untouched glass of tea. No matter how dry her throat now felt, she didn't have the nerve to drink. At her own home, she reflected, nothing would have stopped her from drinking until her stomach was bloated if that's what she wanted to do.

From outside the room came the sound of the maidservant's voice: "It's time for your bath, Young Master. You don't want to be dirty when the Bendoro appears."

She now came back into the room, the baby still in its sling on her back. Noticing the untouched glasses of tea, she tried to sound friendly as she spoke: "Please, have something to drink."

All the guests smiled at the invitation and nodded their heads but still made no move to drink the tea. The father could feel himself sweating. His entire body felt clammy. He was thirsty, too, but this was a different kind of sweat, not the kind of sweat that came from pulling up a net from the sea. He could detect in its smell a completely unfamiliar scent.

"Who was that you were talking to?" the girl's mother asked lightly, though worried about the answer that she would find.

"That was the Young Master."

"And is he the Bendoro's son, too?"

"Yes."

"And where is his mother?"

"She went home to the village."

"And when will she be coming back?"

"She won't be coming back."

"So he would be this baby's older brother?"

"Yes," the servant affirmed.

Everyone now looked at the baby, almost completely concealed in its sling on the servant's back.

"I suppose, then, he's as good-looking as this young boy here," the village headman commented.

"Oh, no, this one is much better looking. He has a different mother."

The headman clutched the sides of his black linen jacket, a piece of apparel that came with his position. He then straightened his head cloth and coughed to clear his throat.

"Shh! Not so loud," the maidservant shushed him yet again.

The tea on the table remained untouched.

"Mbok, Mbok!" they heard someone call. It was the voice of an adult male.

"Coming, Master," the servant said in an even voice. Without another glance at the villagers, she left the room.

They heard her speaking in the other room: "The Young Master Rahmat is having his bath, Bendoro. Please sit down, sir. I'll call him for you."

A quarter of an hour passed before they heard anything more: the voice of the Bendoro addressing someone in a language they could not understand. They assumed it was Dutch. Then it was the voice of the boy, "The Young Master" Rahmat, they heard reply. He, too, spoke in a language the villagers could not understand.

The village headman spoke with an astonished whisper: "Did you hear that? It's amazing what the Bendoro has taught his son. He's so young and already able to speak Dutch! I can't understand a word of it." He then turned to the girl. "And when you have children, they'll get the same kind of education."

The girl paled and clutched her mother's hand tightly.

Outside, the sun was now hidden behind the tops of the pine tree and coconut palms. With the tide rising on the shore, the sound of the waves grew more distinct.

From outside the room came the low voice of the Master speaking to his son, this time in Javanese: "You know you are not supposed to play soccer. It's forbidden. Don't you remember what I told you? It is a game for infidels. It was infidels, you know, who kicked around the heads of the holy men, Hassan and Hussein, after they had been beheaded. Do you want to be a pagan, too? Is that what you want?"

They heard the soft voice of the boy rise in protest as he marched off toward his own room: "What's the problem? We're playing against the Dutch school and we can't lose."

Finally, amid the soft rumble of the waves and the whistle of the wind outside, they caught the muffled sound of leather slippers moving across the floor toward the room where they were waiting.

"He's on his feet," the headman advised in a hushed tone.

The villagers straightened their bodies, listening to the pair of slippers and their muffled slaps as they moved across the floor. The sound grew closer but then, out of the blue, they heard another, quite unmistakable sound, that of a fart.

"What was that?" the girl's mother asked the headman. She knew what it sounded like to her ears, but she couldn't be sure. She shook her head. No, it was impossible; such a thing couldn't happen here, in this house. It couldn't be the same sound that her husband made, for which she railed at him regularly.

The slapping of the slippers ceased. "Why wasn't I woken up?" they heard the man say. "Tell the headman to come here!"

The room was completely still; all eyes were open wide and trained on the door. The headman's breath came in gasps, but no one else took notice as he stood and groped behind his back. From behind his jacket, the headman removed from his waistband a *keris*. The dagger's blade was concealed by a bronze sheath; its handle, sticking out from the sheath, was carved from dark brown wood with a small frog balanced on its end. He raised the dagger before him until the tip was level with his nose.

The manservant who had greeted them earlier came to the door of the room and stared at the villagers, waiting nervously inside. Without formality, he said, "The Bendoro wants to see the headman."

The headman turned quickly toward the manservant, almost knocking over his chair as he did so. He wiped his brow with the back of his jacket sleeve and then walked, heavy-footed, from the room, the *keris* before him at the level of his nose.

"It will be all right, it will be all right," the father mumbled as if in prayer.

"Everything will be all right," the mother affirmed.

After the headman had disappeared from view, the rest of the bridal party pricked up their ears; but all they could hear was the Bendoro speaking to his son, the Young Master Rahmat, in Dutch, until, in a sudden shift of voice, he screamed in Javanese, "What? You mean you don't know?"

"It will be all right," the girl's father mumbled again.

"Yes, it will be all right," the girl's mother reaffirmed.

The girl tightened her grip on her mother's arm. Her mother hurriedly whispered, "Just say to yourself it will be all right."

Her daughter hurriedly whispered the mantra, "It will be all right."

"Yes, my baby," the girl's mother whispered, "it's all going to be all right. You're going to be all right."

"Don't leave me, Ma," the girl pleaded.

"Hush now, you'll be safe here. Just say the words again: It will all be all right."

A half hour passed. The girl's father was drenched in sweat. Grinding forty sacks of corn by hand would have been preferable to this, the mother said to herself. Their daughter squirmed in her chair like a mouse stuck in molasses.

They were able to see the village chief through the doorway to the Bendoro's room. Every once in a while, he would turn around and peer toward them.

There was no sound at all except the footsteps of servants as they padded back and forth outside, surreptitiously trying to see what was happening inside.

Finally, the headman came back into the room, his face very pale. He no longer held the dagger in his hand. He immediately confronted the girl's mother: "This is terrible," he hissed.

The girl's mother immediately paled. "What do you mean?"

"You never told me if she's begun to menstruate."

The mother looked at her husband and then at her daughter. "Well, have you?" she asked.

The girl, her head still bowed, raised her eyebrows and frowned.

"Well, have you?" the mother asked again.

The father now spoke in frustrated anger: "Do you know what that is—the meaning of 'menstruate'?"

The girl looked at her mother in fear.

"I'm sorry, this is my fault," her mother apologized. "You just don't know the meaning of that word, is all. Right? You know what it is? When it's 'that time of the month' and there's blood. You understand, don't you?"

The headman watched the girl and her mother as they stared hopelessly at each other.

Suddenly, the girl's mother pulled her away from the group to a sofa in the far corner of the room, but no sooner had they sat down than the girl's mother jumped back to her feet, so shocked by the softness of the cushions that she was momentarily distracted from her purpose. She had never felt anything so smooth, never experienced such a sensation before.

Bracing her arm on the back of the sofa she stared at her daughter, who was feeling the velvety material of the sofa cushions with her fingers. Seeing that her mother was now standing, the girl, too, rose to her feet.

The girl's mother whispered something, but all the girl could do was shake her head and stare. The mother frowned and shook her head as well. She then turned and looked at her husband, giving him a despondent stare. She left her daughter and went to her husband: "Just tell him yes," she said.

The father then turned to the village chief. "Yes, she has. She really has."

The headman, still looking confused, left the room.

"Why didn't the Bendoro ask for you?" the mother asked her husband.

The man looked as if he were about to cry; he could say nothing to his wife's question and did not reply.

The other members of the bridal party were also silent. None of them had spoken since leaving the village earlier that day.

"No matter what, you are his father-in-law," the girl's mother added.

"Can't we just go home, Ma?" the girl pleaded.

"Shush your mouth!"

Just as the headman came back to the room in which the group was waiting, the drum in the city's central mosque, in the city square next to the Bendoro's home, began to sound, calling the faithful for evening prayers. And then another drum, this one from a room inside the Bendoro's housing complex, began to echo the larger drum's call.

The headman addressed the girl's father: "There, now, my obligation is complete. I have delivered you safely to the Bendoro's home. Now I can return to the village. You'll be all right here." Then he turned to the man's daughter: "You'll be living here now. Your parents will stay with you for a few days, but after that, as the wife of the Bendoro, it will be up to you to manage."

"You're going now?" the father protested.

"Why not? There's nothing else for me to do here. You're the Bendoro's father-in-law, so you must learn to act like an important man's in-law. Don't make a mess of it. You've got a few days to teach your daughter as much as she should know. Do you understand what I'm telling you?" Not waiting for an answer, the headman turned and walked out of the room.

The manservant came back into the room and led the girl's parents away, along with the other family members.

The girl was left standing by herself, alone and confused, in the room.

The tea on the table was cold. The room was dim but then, suddenly, became filled with light. Startled, the girl looked up to see an electric globe glowing overhead. She stared at the light, this artificial sun, until she began to see stars.

Cautiously, she sat down on a chair beside the table. She placed her hands on the tablecloth, feeling the fabric with the palms of her rough hands. Arabic letters—what looked to her like little bean sprouts, circles, dots, and curved lines—ran along the cloth's border. Looking around her and suddenly realizing that no wind could ever penetrate this room's walls, the atmosphere changed from one of frightened wonder to claustrophobia and oppression.

At her own home, the late evening hours would find her at the massive mortar that stood in one corner of the house. Into the mortar she would pour the tiny shrimp that she had dried in the sun earlier in the day. While her father slept she would pound the shrimp until they became reduced to a gritty powder in preparation for the arrival of the Chinese man from the city who came to the village each day, at seven in the morning, to collect however much powder the villagers had prepared. What earnings her mother received from the sale of this powder were stored safely inside a hole in one of the bamboo supports.

There was no mortar in this room. No smell of dried shrimp, either. No fishing nets hanging from the ceiling. No tools hanging on the wall. Nothing except carved boards with meaningless Arabic calligraphy.

The maidservant returned to the room, this time without the baby in its sling, and the girl rose from her chair. The maidservant bowed to her, leaning forward deeply from the waist. What was she doing that for? the girl wondered. Just minutes ago they had been equals. Why was this woman acting so humble now? The change confused the girl, made her feel frightened and apprehensive. What was happening? Where were they going to take her? Why couldn't she be with her mother and father? She wanted to scream.

The maidservant took the girl's hand and led her into the adjacent bedroom. There she placed on the vanity a wrapped parcel that she had been carrying under her arm. Opening the parcel, she took out a towel, a toothbrush, dentifrice, Japanese-made straw sandals, a tortoiseshell comb with a silver handle, several kinds of perfume, and face powder that was in an exotic-looking tin clearly from abroad.

The servant woman then lowered her body into a squatting position on the carpet that stretched between the bed and the vanity. From her lower position, she looked upward at the girl and smiled broadly. "This is your room," she said.

Not knowing what to do, the girl uneasily approached the dressing table. The bottles of perfume, of different shapes and heights, and sparkling with the reflected light of the electric bulb, held her gaze. She reached out her hand toward one, studied its shape with her finger, and then lifted it to her nose. Glancing at the maidservant, she stroked the green tassel on the bottle's stopper, feeling the fine silk threads between her fingers. They were so soft to the touch, she was momentarily distracted.

"What is this?" she asked the servant.

The woman laughed politely. "It's perfume, Young Mistress."

"Mistress? Who are you calling 'Young Mistress'?"

The servant repressed a laugh. She looked at her new and very young employer, then raised her hand and stroked the girl's small smooth chin. Finally, with her right thumb, she pointed at the girl's chest.

"Me?" the girl asked nervously.

Again, the servant tried not to laugh.

"But why?" the girl asked. Her hand reached for the tortoiseshell comb. Raising it toward her head, she noticed its silver handle and how it gleamed in the light. "This is so nice!" she whispered. "Why did you put these things here?"

"They are for you."

"For me?"

Dumbstruck, the girl immediately dropped the comb onto the dressing table. What was this servant doing? Why was she acting so suspiciously? Why were these beautiful things being given to her? Her own parents had never given her such things!

Ignoring the girl's perplexed look, the servant unfurled a long cloth—a lapis-colored silk sarong of exceptionally light weight. "Here, we'll change into this and then go to take your bath."

As if the girl were an oversized doll, the servant removed from her the clothes she had been wearing and then wrapped her, cocoon-like, in the new sarong. Accustomed as she was to the coarse fiber of the fishing nets that she made and lugged about in the village, the girl felt utterly naked to be dressed in cloth so light.

"In the bathroom, you'll find that I've added perfume and flower petals to the bathwater," the servant told her. "You are used to bathing alone, aren't you?"

The servant's question instantly aroused the girl from her trance. She took a step back and looked at the servant for a moment and then down at the light blue silk that encased her body. What is all this? she screamed to herself. But then she asked, "Where's my ma?"

"In the kitchen."

"Take me to her, please."

"Hush."

The girl stamped her foot on the floor: "Take me to her!"

"But, Young Mistress, that wouldn't be the proper thing for the Bendoro's consort to do. When the Bendoro's consort wants something done, all she has to do is snap her fingers and it will be done. For now, it is my duty to take care of you, and until the Master gives his permission, you are not to see anyone. Come with me now, and I'll help you bathe." She placed the Japanese slippers on the floor beside the girl's feet. "Here, these are for you."

At the reference to the Bendoro, now her own husband and master, the girl had lost her will to protest. Never in her life had she worn shoes or clogs, but she immediately lifted her feet as the servant slipped the woven sandals on them.

When the servant then rose to her feet and extended her hand, the girl automatically took her arm.

The two left the bedroom and passed through the back room of the house where the Bendoro and his son had been speaking earlier. There was no sight of them now. This room was also huge, like the other one at least four times the size of the girl's home in the fishing village. Leaving this room, they descended a set of stairs where the girl saw, directly in front of her, a large outbuilding with a tiled roof black from smoke. She hesitated for a moment.

"That's just the kitchen," the servant said to her. The two then turned to the left, skirting the kitchen's outside wall. At the rear of that building they came to a large stone-walled bathhouse, its door already open as if waiting for them to appear.

As they entered the room, the door seemed to swing shut automatically. The girl could hear the sprinkling and splashing of water.

Following her bath, the girl returned to the bedroom to

change into yet another set of clothes. Her entire body felt strange, as if it weren't her own. The perfumed scent emanating from her pores made her head feel light. She had never smelled so fragrant before. That wasn't her body's smell. And the delicate cloth of her apparel made her feel as if she were wearing nothing at all. Silently, though, she did admit she liked the feel of the grass sandals on her feet. But even as she dwelled on these new sensations, the servant's voice never stopped droning in her ear, telling her that things must be done this way or that.

When the servant applied Arabian kohl to the corners of the girl's eyes, she commented, "This will make your eyes look deeper and give you greater presence."

As the girl looked in the mirror, watching as the servant continued her ministrations, she saw her face changing little by little, until finally she didn't recognize herself at all.

When the servant finished and stepped aside, the girl stared in the mirror and whispered, "Is that me?"

"You're very beautiful," the servant sighed.

This was the beginning, the girl thought. This was to be her future world.

That night, as the clock struck twelve in the faraway central room of the main house, the girl was alone in her bed, surrounded by a silence that was broken only by the ticktock of the clock. Although the silence was torture for her, in the brief time she had spent in the Bendoro's house, she had come to enjoy the sensation of her body sinking into a soft mattress. The only feeling she could think of to compare it to was lying in a pool of warm mud.

Lying there, she inhaled the perfumed scent of her body and clothes. Before coming to the Bendoro's house, she had never dreamed there could be such a refreshing scent. In her village, no matter where one went, there was only one odor, that of fish and the salty sea.

She recalled that her father had once rescued a man lost at sea. The people of the village had nursed the man to health. They had given him food and clothing and herbal medicines to speed his recuperation. What was his name? She couldn't remember now, but he had told her about flowers and how perfumes could be derived from them. But in her village on the coast she had never come across a flower that smelled so good.

The girl peered over the edge of the mattress and looked down at the floor at the foot of her bed, where the maidservant was sleeping soundly on a woven mat of pandanus leaves similar to the one she might now be sleeping on if she were at her parents' home in the village. Though she missed her mother's constant presence, she was thankful to have this woman here to watch over her. She was a good woman, that was easy to tell, and even in the short time that she had spent with her, she had grown fond of her. The woman had a way with words.

The girl smiled, thinking of the servant's retelling of the tale of Joko Tarub: One day, when sitting on the lakeside, the young man had spied a goddess who had descended from heaven to bathe in the lake's clear waters. Instantly falling in love with the goddess, Joko Tarub swore to do anything in his power as long as he could keep the goddess for his bride. First he stole the goddess's clothing so that she was forced to follow him home. And then, through a mixture of both guile and devotion, he somehow managed to convince the goddess to be his bride. Imagine how happy a goddess must be to inspire such longing, the girl had thought, to be everyone's ideal.

The night grew deeper, but still her eyes wouldn't close. She couldn't decide whether she was happy or not. From the central room of the house came the booming sound of a man reciting from the Koran. The man's voice was deep and strong, resounding like the echo of thunder from a mountain cave. She had never heard a person recite so beautifully before.

The night air, which had felt cool and refreshing before, now began to grow cold as the ocean wind, having fought its way through the tops of the large trees that lined the coast, circled and entered her room through the gaps of the roof tiles overhead.

Two hours later, she was still awake when the Koranic chanting ceased, and with it, or so she felt, the world had stopped turning and her heart had stopped its beating. She heard the heavy slap of sandals, growing louder as they came closer to her room. She heard the door to her room open and then again the slapping of sandals, now with a more cautious gait. Through the lashes of her half-closed eyes, she watched the man she was to call her husband approach her bed. He was tall and of fair complexion, with a thin face and sharp nose. He wore a tunic of white silk and an expensive black Buginese sarong, the lower hem of which was circled with several thin white bands. On his head was a *kopiah,* the kind of rimless hat she had seen worn by men who had made the pilgrimage to Mecca. She continued to watch silently as he roused the maidservant with his foot, and then as the servant hastily rolled up her sleeping mat, with her pillow inside it, and crawled backward toward the door, where she rose in a stooped position and then disappeared through the doorway.

The girl quickly turned her body toward the wall. Her heart seemed to have stopped beating; her body was bathed in cold sweat. If it was fear she felt, then she no longer knew the meaning of the word. She was too afraid to think, too afraid to even cry.

Although she couldn't see the man, she could feel him open the mosquito net that surrounded her.

"My bride," he whispered.

A prickling sensation spread across her body, as if it were covered by ants. She couldn't reply.

"My bride," he said again.

Automaton-like, she turned her body toward the voice and then sat up, her torso stooped at the waist, her head bowed, and her arms positioned at her sides with her palms resting on the mattress for support.

"Yes, Master," she whispered.

"I am your husband," he told her.

"Yes, Master," she repeated.

"Say that for me."

The girl didn't understand.

"Say 'Praise be to God.' "

"Praise be to God," the girl repeated.

After that, she didn't know what was said. All she remembered was lying back down, resting her head not on her pillow but now on her husband's arm, and feeling his soft, gentle hands kneading her own small hands.

Then a soft voice said to her, "Your hands are rough."

"Yes, Master," she whispered automatically.

"You mustn't work," he told her. "Your hands must be as soft as velvet. There must be nothing coarse about the principal consort of this house."

"Yes, Master."

She couldn't say how many times she repeated those two words, but then, even if she had wanted to, she couldn't have kept count—she had never learned to count past fifty.

As dawn approached she heard the screech and hoot of an owl on the rooftop; the sound made her body shiver, but with her head close to the Bendoro's chest, she could also hear the beating of his heart, its pounding reminding her of the distant explosion of firecrackers on Chinese New Year's.

"Are you happy here?"

"Yes, Master."

"Do you like the feel of silk?"

"Yes, Master."

She felt his soft hand stroke her hair and ever so slowly remove her worries, her feeling of claustrophobia, and her fear. Each stroke of his hand brought comfort and greater calm to her trembling heart. Such gentle hands they were: those of a scholar, whose only tools were books and a bamboo pointer to trace the lines as he read. His hands were not those of her father or even her mother, ever ready to slap some part of her body when she made a mistake. That said, while her parents' rough hands may have inflicted pain on her body, they had never ever brought pain to her heart. No sooner had an incident passed than her parents were nice to her again. But these gentle hands . . . She marveled at how they could still her heart and make her blood pulse.

After the Bendoro had fallen asleep, the girl lifted her head to study his features. His skin was so fair, a sign of high birth, she thought, the complexion of a person who had never had to work in the hot day's sun. And his skin was so soft, almost like that of a child, it seemed to her, with a thin layer of baby fat. She wanted to explore his skin, to feel its softness, as she used to do with her baby brother in the village, but she didn't have the nerve. She lay there silently, afraid to move, until the roosters at the back of the house began to crow. Immediately, her husband, the Bendoro, started to rise and she, too, with him.

"Time to bathe," he told her.

In her village, she was used to waking at the first crowing of the cocks. She would wander out behind the house and look out at the ocean where, inside the veil of darkness that covered it, the lights of fishing boats flickered as they made their way to sea. One of those lights would be her father.

But to bathe, so early in the morning? That was not part of village life.

She was afraid to go to the bathhouse alone, but fearing the Bendoro even more, she left the house by way of the back steps and made her way toward the kitchen. Before she could enter, she was startled by the sudden appearance of her servant, who, in a reproachful manner, led her away from the kitchen and toward the bathhouse.

In the bathhouse, a small electric light illuminated the colored patterns of the floor tiles beneath her feet. They were eye-catching, as pretty as her favorite pieces of coral at home. She wanted to break off a section of the floor just to take it home with her and look at it and run her hand over its surface in her evening's free time. That's how beautiful it was.

Scented bathwater in a Chinese porcelain urn encircled by serpentine dragons was ready for her use. Just as the previous evening, before she had time to think, her servant was showering her with the fragrant water. What water remained in the urn would be saved for later use.

Following her bath, the servant demonstrated how to purify herself before the morning prayers. "You must always use holy water before you pray," the servant advised.

The girl was puzzled. "But with all the water I've used already, aren't I clean enough?"

"That's the way it's always been done."

So, for the first time in her life, the girl ritually purified herself with holy water, thereby making herself ready for prayer.

The servant led the girl back to the bedroom where she combed her hair and fixed it in place. She then escorted her out of the bedroom and across the back room of the house to a doorway in the room's back wall. Compared to the size of the room, with its high ceiling covered in cream-colored sheets of appliquéd metal, the doorway looked very small.

The servant pointed toward the door with her thumb: "This is the *khalwat*."

"Kal-wat?" the girl asked.

"Yes, a room for prayer. But don't say it wrong. It's '*khalwat*' with a 'kh.' "

Without further correcting the girl's pronunciation, the servant opened the door to the room.

The prayer room was also large, a massive rectangular space made bright by two electric lights hanging from a low cable that spanned the room. There was no furniture inside, just two carpets, one near the door where they had entered, the other on the room's opposite side.

From a storage closet in the corner of the room nearest the door, the servant removed a white prayer cloak with which she covered the girl's head and body.

"Sit here quietly," she advised. "And don't move. The Bendoro will be sitting over there. You must pray with the Bendoro."

"But I can't."

"Then just follow his lead."

"I can't," the girl insisted.

"The Bendoro's consort must know how to pray. She must be able to please the Master. You had best remember that."

The servant then slipped quietly away.

Feeling like a mouse caught in a trap, the girl sat alone in the prayer room, the likes of which she had never seen before. It was eerie and frightening. From time to time, a swallow would fly into the room through the air vent at the top of the opposite wall and then, just as quickly as it had come in, fly back out again. The girl suddenly realized it was silence that made her afraid, and also situations in which she was not allowed to move. With no one with whom she could share her concern, she sniveled to herself.

The thick stone walls were heartless and mute. What's the use of my being here? she wailed silently. She might as well have been a part of the prayer room's wall for all the good she could do.

When the girl heard the Bendoro enter the room through a side door, she lifted her head to look at him. He had on his white silk tunic and black Buginese sarong, but now he was wearing a turban. An embroidered shawl was wrapped around his neck. His feet were bare. In his right hand, he carried a rosary, and in his left, a collapsible book rest on which to place the Koran. Without saying a word, without even pausing to see if anyone else was with him in the prayer room, he went directly to the carpet at the front of the room. There, he placed the book rest on his left side and, with his right hand telling the beads of his rosary, began to pray.

As if commanded by some mysterious force, the girl rose to her feet and, from her place on her own prayer rug, imitated the Bendoro's every action. Her mind, however, was on her village: the sea, her playmates, the children of the village—all of them naked and dirty, rolling about on the warm sand in the mornings. She had once been a member of that naked band. She found it difficult to say whether she now felt all that much cleaner for having been bathed in scented water. She still felt like the child she had once been, an imp running along the shoreline as far as the river's mouth and then scampering back home again, her feet coated with fishy-smelling mud.

Far from her, at the front of the room, the Bendoro bowed. Mechanically, she followed his actions. When he knelt, she knelt, too. When he sat, she sat, too. She had once had to carry, all by herself, a stingray that weighed at least sixty pounds; she had taken it not to the fish market for sale at the daily auction, but to the home of the headman as a contribution on behalf of her family for a village feast. She had been bathed in sweat that day, and the serrated tail of the fish, hanging down behind her back, had knocked against her legs until they were lacerated and started to bleed. She felt pain that day, but knowing that the fish would be a meal for the entire village, she had kept going. But now, merely having to imitate her husband's actions felt like an even greater burden for her. In the village, she had been able to say whatever she wanted to say, to cry when she wanted to cry, and to scream with delight when she felt happy. But now, in this house, she had to be silent; there was no one willing to hear the sound of her voice. All she could do was whisper. And in this prayer room, even her movements had to follow a prescribed script.

A cold sweat covered her entire body.

In the days before she had come to this house, she had been able to look wherever she wanted to look. Here, in this place, she could only stare at the floor because she no longer knew what she was permitted to look at or where her gaze must fall.

A shiver ran down her spine when the Bendoro altered his position to sit facing her. When he unfolded the book rest and took from the Holy Book a small bamboo place marker, she felt that his eyes were sending her a command. In all her life, she had never felt such a chill. Earlier thoughts of his soft hands and their gentle caress vanished.

She heard the sudden crowing of a rooster behind the house and prayed silently for the sun to rise, just as it had the day before. When the Bendoro uttered the final prayer—*Bismillahirohmanirrohim*—he stared at her from his position on the prayer rug, but she was unable to repeat the phrase. She had never been taught it. Without quite realizing it, she began to cry, her tears wetting the eyehole of her prayer gown.

Again she felt the Bendoro staring at her. The Bendoro repeated the prayer. When he coughed, she automatically raised her eyes; but when she caught his gaze and saw him raise his bamboo pointer and gesture for her to go, her heart shrank within her.

She knelt and bowed and then retreated, backward, toward the door. There she stopped momentarily and looked back across the room at the Bendoro. For the second time, she saw him gesture with the bamboo pointer for her to leave.

The girl's legs felt numb when she tried to stand. Her arm felt leaden as she tried to grip the door handle. But then the handle turned, as if by itself, and she was startled to find herself outside the prayer room, in her servant's arms. With what strength she still had, she broke free from the servant and ran to her bedroom where she threw herself on the bed.

"Mama, Papa," she whispered over and over as if her words could make her parents appear.

"Young Mistress," the servant said.

"Take me to my mother," the girl demanded. "I want to go home, to the village."

"Don't cry," the servant soothed, but the girl was already foundering in tears.

"The Bendoro's consort must be wise. She must learn to paddle against the current if necessary," the servant advised.

"I want my mother!" the girl shouted.

"Hush. In a moment, the Bendoro will be here."

The girl suddenly fell silent. The stillness of that early morning held back the sobs that rose and fell within her, that seemed to carry on their crests pieces of her very soul.

After a time, she regained some of her calm and asked in a more controlled voice: "Where is my mother?"

"She's in the kitchen."

"If I can't go there, then bring her here," she told the servant.

"She's still sleeping."

"Not at this time of day; she'd already be awake."

"Of course, you're right. In the village, she'd have been up long ago, ready to send her man off to sea. Isn't that right? But here, it wouldn't be wise for the consort of the Bendoro to leave her room before the proper time. At this hour, Young Mistress, even the chickens are still in their coop."

When the sonorous sound of the voice emanating from the prayer room died, the girl heard the slapping sound of her husband's sandals. The sound grew louder as they came closer to her room, causing the girl to tremble. Again, it was fear itself that made her afraid. She sat silently on the bed, staring forward as the servant slipped her prayer gown over her head then smoothed the silk wrap she was wearing underneath. Just as the Bendoro arrived at her door, the servant stole quickly from the room.

"Come here, my bride," the Bendoro said to her.

She recognized the tone of his voice—soft, gentle, and polite—and as if drawn to its source by an invisible cord, she rose slowly, lifelessly, and walked somnambulantly toward the door. The Bendoro stretched out his hand and took hers in his own.

Together, they descended the set of stairs outside the back room. Turning to the right, the girl was suddenly able to see the free world once more—or at least as far as the high wall that surrounded the property. It seemed to her like ages since she had last seen a tree. In the dawn's murky light, beneath the pale moon still looming overhead, she saw a tree that towered above all others. She thought it looked like a sapodilla, but of all the *sawo* trees she had ever seen, none had ever looked like this one; there was something frightening about it. She tightened her grip on the Bendoro's arm while he, with his free hand, gently massaged her shoulders.

They breathed in the fresh morning air of the back garden,

which was far larger in size than the whole of the village where she had been born and raised. But unlike her village, this garden and her new home were surrounded by a high wall.

The ground's sand cover, so soft beneath her feet, rose in tiny waves as she moved her feet forward. Mango trees stood in straight rows, like soldiers in formation, while lonely banana plants leaned against the wall as if aware of their own insignificance.

"Do you like going for walks?"

"Yes, Bendoro, I do," the girl answered, thinking as she said it how, at this time of the day, she would usually be stumbling back to her sleeping platform after having just seen off her father and watched his boat sail away until the light from its lantern was swallowed by darkness. Then she would nestle and doze in cozy comfort until her mother was forced to shake her awake: "My, my, what kind of girl are you? Have you fed the chickens? Wake up late in the morning, and a crocodile will find you snoring! So get a move on." And soon she would be on her feet, scattering feed for the chickens that were already scurrying about outside.

"What do you eat in the village?"

The girl couldn't answer. The language the Bendoro used was different, and not having been taught to speak the language that people in the city used, she was afraid to reply and thus refrained from speaking at all.

"Do you eat corn?"

"Yes, Master."

"Do you have rice very often?"

"No, Master."

"Well, you can be thankful there's always rice to eat here. Praise Allah, God always provides."

They continued their leisurely walk.

The Bendoro spoke with a teacherly tone: "That mango tree is two years old, planted at the same time the electricity was installed. But one doesn't plant a tree for one's needs alone. God is so beneficent. Even He did not create nature and humankind for Himself alone." Not hearing an assent, he looked at the girl and asked: "Are you still sleepy?"

"No, Master."

"You're hungry."

"No, Master."

"Tell me something about yourself."

Again, the girl was dumbstruck with fear; she felt as if she couldn't breathe. Why couldn't she make herself open her mouth? If she were at home, she'd have no problem screaming at her pet chicken Kuntring or calling out for her playmates, or laughing along with Pak Karto, the neighbor man she always went to for help when she had something too heavy to carry.

"You don't have to if you don't want to. I know about the villages on the coast, and they're all pretty much the same. About ten years ago, I visited your village. It was dirty, the people were poor, and nobody prayed. A person of faith would never approve of such filth. People who live amid filth incur God's wrath. Wealth does not come easily to people like that; they are condemned to be poor."

"Yes, Master."

"Cleanliness is an important part of faith and is reflected in spiritual purity. Do you understand what I'm telling you?"

"Yes, Master."

"Spiritual purity brings people closer to God."

"Yes, Master."

"So, what would you like to do today?"

She didn't know what to say. In the Bendoro's eyes, she was one of those villagers he had spoken of. That was it, she now realized: She was one of those nameless villagers, just a girl from the coast. Is that what she would always be?

She suddenly felt incredibly tired and drowsy and wanted nothing more than to lie down on the soft mattress in her bedroom, alone. But she didn't have the courage to speak.

The Bendoro led her to a bench under a tree she didn't recognize. After sitting down, he removed from the pocket of his silk jacket a small parcel and then, without the girl quite realizing what was happening, slipped a ring onto her ring finger and a bracelet on each of her wrists.

A few minutes later they were back in the house and the two of them were seated at the dining table, an array of food before them: a sliced but still warm loaf of bread, newly delivered from the bakery; jars of marmalade; stoppered bottles of chocolate sprinkles and brown sugar crystals; a pitcher of freshly squeezed orange juice; a plate of shrimp crackers; and a tureen of cooked oatmeal. Steam rose from coffee in Japanese porcelain cups. The gloss of highly shined cutlery—spoons, knives, and forks, implements she hardly recognized—made the girl's head spin. The glare of a silver fruit bowl assaulted her eyes. The girl's mind reeled. She was hungry, but what were all these shining implements for? And why were there so many of them?

At the girl's side, her personal servant inquired, "What would you like to eat? Some porridge or bread? Or maybe you'd just like juice?"

Anything at all, the girl thought, as long as she could eat it without anyone watching. The servant spoke to her again: "Ask the Master what he wants and then serve it to him."

The girl glanced at the Bendoro, hoping that her eyes would speak for her, and then bowed her head again. When he then pointed at the bread, the girl rose and looked questioningly at the servant.

"Now ask what he would like on this bread: chocolate sprinkles, brown sugar, or marmalade."

Another shiver ran through the girl. She didn't know which items were which.

Her husband said softly, "I'll have the chocolate."

The servant took the girl's hand and guided it toward the bottle of chocolate sprinkles. She put the girl's fingers around the handle of a small butter knife—the shape of which seemed so strange to the girl—and helped her to lift the sprinkles from the jar and spread them across two slices of bread that were already gleaming with the rich yellow of Friesland butter.

That morning, the Girl from the Coast returned to her room with a hungry stomach. She had wanted to eat another slice of bread and chocolate, but as the Bendoro had eaten so little, she hadn't dared to take any more. Maybe it was just that the bread had tasted so good, she rationalized. That's why she had wanted more. She wasn't really hungry; it was just her stomach acting independent. But the hunger she felt kept gnawing away at her insides, refusing to go away. Even two years ago, when most of the village had been swept away by a tidal wave, leaving the few surviving boats buried in mud, she had never felt such hunger.

She thought back to that time, hearing the boom of the bamboo clapper, as if it were just outside the door, that the headman had beaten until the last child was whisked away from the clutches of death that were set to strangle the village. She could see overhead the giant leaves from the coconut trees, flying through the darkness, their stems ready to puncture any human head that got in the way. In the morning, when the inhabitants emerged from their hiding places and returned to the village, not a blade of grass was left standing. Trunks of palm trees lay crisscrossed, atop one another, forming a solid barrier on the beach. Of all her parents' trees, only one had not been uprooted, and it had been beaten down so low she was sure that a light tap of her finger would have severed the trunk. More surprising, the tree hadn't lost its fruit; but the once-green coconuts were now a dirty brown, and two weeks later they dropped from their stems, rotten and inedible.

At that time, and during the week that followed, she had felt hunger, real hunger. The village's fishponds and even their embankments were gone without a trace. And even if they hadn't been destroyed, there were no young fry remaining with which to restock them. The hunger she had felt at that time was an empty feeling, caused by the absence of corn or rice. But the sea still gave her sustenance in the form of shellfish, crabs, and seaweed.

Now, in this house in the city, she found herself with plenty of food, far more than enough, in fact, but she couldn't eat any of it. Here, in this place, there were too many restraints, too many mysterious hands stopping her, a coven of all-powerful spirits that made her draw back in fear.

"Mama," she sighed, and as if in answer, she heard the voice of her servant reply, "Here she is."

Looking up to see her mother at the door, the girl leapt to her feet and ran to her mother, immediately throwing her arms around her. "Ma! Ma! I want to go home," she cried.

"Hush."

At her mother's side, the girl's servant spoke in a whisper: "Your daughter must remember that the Bendoro's consort has to be strong and to always wear a smile no matter what she might be feeling."

"Yes, of course," the mother answered.

"Please tell your daughter that," the servant insisted.

"Of course, I will," she muttered before looking kindly at her daughter. "It's all right. Be quiet now, my baby. There's no need to be afraid."

"But, Ma, I don't like it here."

"That's because you still have so much to learn. In time, I'm sure you'll come to like it here."

"Take me home, Ma."

"What did she say?" It was her father's voice.

The girl looked around to find her father suddenly standing beside her.

"What did you say?" His voice was harsh and threatening.

"You must never raise your voice to the Bendoro's wife," the servant told him.

The girl's father dropped into a chair. The strength that he used to fight waves and strong winds dissolved instantly, of no use to him in this bridal chamber. His chest rose and fell; his hands lay helplessly on the arms of the chair.

"If the Bendoro's wife should like," the servant added, "she could have you removed from this room."

At this remark, the girl wailed and broke free from her embrace around her mother's chest. Sobbing, she knelt before her father and put her arms around his legs. "Forgive me, Papa, just take me home."

Two tears hung suspended from her father's eyelids. Weakly, he raised his right hand and stroked his daughter's hair. He then rose, pulling her along with him to her feet, and sat her down on the chair where he had been seated.

"Good luck to you," he whispered to her.

"Say thank you to your papa," her mother urged.

"Thank you, Papa," the girl repeated.

The girl's father then left the room, not bothering to look back.

For lunch that day, the Girl from the Coast ate alone in the dining room, with her servant waiting and observing her from her position in one corner of the room. From time to time, she would approach the table to demonstrate the use of a particular knife, fork, or spoon. Such a fuss it was, the girl thought, for each of the trays and bowls to have their own serving utensil.

"The Bendoro won't be home for lunch," the servant remarked. "At this time of day, he's usually with the Regent."

"Why do you always have to be following me around?" the girl asked the servant.

"I'm not following you. It's my duty as your servant to help you."

"Why do you talk about yourself that way?"

The question both startled and impressed the servant. The girl was very new to the ways of the house, but her voice already possessed a tone of command.

"But I am your servant, Young Mistress."

It was now the girl's turn to feel startled. At that moment, she had suddenly begun to understand that in the Bendoro's house, her new home, there would never be anyone she could address as her equal. A nearly unbridgeable barrier had been erected between herself and the servant. Here was this incredibly kind woman, who almost never slept for having to watch over and care for her; who was always ready to carry out whatever she might request and explain whatever she did not understand; who could tell her stories when her heart cried for entertainment; and who could stroke her shoulders so lovingly whenever she wanted to cry. Yet she could not call this woman her friend. Why was that? she wanted to scream. Why was this woman her servant? Who was she to deserve such a helpmate? And what had this woman done to deserve ending up working as a servant for her?

"You seem to be daydreaming," the servant remarked. "You should eat more, Young Mistress."

The girl stopped eating and put her utensils on the table. She then rose from her place and, without looking at the servant, went directly to her room and her beloved mattress, where she began to cry. She felt like a chick that had been removed from its flock, having to live alone, with no friends, among a group of strangers she would never get to know. She wasn't allowed to have friends. All she could do was give orders or wait for them to be given to her. Such a cold and silent place—colder than any weather she had ever known on the coast, even on mornings when the air was so chilly the palm oil for cooking congealed in its bottle. She cried until her tears had drained and she had fallen asleep.

A soft shake from her servant finally woke the Girl from the Coast, and she was led away, once again, to the bathhouse for her bath and then back again to her room.

"I want to see my father," she said upon her return.

"He hasn't been seen since this afternoon. No one knows where he's gone. The Bendoro will be most angry if he finds out, and mad at us, too, for not knowing how to look after his guests properly."

"And my mother?"

"Your mother seems to be very upset. She wanted to come here earlier, but I forbade it since you were sleeping."

"Please call her here for me," the girl requested.

"Let's straighten yourself first, Young Mistress."

"Please call her now," the girl insisted.

The servant left, only to return a short time later with the girl's mother beside her. A look of worry was on her face.

"Where's Papa?" the girl asked, but her mother didn't reply. Instead, she approached her daughter and helped the servant to dress her and apply her makeup. Kohl lined her eyelids. French rouge brightened her cheeks.

"Look in the mirror," the servant urged.

The girl stared at her reflection, then suddenly covered her face with her two hands.

"What is it?" her mother asked when she saw her daughter turn away.

The girl lifted her left hand to the mirror and screamed: "That's not me! It's the devil!" But then, just as suddenly, she remembered her mother's fears and forgot her own problems. "Where did he go?" she asked calmly.

"Back to the village, no doubt," the servant answered for her.

The Girl from the Coast had never loved her father as much as she did at that moment. Quite likely, she thought, her father was now inspecting the sails of his boat, making sure it was ready for him to go out to sea later that night or early the next morning, strong enough to confront the ocean's wind and pounding waves and safely return with the catch needed to feed his family.

What would she say to the Bendoro if he asked why her father had gone home without first saying good-bye?

As if reading the girl's mind, the servant provided an answer: "If you were to ask the Bendoro's pardon," she suggested, "I'm sure he would give it to you."

The girl's mother conveyed the same question with her eyes. The girl hesitated momentarily but then nodded her head. Even so, she was of two minds. Who was the Bendoro? Was he so powerful, more powerful than the sea, that her father felt he had to flee? He had lost two of his sons, two of her brothers, at sea, yet he had never attempted to leave the village. Why would he run away now? Even she wasn't afraid of the sea. Why then this incomprehensible fear of the Bendoro? Why? The Bendoro was tall and slender with a pale face and soft skin. Her father was muscular, much stronger than her husband. Why then was he, and everyone else, for that matter—even herself—so afraid of this man?

"What are you thinking of?" the servant asked. "I'm sure your father is safe at home."

The girl erased from her mind her thoughts of her father. He would be all right.

"Listen to me, let me teach you," her servant began. "You must speak to the Bendoro like this: 'Forgive me, Master . . .' That's all you'll have to say. And then the Bendoro will ask, 'What is it, my bride? Is there something you want?' "

The girl stared at the servant, not blinking.

"And then you'll say to him, 'My father was forced to leave, Bendoro. Forgive me and my family, Bendoro; he was in such haste that he forgot to ask your leave.' And the Bendoro will laugh. 'That's no problem, no problem at all,' he'll say. And then . . ."

"And then what?"

The servant turned the girl's head toward the mirror. "Look at that. That is no devil. That is a goddess from heaven!"

The girl studied her image in the looking glass but did not find herself there. No, that's not me, she said to herself. That face was not the one she had come to this house with; it was a mannequin's face, with no evidence of yesterday's child in it. She could see no childish glee in her eyes. The child there was gone forever.

Even the girl's mother was hard pressed to recognize her daughter's reflection. No, that wasn't her child anymore. Only a few days had passed since they had set out from the village, yet the energy and liveliness that her daughter once possessed was no longer in evidence.

There suddenly came to the girl the sound of her own laughter, the waves of glee that a joke or something else humorous often produced in her. But that laugh was a child's laugh, something she had not heard in this building, the Bendoro's home, and something she suspected that she would never hear again.

"What man would not desire the woman you see here?" the servant asked. "Just look," she said to the girl's mother. "With her small body, no heavier than a cotton ball, and her tawny skin, as smooth as a flat iron to the touch. It's only her hands that need some work, but if we soak them in saltwater, they'll soon lose their roughness. And with her supple eyelids and almond-shaped eyes, she looks for all the world like a Chinese princess. Who would not recognize such beauty?

"Tonight," she said to the girl, "I will tell you the story of the battle between the Chinese princess and Amir Hamzah. I can't tell you how many people I've seen break into tears when they hear how the princess was shot in the shoulder and rolled on the ground in her own blood and no one came to help her."

The servant began to hum the section of the song-tale where the Chinese princess falls from her horse on the battlefield, but then, just as suddenly, she stopped. "I'd better take your mother back to the kitchen," she pronounced. "You never can tell when the Bendoro will appear."

The two older women left the room, leaving the girl alone once more, standing dispiritedly before the mirror.

The mirror at her family's home was a simple one. In her village, the larger the mirror a family owned, the greater the family's prestige. Families placed their mirrors where other people would see them. Guests would invariably note the size and thickness of a mirror. Intricately carved frames were commonplace. Almost everyone in the village could carve; the skill was nothing special, just something to do in one's spare time. It was only outsiders who noticed the frames. For the villagers, it was the mirror itself that counted.

But this mirror, the one before her, had no appeal for her; the image she saw in it aroused in her suspicion and antipathy. Here, in the city, everything was supposed to be better than it was in the village. But she was learning that it wasn't true. That finely adorned image she saw in the mirror was simply not the same face that she so often saw in the mirror at her family home. Maybe the mirror at her family home was simple and lacking a frame, but she knew it and could always be sure of its honesty. In that mirror she could clean the mucus from the corners of her eyes and wipe her cheeks clean of the soot from the kitchen hearth. But here, in this mirror, imported Arabian kohl darkened her eyes. People said her skin was soft and smooth and the color of lansium fruit. At home, when she wiped her face clean of sweat, that natural color was evident in the mirror. But here, in this mirror, a layer of rouge covered her skin, changing her natural color to the soft pink of a rose-apple. And here, too, a thin black line that looked to her like a fish spine ran through the center of her wide eyebrows. No, the face in this mirror was not her own. Here, in this house, she wasn't permitted to see her own face.

She looked at her necklace, bracelets, and ring, all of them made of gold and studded with gems. She thought again of the village and how everyone there detested Pak Kintang—a man who measured the value of everything in terms of its weight in gold, but when one of the village elders died, Pak Kintang hadn't contributed anything at all. In the village, gold and pretense went hand in hand.

The girl mused: Who else had talked to her about gold? She searched her memory until finally there came to her the face of a man—a man from the city with a sallow face, sunken cheeks, and a constant smile. He was a moneylender who had come to the village to convince the villagers to invest in gold. At the time, her father was out at sea and her mother had invited the man into the house. The girl remembered him taking a seat on the sleeping platform and saying to her mother, "You should buy some gold, Ma'am. No need to pay me all at once; credit will do. You have an unmarried daughter, don't you? That means you should be collecting gold. With gold, you can get anything, anything at all!"

She had been playing at her mother's feet when she saw the village elder, an ancient man, enter the house, walking unsteadily with the help of a cane. He coughed as he raised his cane and pointed its tip at the city man. "Was that gold you said we needed? Look at the boats out there, the ones without sails, the ones with leaks half-covered in water by the shore. Boats! It's boats we need. Don't listen to him," he told her mother. "Boats provide everything we need. Gold just takes it away." With his cane, he then began to drive the man from the house, and when the man with the sunken cheeks had reached the doorway, the village elder turned to her mother and raised his cane toward her: "If you listen to him, you'll ruin your husband. Do you understand? Remember this: Anyone who comes here to talk about gold has the devil inside him. Keep him away. We must keep this village safe."

And now, before her, on the dressing table, were gold and gem-studded pieces of jewelry, shining brightly beneath the light of the lamp. She stared at them closely, until she was startled by a voice whispering in her ear: "Such things as these, most people can only dream of owning."

"You startled me," she said to the servant.

"You like the jewelry, don't you." This was a statement, not a question.

The girl had never owned any jewelry. She had to admit, however, she did admire their beauty.

"The workmanship is very fine," the servant continued. "They were specially made in Solo."

"If you want them," the girl told her, "then take them."

The servant's eyes glowed brightly and she clutched her hands before her mouth. Her voice trembled as she spoke: "Who wouldn't want such things, Young Mistress? But you shouldn't talk that way. It makes me afraid."

"What's there to be afraid of? It's only gold."

"But I'm afraid, Young Mistress, afraid of doing something wrong. I am who I am, and I am a servant. If there were no servants there could be no masters. This is God's will, my destiny. My grandfather wasn't a servant and none of his children were, either. But I am, for that is what I was destined to do—to serve the Bendoro and to serve you."

"Take them," the girl said again.

"How could I? Even your own parents would be afraid to accept them."

The girl was struck by this comment. But gradually, despite the burden weighing on her mind, she began to understand that everyone was frightened, everyone except for the Bendoro, that is. Why was everyone afraid of him? He didn't seem to be harsh or cruel; in fact, he was gentle and polite.

The servant spoke more confidently now: "My sister once wanted a small chain of gold coins to use as a clasp. She was very beautiful, and one day she went to Lasem hoping to snare for herself a rich Chinese man who lived there. The front fence of the man's house was a long line of steel spears, and the house itself was huge, with blue roof tiles on a curved roof and serpentine dragons on its peak."

"Which house was bigger, that one or this?"

"That one."

"And which was better?"

"That one."

"What happened to her?"

"She went into the house and never came out again."

"Did she get the chain she wanted?"

"Who knows? She never appeared again. And that was twenty years ago."

What was the servant trying to tell her? The girl suddenly felt a rush of panic and clutched the servant's hand: "Will I ever be able to leave? Here, take this jewelry away."

The servant opened a drawer in the vanity, took out a key, and handed it to the girl. "After three months, you'll be able to go wherever you want, as long as it's with the Bendoro's permission. Put this jewelry in the armoire. I myself wouldn't dare touch them."

"Why is it that people like gold?"

"Because, well, what can I say? Because with gold, you don't look like everybody else. You don't look like a servant."

"Who do you mean by 'everybody else'?"

"I don't know how to answer you. When I say 'everybody,' I guess I mean everybody like myself."

"But what's wrong with you?"

"Well, people like me, they have to work hard and almost never eat."

"Then why don't you take these things? Then you wouldn't be like everyone else. You wouldn't have to work so hard. Sell them. Then you'd have plenty to eat. Or wear them if you wish."

"But, Young Mistress, they're for you to wear, for the Bendoro to see."

With her mistress acting so friendly toward her, the servant seemed at ease, but this mood was cut short when they heard the call of a voice they knew so well: "Mardi!" It was the Bendoro calling someone.

"The carriage! Prepare the carriage for me."

"Yes, Master," came the familiar reply.

From somewhere at the back of the house came the sound of

a commotion. Only then did the Girl from the Coast realize that there were many more inhabitants in the house than she had first guessed.

"Who are all those people?" she asked the servant.

"Relatives of the Bendoro, nephews mostly, who have been placed in his safekeeping."

"What do they do here?"

"They work here, but in the afternoon they study."

"Where have they been keeping themselves all this time?"

"They spend most of their time at the prayer house."

"Where's that?"

"Outside, to the left of the house, that building is the prayer house. That's where they study and where they learn to recite the Koran."

"I haven't heard them practicing."

"Their teacher was fired. He was a lazy and greedy man."

"I hope that's not what he was teaching."

"It might very well be for all the good he seemed to do, but I couldn't really say for sure. Here, let me fix your hair."

The girl, having been made aware yet again of their different stations, felt her heart shrink; but she could say nothing as she watched the servant brush out her hair, thicken it with a fall, twist and braid it into a bun, and then finally fix frangipani flowers in its curve.

"In the village, no one puts flowers in their hair," the girl protested.

"That may be, Young Mistress, but in the city a married woman is expected to do so."

Yet again the girl was reminded of her station: She was the wife of an important man.

"I like it better in my village," she pouted.

"Isn't that the way everyone feels about their home?"

"Why don't you go home?"

"At my age? Who would feed me? Life is hard where I come from."

"Why's that?"

"Young or old, it's all the same; the only difference is that when you're older, life's even harder. For a person my age, everything is difficult."

"What, do people beat you?"

The servant began to straighten the pleats of the girl's batik wrap. "Beat me? Not really," she paused, "but just about anyone and everyone has the right to beat people like me."

They heard the Bendoro's voice again: "Mardi!"

"Yes, Master."

"Is it ready?"

"The Master must be in a hurry to go somewhere," the servant whispered. "I suppose the wedding of an official," she guessed.

"Would they be using a dagger, too?"

"No, it's only commoners who get married that way . . ." The servant stopped as if remembering something. "No, that's not right. That only happens when the groom can't be present. That's when a *keris* can be used in his place."

"Why do people have to get married?" the girl asked.

The servant laughed and shook her head. "My, the things you say! For most people, like me for instance, we get married just to make life more difficult for ourselves. But it's different for the *priyayi*. The upper class get married for pleasure."

"Why would you get married if it makes life harder?"

"That's what you call fate, Young Mistress." She sighed. "My grandfather told me that his father, my great-grandfather, was hanged when the Dutch Governor-General built the cross-Java

Postal Road." She pointed her hand in the direction of the sea. "That's why my grandfather ran away. That's why he was never a servant."

"Why did they hang him?"

"He was a foreman, I was told, and was ordered to build a section of the road in just one week's time, but it was in a swampy area and most of the workers came down with fever. Anyway, a week passed and the Dutch came to inspect the work, and because the road wasn't done, they hung them all."

"No, that can't be!" the girl cried.

"Oh yes, it can," her servant asserted. "And that's what fate is for most of us folks. When my grandfather ran away, he joined the rebels who were being led by Prince Diponegoro. Then, when Prince Diponegoro lost the war, my grandfather fled again, this time with a Javanese noble who had joined the rebels, too. When the nobleman finally surrendered, my grandfather surrendered, too. And when the noble was appointed to a government position, my grandfather became his retainer, no more than a slave really, just like me.

"Whenever the noble went out on patrol, my grandfather went along. One night, when they were on patrol, the nobleman was killed by a band of robbers. My grandfather managed to escape, but when he returned home alone, he was beaten and thrown into prison. Five years he spent there. When he got out, he couldn't work as a retainer any longer, so he started to farm. All of his children became farmers. None of them could be retainers."

The Girl from the Coast bowed her head, avoiding the servant's gaze.

"You're lucky, Young Mistress, and should give thanks to Allah. Not every woman has a chance to live in a house like this, unless it's as a servant."

"I like my own home better."

"That can't be true."

"I'm not afraid there."

Hearing the slap of a pair of sandals on the floor outside the room, the girl took hold of the servant's arm.

The older woman whispered, "Smile. You must learn to smile and always be standing, ready to greet the Master, just inside the doorway."

The servant led her to the door. Thus, when the Bendoro called out for her, it was from there that she replied: "Yes, Master."

"I won't be home tonight," he said, without looking inside. A moment later, she listened to the sound of his sandals fade as he walked away.

That night the Girl from the Coast asked the servant if she could sleep with her mother, but the servant objected.

"If I can't sleep in the kitchen," the girl suggested, "then let her sleep here with me."

"That wouldn't be right, not for the Bendoro's consort."

"But she's my mother," the girl protested.

"That may be true, Young Mistress, but she is a commoner and no more than a servant in this place."

"But that's not right. I should be a servant to her. In our village, I carry out her orders; I do whatever she tells me to do."

"That's what's wrong, Young Mistress. The ways of the nobility are different, and besides, this is the city, not some fishing village."

"Then what am I supposed to do here?"

"Only two things, Young Mistress, nothing more: Serve the Master and command the servants and other people who live here."

"What must I do for the Bendoro?'

"Whatever he wants you to do. You must follow his every wish."

"I can't. I don't know how."

"In time you will, all in time."

"You think so?"

"It's very easy."

"What am I supposed to tell the people here to do?"

"Whatever you want them to do."

"There's only one thing I want."

"Then that should be easy."

"To go back home with my mother."

"That's the only thing you can't do."

"But that's the only thing I want."

The servant rolled out her sleeping mat beside the girl's bed. "Listen to me. There's only one thing that Allah wants, and that's for people to be good. That's what religion is for—so that people can turn to Him. But that's not how it is in real life. There are lots of bad people in the world. Allah has just one wish, and we can't even grant Him that."

"And so am I one of those bad people, too?"

"Who's to say what's in a person's heart? Not even the devil knows, especially not when we ourselves don't even know. If we could, we probably wouldn't have to live in this world at all. But enough of that; it's time for you to go to sleep."

"Tell me a story first."

And so it was that, in this way, the servant woman began to calm the girl's restless nature and teach her the ways of a nobleman's consort. How many times had she told her stories before? She herself couldn't remember. Four women had preceded the Girl from the Coast as the Bendoro's consort, and she had told them all the very same tales. For every new mistress of the house, she always repeated her tales of princes who fell madly in love with village girls; of village girls who came to live in a palace and all about their rich lives and their many servants. She also told them about the sons they bore; about Allah's beneficence and His scorn for the wicked; about the Dutch Governor and his hangman's pole; about the mass graves along the coast; about Prince Diponegoro's uprising; about the homes of the city's nobility; about the marriage celebration of Kartini, who had established schools for girls, and about her burial only a few years later.

And when she had finished whatever tale she was spinning, the servant would rise from her place on the floor to look at her mistress. And when she saw her mistress fast asleep on her soft bed, she would give her thanks to Allah for having acquitted herself of her duties for the day with results the Master would find pleasing.

A week passed before the Bendoro returned home, and the Girl from the Coast felt happy during that time. Her servant felt happy as well for the opportunity his absence presented her: She needed time to tame this new wife's heart. From past experience, the servant knew that she needed at least a week to gain the new wife's friendship and to mold her for her new role as mistress of the house.

One evening, a recitation teacher came to the house to teach the girl how to pronounce the curvy letters from which holy words were formed. And she repeated these, one by one, after the man. She pronounced all the words and letters but wasn't taught their use or meaning.

One night, while lying on the bed and listening to the incessant buzz of mosquitoes outside the mosquito net, the girl rolled over, putting her back to the wall, and looked over the edge of the mattress onto the floor where her servant was lying, with her eyes wide open and staring at the ceiling.

"Have you ever been married?" she asked the servant.

The question startled the servant, causing her to quickly sit upright. "Yes, Young Mistress, twice, in fact."

"Do you have any children?"

"I should have, Young Mistress."

"What do you mean? Did your husbands die?"

"Yes, Young Mistress, but such is the tale of so many people like me. I got married when I was very young, but because I was married, I was considered to be an adult. At that time, the Dutch made all the villages contribute labor to government projects, so the village chief sent me and my husband to Jepara, where we worked on an estate planting cacao. Four months we were there, and I was pregnant at the time but lost my baby before he ever had a chance to breathe fresh air. It was the foreman who did it. He kicked me in the stomach.

"What happened is that I was feeling dizzy one day and had sat down to cool myself in the shade of a tree. That's when the foreman came and then, out of the blue, a Dutch official and some soldiers, too. The foreman kept pulling on my arm to try to get me to stand, but I was too weak. That was when he kicked me in the stomach. Then everything started to blur, but I could hear my husband running toward me, screaming like a crazy man. I blacked out."

"That's terrible."

"That's what happens to people like us, Young Mistress."

"Not in my village, it doesn't. Nothing like that ever happened there."

"I've heard that. My husband once tried to get me to run

away. He said we could stay in a fishing village or go off to some island. But I told him I didn't think that would be the best thing for our child. And look what happened instead." She now addressed the girl: "Does your father own a boat?"

"Yes, he does," the girl answered.

"That's what my husband wanted: to own his own boat. We were going to sail away to one of those fishing islands off the coast. Did your father ever take you out to sea? Have you ever been to one of those islands?"

The girl thought for a moment, then answered slowly: "Yes. Three times, maybe more. I was very young."

"So then, you've run away, too. Do you remember the times?"

"I remember staying overnight on a small island and in the morning finding the shoreline covered with jellyfish. I slit their sacks and took out the larger fish inside and grilled them on a fire. But my father never called it 'running away.' "

"I don't suppose he would, but it happens to most everyone, everyone like us."

Sadness and curiosity marked the girl's voice: "What happened to your husband?"

"I don't know. When I came to, I was covered in blood—my blood, my baby's, my husband's, and the foreman's."

"Was there that much blood?"

"I can only tell you what people said. I don't remember myself. People said he ran amuck and stabbed the foreman in the stomach, slit it right open, and then fought off anyone who tried to help the man. The soldiers finally went after him, but he fought back, attacked them with his machete. Finally, after they had surrounded him, and he couldn't get close enough to stab anyone, he threw his machete at one of the soldiers. Hit him, too, they say, but the man didn't die. My husband was so thin he didn't have any strength left. All that was left of him was skin and bones; no meat on him at all. And his skin was covered with sores and welt marks where he'd been whipped."

"Did you see him after that?"

"No. When I woke up, it was all over. The only people there were three women, friends of mine, who tried to help me but couldn't do much of anything, so they just waited there with me. When it was getting dark, an oxcart came, and some men got down from it. They kicked my three friends and ordered them to leave. And then the bunch of them—there must have been four men because there was one for each of my arms and legs—picked me up, said 'one-two-three,' and then threw me up in the air and onto the back of the cart. I don't remember after that."

As the woman finished her story, she saw that her mistress was crying. "What is it? Why are you crying?" she asked.

The girl couldn't answer.

"Tell me why."

"What, am I not supposed to cry?"

"But why should you cry?"

"I'm crying for you!" the girl wailed.

In a flash, the servant was on her feet. She opened the mosquito netting, put her arms around the girl's legs and kissed her feet. "Oh, my dear. I have so many bad memories. Outside this place, I tell you, there's only cruelty—cruelty to people like ourselves."

"Where did the oxcart take you?"

"Where else do they take commoners? To jail."

"Was it bad in there for you?"

"I couldn't walk for three months. Even so, they still chained my legs. After they finally removed the chains, they took me away, I don't know where. I just remember being laid out on the cold floor and then three Javanese government officials taking turns asking me questions. There was a Dutchman there, too, watching me, but he didn't ask me anything. All he said was 'dog.' "

The girl didn't know what comfort she could give her servant. All she could do was speak: "Where I come from, the people say the sea can be mean. It gives us our food, but it can be mean."

"Maybe so, but it doesn't torture people on purpose."

"No, it doesn't do that," the girl agreed. "It collects the debt that's owed to it, nothing more. At least that's what my father says." The girl sat up. "Why do you sleep on the floor? Why don't you sleep here, beside me?"

"I am your servant. It would be a sin against the Master, and against Allah, too, to place myself higher than the Master's knees."

"But I never had a servant before I came here," the girl insisted.

"I know that, Young Mistress."

"I don't know what I'm supposed to do."

"I know that, too."

"And why am I even talking about myself after all you've had to go through? How did you get out of jail?"

"One morning they just kicked me out. That's all."

"So what did you do?"

"I set off on foot. I didn't know where I was going, didn't even know the name of the city I was in. I couldn't go back to my village; I was afraid they'd put me on another work crew. The first few nights, I slept beneath the big banyan in the city square—yes, the one over there." The servant pointed in the direction of the city square. "In the morning, I'd hide in the market." She pointed toward the south. "It was here, in this city, that I had been imprisoned, but then I met a man, one of the Bendoro's drivers, and we got married. Five years we were married and lived here, but I never got pregnant again. And then one day, my husband fell from a coconut tree and died."

"But you stayed on?"

"Yes, Young Mistress, I did. I liked taking care of children. I can't tell you how many I've helped raise in the fifteen years that I've been here."

Neither the girl nor her servant spoke for a moment as they listened to the crashing of the waves on the shore. The steady whistle of the wind reminded the girl of her father. "Who's cooking for Papa now?" she suddenly asked.

The servant said nothing as the girl continued to speak: "It should be me. What with Ma here with me, Papa is alone."

"Don't think about men," the older woman advised, "even your own father. Men can always take care of themselves, even in hell no doubt."

"But he is my father," the girl said.

"But now, Young Mistress, you are the Bendoro's consort and you live here, in this big house. And nobody is going to bother your father, not even with him living out in that fishing village on the coast. None of the overlords; none of the soldiers, either. Your father will never have to run away again or to take his family to some small fishing island. Not now. Your father will have the respect of everyone in the village. Everyone will listen to what he has to say. Don't worry yourself needlessly, Young Mistress."

"How can you know all this?" the girl asked.

"I know lots of things, Young Mistress, too many things." She smiled. "Sometimes even the Master asks me questions."

"Do you like me, Mbok?" The girl now used the familiar term of address for an older woman.

"More than you'll ever know, Young Mistress."

"Then take one of my bracelets, or a necklace."

"You must stop suggesting such a thing. I could be run out of this place for that. And if that were to happen, I wouldn't know where to go. The world is wide, but where would I go? I just don't know."

"I love you, Mbok. I just want you to promise me to tell me if I do anything wrong."

"As long as you keep the Master happy, Young Mistress, you can do nothing wrong." She turned her pillow over, plumped it up, and slapped it down. "To do any wrong toward the Bendoro would be to invite trouble in your life. Do you understand what I'm telling you, Young Mistress?"

There was no answer. The Girl from the Coast was asleep.

After the Master's return, days and then weeks went by without the girl's servant visiting the girl's room again. Meanwhile, the girl's mother returned to the village, taking with her a gunnysack of rice, several score rupiah, some used clothing of the Bendoro's for her husband, a kilogram of tamarind paste, and a number of tins of spices.

The Girl from the Coast wasn't able to see her mother until a few minutes before her departure. When the girl's mother came to her bedroom to say good-bye, the girl offered her her gold jewelry several times, but her mother feigned not to hear the offer and talked to her about other things: about the girl's father and his work in the village; about their need for a new net to replace the one they had, which was old and worn out; about the cost of sailcloth, which had fallen in price; about the rise in the price of resin, which meant that her father had to put off resealing his boat.

"Is there something you'd like me to tell him?" the girl's mother finally asked.

"Just ask him for his blessings," she said.

"Do you like living here?" her mother asked.

"You and Pa want me to live here. I'd rather be home, in the village."

"A woman must be with her husband. That's the way it's been for me," the mother consoled. "It doesn't matter if you live in a rundown shack or whether or not you're happy; you have to learn to please your man."

The girl pressed on her mother two lengths of dress batik, which she accepted without comment. But then, finally, she said, "I have to go."

"But Ma!"

"Don't raise your voice like that. You're not a little girl anymore."

"Yes, Ma."

"Now when you cry you must learn to cry alone. Nobody else is going to see or hear you. You have to stop thinking about yourself and learn how to make other people happy."

After watching her mother leave from her place beside the door to her room, the girl turned and went inside. Catching sight of her reflection in the mirror, she studied her features, and the look on her face, but then quickly averted her eyes and went to lie down on her bed.

What now? the girl screamed silently. Haven't I suffered enough? But she had no rights now, she had come to realize, not even the right to scream from fear or pain. During the weeks since her arrival at the Bendoro's house, she had gradually been taught to understand that the one and only thing she could do—in fact, had to do—was to serve her husband, the Bendoro. It's not that she wasn't accustomed to helping others. At home, in the village, she had always helped her parents and lent a ready hand to relatives and fellow villagers. She herself sometimes had to gather her father's net, heavy with its metal sinkers, and hang it from the crossbeam in the house to dry; using a wooden pole for a lever, she would, all by herself, hoist the net onto a pulley and raise it to the joist. She also had to help grind the dried shrimp. Now her mother would be performing that task alone, all for the few cents that she would receive from the Chinese trader from town. That was work. But here, in this house, what did people actually do?

"We are here to serve the Bendoro, Young Mistress," the servant stressed.

Was that work? Serving the Bendoro was work? This was something the Girl from the Coast could not comprehend.

A batik teacher was called to the house to teach the girl how to transform a piece of white cloth into a fabric of multicolored patterns; thereafter, mornings would find her with a pencil tracing intricate patterns on cloth. The calluses on her hands disappeared, and her skin grew soft from the lack of hard work. Once a week another teacher came to teach her cake making. And every third day, her religion teacher would come to tell her tales of mystery that had been handed down from some far-distant desert kingdom.

In time, the girl's thoughts of home—of her mother and father, her younger siblings and her relatives—grew less frequent. But when she did think of them and her life in the village, she would ask her servant to repeat for her all the fisherman's tales she knew.

The Girl from the Coast gradually became accustomed to a way of life that was filled with tools to make work easier. She became familiar with the sound of Dutch being spoken by the young relatives of the Bendoro when they left the prayer house to the left of the main house. She could hear their voices through the wall of her room, and when they spoke in Javanese she learned of many things she didn't know before: One of their classmates, who had gone to school in Holland, had returned home, not with a degree but with a young Dutch woman on his arm; a Dutch warship was now anchored a number of miles offshore; the cliffs on the coast north of Lasem had caved in, resulting in a large flood; three pirate boats had attacked a fishing village near her home and wiped out more than a tenth of the population before carrying off all the gold, silver, and other items of value that were to be found; a number of young men from the city had joined the government army and gone to fight overseas.

"If you were to go back to your village now," her servant told her one day, "everyone there would think you were a princess."

The Girl from the Coast also took lessons in embroidery, knitting, and sewing. Her quick mind and apparent skill at most anything she set out to do excited praise in all her teachers.

Several times during the weeks she had been at the Bendoro's house, she had gone to the kitchen to try to help with the work there, but she didn't do that anymore. The looks the kitchen staff gave her told her that her company wasn't welcome.

"You'd best stay out of the kitchen," her servant advised. "The kitchen help are nothing more than servants, but you'd never know that from their attitudes, grumbling and griping all the time. They can't see the good fortune in front of their own faces. They should live in their own shacks and see how they like it then."

During this formative time, the Bendoro did not visit the girl's bedroom.

"The Master is very busy helping the Regent," the servant told her. "They say that the Regent is now going to marry a princess from Solo. It's such a shame about Kartini's death. Just twenty-something and dead from childbirth! Now she was a person to look up to. Such courage! No one had more. She wasn't even afraid to speak her mind to the Dutch. All the important people respected her."

Even the Girl from the Coast had come to know of the young woman named Kartini. When she had visited the city several years ago, the girl learned, she had traveled in a royal carriage. All the people of the district had been ordered out to the highway to greet her, where they stood waving the Dutch tricolor paper flags with their dark brown hands. Now, she finally understood the story her father had brought back with him from the city several years ago when he and several other men from the village had gone there to represent the village at a gathering in the city's central square. All she knew at the time was that they had been there to witness festivities for an incredible young woman from Jepara who had married the Regent. That young woman, she surmised, must have been Raden Ajeng Kartini. And now she was dead. Such a short life, but she had managed to do so much in that time: acquiring an education and fluency in Dutch despite the many barriers; establishing schools for girls; setting up cooperatives for artisans. It was no wonder her name was now held with such respect.

The Girl from the Coast didn't particularly like hearing about the great wedding celebration that had been held for Kartini and the Regent. What did that say about her own marriage ceremony, with a dagger instead of a groom? But she marveled at the stories of Kartini's love for children, regardless of whose they were. Her servant had told her about the Bendoro's children; and what caused it, she wasn't quite sure, but the more time she spent in his house, the more she wanted to take care of his children. But that, it seemed, was not to be; the children of previous consorts were intentionally kept away from her sight. Even the older child, the Young Master Rahmat, she rarely saw, though she did sometimes hear him speaking in Dutch to his teacher in the back room of the house.

The days passed and the Girl from the Coast spent her time practicing her new skills. Her skin, no longer baked by a coastal sun, became reddish yellow in color; her young girl's features had disappeared and had been replaced by a more womanly expression.

As the wedding date of the Regent approached, the Bendoro spent less and less time in his own home. Months passed when she almost never saw the Bendoro; during this time, he never set foot in her room. The city was bedecked with colored flags and palm-leaf decorations. The princess from Solo, it seemed, was to be given an even greater welcome than the one that had been shown to Kartini.

The city arches, marking the official gateways of the regency, were decorated with palm leaves and banana trunks, as were the roadways into town. On the shore of the city's northern border, the masonry wall that surrounded the sacred anchor, symbol of the city, was being restored.

And then one night, some six months and a few weeks after the Girl from the Coast arrived at the Bendoro's home, the city came alive with celebration. On that night, her servant escorted her from her room and out of the house across the central garden to a pavilion on the far right side of the compound. They went inside and climbed to its uppermost floor and there, from the open air vent, watched the festivities in the square below. The city was bathed in light and the square was filled with spectators. She wanted to join the party makers below, to be a part of the crowd of people she had known since she was just a baby. But now that was not possible, for she was higher than them all.

Late that night, she returned to her room, her mind awhirl. She thought of the Regent, a man much older than the Bendoro, and his Solonese bride, a woman greater in years than she, whose wedding celebration had been an event for all the city to see. But her own wedding to the Bendoro—how had that been celebrated? Certainly there had been no grand welcome celebration.

At three o'clock in the morning, she awoke to find the servant gone from the floor below her bed and the Bendoro sprawled on the bed beside her.

At five in the morning, the servant came back to the room. Seeing her mistress still lying on the bed, she went closer and heard the young woman calling to her in a whisper, "Help me, Mbok, please . . ."

The servant pulled back the mosquito net and placed the folds over a hook to keep the curtain aside. "Are you sick?" she asked.

The girl could only moan.

The servant felt the girl's legs. "It's all right, Young Mistress. You don't feel feverish."

"But I feel sick," the girl told her. Lifting her arms toward the woman, she said, "Please take me to the bathroom."

The woman took hold of the girl's arms at her elbows and pulled her into a sitting position. She fixed the girl's hair, which was now in complete disarray, and straightened the girl's blouse and batik wraparound cloth. She smoothed out the wrinkles in the bedsheet with her hand.

"You're not sick, Young Mistress," the servant said again as she helped the girl from her bed.

"But Mbok . . ." she lamented softly.

"It's all right, Young Mistress, it won't be like that again."

The girl's mind reeled with darkened images of the night before: her husband coming into her room and lifting the cloth that covered her lower body.

"What happened?" she asked, for she herself was not completely sure.

After the servant had helped her mistress to her feet, she pointed at the bedsheet and several small reddish brown stains. "Don't worry. A little pain, a few drops of blood. You've been here over six months. That's nothing."

"But Mbok . . ." the girl moaned again.

"Yes, Young Mistress."

"I'm afraid."

"Of course you are."

"Take me to the bathroom."

The servant helped the girl walk away.

"Mbok?"

"Yes, Young Mistress."

"I want to see my mother. When can she come back?"

They continued their slow journey toward the bathhouse.

"Mbok?"

"Yes, Young Mistress."

"Do you think I'm pretty?"

"You're beautiful, Young Mistress."

"But weren't the others prettier?"

"In this world, Young Mistress, when beauty passes, everyone steps aside."

At the inner courtyard, they rested momentarily.

"But the others," the girl continued, "weren't they nice, too?"

"You're much nicer, Young Mistress."

"Mbok?"

"Yes, Young Mistress."

"Do you love me?"

"Do you still have any doubt?'

"No, I wasn't doubting you. But, what about . . . ?" She didn't have to finish.

"The Master loves you, Young Mistress. You don't have to worry about that."

"But . . ."

"Yes, Young Mistress?"

"I'm afraid."

"What are you afraid of?"

"Do you think I'll always be pretty?"

"Of course you will. Why not?"

"When you were young," she asked the servant, "were you pretty?"

"I was never pretty, Young Mistress."

"I'm so afraid."

The two women vanished behind the door to the bathhouse.

PART TWO

A year had passed, and now, on nights when the Bendoro did not come to her room, the Girl from the Coast felt lonely. She no longer required the constant ministrations of her personal servant; beyond the older woman's expectations, the girl had adapted surprisingly well to her new life and home. Nonetheless, the woman remained for the girl a friend and source of wisdom.

The girl now spent much of her time outside her room: in the morning, taking lessons, talking to relatives of her husband in the household; in the evening, taking solitary walks in the back garden; and, at night, participating in recitations of the Koran with the servants and, sometimes, the neighbors.

In the year that she had been at the Bendoro's house, she had never once set foot in the front or central room of the house, nor in the inner rooms. The prayer room was the only exception. No one had ever told her not to enter these rooms; it was a rule that she herself had sensed to be in place. There seemed to be a silent power forbidding her.

One evening, when her husband ordered Mardi to prepare

his carriage, the girl suddenly felt a stab to her heart. He was to be gone for at least a week. Upon hearing her husband's command, she immediately changed her clothes, fixed her makeup and hair, and then sat down in the chair in her room to wait for her husband to come say good-bye. She waited and waited but he didn't come. This had happened often during the past year, and she suspected that his departure this evening wasn't likely to be the last time, either.

After she was sure that her husband had gone and his carriage was speeding away, taking him to wherever it was he went, she stood and left her room. She descended the stairs off the back of the house and turned right to enter the back garden. There, she walked directly to the bench where she had sat with her husband for the first time. She hoped the cool evening air would help to still her confused and anxious heart. She wanted to be alone, enveloped by nature and one with the world, a feeling that had always been present inside her when she was living in the fishing village. She wanted to think only of pleasant things and to suppress the restlessness of her heart. No more than ten minutes had passed since her husband had left, yet she already missed him. How greatly she regretted that they never had enough time together, no more than a few nights in a week.

Whatever happened to her, the Bendoro had once advised, she was not to dwell on bad things. It's foolish to do that, he had told her. One should think of beauty and the good things in life to keep one's heart pure and one's mind clear. Only an ass dwells on misery, he also said, and for that reason, until the day it dies, the ass remains a beast of burden. She didn't know what an ass was, but her servant told her it was one of those runt-horses you could see daily in the city, transporting people and limestone cargo. Was she an ass? No! The Bendoro would never have an ass for a wife. That wouldn't be seemly at all.

Over and over again, she tried to convince herself that she was not a beast of burden, but her heart would not be lifted.

The minutes passed, and she made no move to return to the house. After about fifteen minutes, her servant came out to find her. "I've been looking for you everywhere," she said immediately. "Your teacher is here, Young Mistress."

"Tell him I'm not having lessons today. I have a headache."

"He won't go until he does what he's been told to do. That's how he makes his living."

"Go away!" the girl snapped, but then, apparently startled by the shrillness of her own voice, quickly added: "I'm sorry, Mbok. Forgive me. I'm just upset."

The servant said nothing to this rebuke but left immediately. Now the guilt the Girl from the Coast felt for having yelled at the servant plunged her into deeper confusion. She rose quickly and followed the servant.

When she found the recitation teacher waiting for her, she told him, politely but firmly, that she would not be studying that evening.

"But, Young Mistress," he replied. "What will I say if the Master becomes angry with me?"

The girl wouldn't be dissuaded: "I won't be studying today, tomorrow, or the next day, either, not until the Bendoro returns."

After the teacher had gone, the girl retired to a chair in her room. When she saw her servant quietly enter, she pleaded: "Forgive me, Mbok. Don't be mad. I didn't mean to shout at you."

"A woman gets jealous sometimes," the servant told her. "That's natural. But even if you are feeling bad, you shouldn't try to make other people feel the same way."

"Thank you, Mbok," she replied, but then began to wonder: Jealousy, is that what she was feeling? Never having felt the pangs of jealousy before, the girl did not know they might be the cause of her pain.

"But where does the Master go for days on end like this?"

"That's a man's business, Young Mistress, and it would be best for you not to interfere. Women don't know about such things. Our work is here in the house. This is our territory, the area under our control."

"But I don't even know the area. Since coming here, I've never even been in the front or center rooms."

"Then let me show you, Young Mistress."

"What for?" she asked. But the servant's invitation had stirred her curiosity, and she rose from her chair.

The servant then led her out of her room and through the back room, past a huge set of doors—several times larger than any table she had ever seen in the fishing village—and into the center room. The room was huge. Looking upward at the expansive ceiling, she saw that it was covered with colorful flowered squares of tempered metal. In the very center, there was a much larger and more intricate design, a circular band of interwoven sheaves of rice, some of the heads of which fell out of the circle and onto the adjacent squares. From the center of the wreath, a brass pipe hung downward, and suspended from it was a chandelier with each of its electric lights ringed by crystal droplets, like diamonds on a woman's ear.

Beside the door was a small low table on which the girl noticed a large glass apothecary jar filled with water and something black clinging to its bottom. The girl looked closer. It was a mass of leeches.

"What is this doing here?" the girl asked.

"The Master uses them once a month to drain his blood."

"Why does he do that?"

"A Chinese healer told him to."

"Is he sick?"

"Yes, he is. He's called in several Dutch doctors, from Jepara and Semarang, but none have been able to find a cure."

"What's wrong with him?"

"Nobody knows."

The girl suddenly lost the desire to explore the house any further and stood quietly in the center of the room, her eyes still studying her surroundings: the glass display cases that lined the room's wall; the many plaques of calligraphic art; numerous carpets—of blue, black, red, and white—showing desert scenes with camels and horses. Separating the central hall from the traditional reception hall beyond was a mammoth set of doors. They were open, but their lower halves were hidden from sight by a large folding divider the double frame of which was made of intricately carved mahogany. Inside the frames were thatch screens of exceptionally fine bamboo fiber, in which was woven an ocean panorama of golden thread.

The girl looked around her, almost in awe. "It's so clean here. Do the children in the house ever play here?"

"No children are allowed in here. They stay in the kitchen. When they want to play, they play outside, in the front yard or across the street in the city square."

"Where is the baby that you were taking care of when I first came here?"

"He was taken away so that he wouldn't disturb you."

"I could take care of him," the girl suggested.

"Young Mistress, don't ever say that in front of the Master. Children are a very delicate subject in this house and a frequent source of argument, even though it's the servants here who have to look after them."

The girl didn't understand what the woman was telling her but chose not to pursue the issue further.

"In time, you'll have a son of your own, Young Mistress."

The very thought of having a child made the girl smile with pleasure and forget her feelings of jealousy. Her motherly instinct had been aroused. Even stronger was her desire to be a greater part of her husband's life.

"So who does the Master spend time with here?"

"No one. He receives visitors in the central room, but never any women guests."

"Why not? In my village, men and women call on one another."

The servant gave her mistress a look of pity. Long years of experience had taught her a great deal about the differences between ordinary people and members of the upper class on this part of the coast. A man such as the Bendoro who took a common woman for a wife was not considered married, even if the couple produced a dozen children. Such marriages were "practice marriages," rehearsals for the man's real marriage, a proper marriage to a woman of the same class. The Bendoro's marriage to a common woman made it impossible for him to receive as his guests married couples of the same upper class; the presence of his commoner wife would be seen as an affront.

"Why aren't you saying anything?" the girl asked.

"I was thinking, Young Mistress."

"About what?"

"About how much more fair it would be if everyone had a house this large."

"But then there would be no one to look after it!"

"That's right. A house would be a burden for everyone. Look at that . . ." The servant turned and pointed to a small table, on top of which was a small sandalwood box carved with butterflies and flowers. "That's the Master's medicine box."

"I don't understand what's wrong with him. He doesn't look sick to me."

"Would you like to see his room?"

Before the girl could reply, the servant opened a large door on the right-side wall. When the girl poked her head inside, the first thing to catch her eyes was a wooden stand with a row of ceremonial lances and spears. She immediately leapt back and turned away. "No, no, thank you very much."

The servant closed the door, and the two walked back toward the girl's room.

Outside, it was growing dark; the drums of the mosque and prayer house were calling.

At the door to her room, the girl suddenly found herself unable to contain her fears and anxiety. She stared at the servant, then spoke in a rush: "Is another woman going to take my place?"

"No, no, I don't know!" the servant hastily replied. Turning away from the girl's eyes, she quickly descended the back stairs and disappeared into the kitchen.

The past year had brought about a sea change in the girl's feelings. When she left her small fishing village she had taken with her fear and great uncertainty about her future. Arriving in the city and coming to the home in which she now lived meant entering a world completely absent of certainty. Previously, she had known the value of a service rendered, regardless of its recipient. But here, in this place, her services had no value; they were just part of the devotion shown by a loyal servant to her Master. She had once been able to speak freely to anyone and could, if she had so pleased, cast aspersions on the Bendoro, or anyone else for that matter. Now she was unable to speak, so careful did she have to be of not offending the Master's sensibilities.

Her servant was forever having to remind her, "No, Young Mistress, the Bendoro's consort cannot talk to just anyone. Just tell the people here what you want and don't be hesitant about it. What they might think or feel is irrelevant. They are here to serve you, just as I am, Young Mistress."

Gradually, the girl had come to see that in the Bendoro's house she was the proverbial queen whose wishes were her servants' commands. There was only one person who had the right to tell her what to do, and that was the Bendoro, her husband, her master, and her lord. Her young mind found it difficult to comprehend such a situation, where life was nothing more than orders and commands. She sensed that something important was missing: the simple pleasure that comes from working together. No one did that here. It was all just orders and commands, and there were those who issued orders and those who carried them out.

One day, feeling lonely, she asked her servant: "Why is it, Mbok, that no one laughs or smiles when I'm around?"

The woman looked at her with surprise. "Why ever would they do that? They're servants, here to do what you ask. And besides, it wouldn't be good for you to indulge in their laughter or smiles. The principal consort, Young Mistress, is like a mountain that cannot be moved, except by the Bendoro's hand. And the Bendoro cannot be moved by anyone with the exception of God the Almighty."

The girl pondered this.

"What is it, Young Mistress?"

"I must be stupid. I just don't understand."

"If it were that easy to understand, Young Mistress, everyone could be nobility."

"So where does that leave me?"

"You are the Bendoro's consort. Your position and power rest in his authority. As you yourself must know, Young Mistress, the path to honor and nobility is not open to everyone."

What the girl had once known in the village was that only the strong and powerful sailors were thought to be worthy of honor and respect. They sailed the seas and caught hundreds, perhaps thousands, of fish in their nets. And the fisherman that was shown the most respect was the one who brought the biggest fish home. He was the hero, but he would not sell his prize catch. He would divide the meat among the neighbors, leaving the backbone for himself, which he would place above the doorway of his house.

As a child, the girl and her friends used to stop outside the doors of the fishermen's homes and stare at the long and broad backbones of fish hanging above them. In her imagination she would add the fish's teeth and eyes to its bare skull. With the fish sometimes being two or even three times larger than herself, she could only guess how strong it must have been. Just once, she would have liked to have seen a creature like that brought alive to shore. But that had never happened; they were always dead. She had once begged her father to bring a big live fish home, but he had immediately silenced her with the harsh tone of his voice: "Even if you have the strength, never look death in the face unless you have to."

Although she wasn't sure of what he'd meant, a shiver of fear ran through her. That night, after her father had gone off with his friends to team up with the other fishing crews, she had joined her mother on the sleeping platform. She hadn't said a word but, during the night, had snuggled next to her mother, silently squeezing her until she had become disturbed and snapped at her: "You spoiled child!"

No, she hadn't been able to sleep a wink that night. Visions of monstrous fish, rulers of the oceans and all the smaller fish in it, kept swimming through her mind. She tossed and turned so much that her mother finally awoke and stared at her in the room's murky candlelight.

"What is wrong with you?" she asked.

Finally, the girl related for her mother the words her father had spoken to her and the thoughts that had kept her awake that night.

"Stupid girl!" her mother whispered, while softly slapping her cheeks. "Go to sleep. What are you thinking? You should never talk to your father about that. What are you trying to do? Make him afraid? Those fish are dangerous. And out in the sea, who's there to help? You could scream for a year and no one would ever hear you. The waves are louder than your screams. There are more big fish in the sea than fishermen. Their teeth are stronger than your father's spear. Do you understand what I'm telling you, child?"

Hearing this, the girl's hair stood on end. From then onward, she began to pray daily for her father's safety. From the experience, she had gleaned a hint of her father's courage—her very own father—and, thereafter, had never again suggested that he try to capture one of those giant and fearsome fish alive.

Her young mind began to make comparisons between the old and the new, between all that had been and all that was now. In the end, however, she was forced to quit this exercise; for she truly didn't understand anything at all, or so she thought. All she had were questions, the answers to which were forever outside her grasp.

"Why is everyone afraid of the Bendoro?" she had asked the servant one day. Why couldn't she be given a clear answer? Or was it that she was unable to understand the answer that was given to her?

She wanted to ask about courage. Where was the courage in the Bendoro? What with him being so thin and soft-skinned, so pale and delicate—where were his extraordinary features? But she couldn't ask such questions; she didn't dare. She listened in silence to the older servant as she patted herself on the chest like a person trying to convince herself that her memory could be trusted: "As you can see in the shadow plays, Young Mistress, on the battlefield, the giants are always defeated by the thin and delicate noblemen. And ogres, too, for all their fire and sharpened teeth, are felled by nothing more than the touch of a noble warrior's hand. While the ogre is jumping up and down, turning cartwheels and bounding to and fro, the noble warrior acts calmly, hardly moving from his place."

"That's in the *wayang* theater?" the girl asked.

"Don't you have shadow plays in your village?"

"We've heard about them, but in my village, nobody puts up pictures of *wayang* characters on their walls."

"Why not?"

"Once, when a man from the city came to the village with shadow puppets, the village elder got mad and hit the man with his cane. This made the man very angry. He cursed and clenched his fists; for a minute it looked like he was going to beat the old man. But then, suddenly, he seemed to lose heart and so he shoved him instead, making him fall down on the sand. 'Crazy old man!' he screamed at him. 'What did I do wrong? What's wrong with my shadow puppets?'

"When this happened, the two of them were on a small path that was hidden by bushes on each side. I was there and saw what happened, but nobody else in the village could see. Anyway, there was the elder, growling and moaning on the ground, so I went up to him to try to help him to his feet. When the city man saw me doing this, maybe he felt sorry for the old man and he helped me to lift the elder.

"After he was back on his feet, the elder then said to the city man: 'The problem with you, city man, the thing you're doing wrong, is that you're trying to trick us with those puppets of yours.'

" 'I'm not trying to trick you!' the city man shouted.

" 'That's exactly what you're doing,' the elder screamed back. 'You're here to sell us fairy tales. You're here to deceive the village people with bits of buffalo hide that you've carved and colored. You'll tell them your puppets are powerful, without comparison. But that's crap! The only power here is the sea, not any of those shadow puppets.' "

At this point, the girl's servant interjected, "That village elder of yours certainly was full of himself. If he were here and said that, he'd have the wind taken out of him so fast he'd never speak up again."

"But the fishermen in the village feel the same way the elder does, maybe even more so. They don't like the shadow theater at all. They won't even say the word *'wayang.'* "

"Then they don't understand, Young Mistress: The characters in the shadow theater are our very own ancestors."

The girl disagreed: "Our ancestors are gone, Mbok. It's the sea that is still here."

"But, Young Mistress," the servant argued, "if it weren't for our ancestors, even we wouldn't be here."

"The elder once said that everything comes from the sea, that there is nothing more powerful than the sea, and that our ancestors wouldn't have been here either if there first wasn't the sea."

"I don't know, Young Mistress, I just don't know," the servant mumbled with a distinct tone of annoyance in her voice.

Though the Girl from the Coast didn't realize it, all of her questions were, in fact, an expression of her jealousy. She wanted to know everything about the Bendoro, her master and husband, but lacked the courage to ask him herself.

"Don't be cross with me, Mbok. I was only asking," was her constant defense with her servant.

"But you make me confused," the servant would reply. "I've never heard such questions in all my life."

There were so many things the girl wanted to know: where the Bendoro went for days on end; whom he saw; what he talked about; what he thought of her. But from the scant amount of answers she found, she was forced to conclude that in the Bendoro's house, knowledge was very costly. And she had so much to learn: how to make batik, how to embroider, how to read, and how to recite the Koran. Learning about her husband and what he thought of her was yet another subject for her to tackle. In the village, she often heard women criticize their husbands and, at times, their criticisms led to arguments. But here, in this place?

"Have you ever lived in a fishing village?" the girl asked her servant.

"Yes, I have, Young Mistress."

"Husbands and wives act different there," the younger woman commented.

"I know. They eat together, sit together, drink together. And when the husband isn't off at sea, they talk about things together."

"They do, yes, they do, about everything: the seasons, the moon, the wind, the stars . . ."

"Indeed, Young Mistress."

"And about sails and oars, about how the man's net might have gotten caught on some coral or how he stepped on a sea urchin."

The servant smiled at her mistress.

"In the city, don't husbands and wives ever speak?"

"Well, in the city, in most every city, I'd say, it's usually the men who are in control. So the women there find themselves in a man's world. Maybe that's not the way it is in a fishing village."

"Then what do women have in the city?" the girl asked.

"I'd have to say nothing, Young Mistress, except for . . ."

"Except for what?"

"Except for her duty to guard her man's holdings."

"So what do women own?"

"Nothing, Young Mistress. She herself is property."

The Girl from the Coast knew this was true: In the Bendoro's house she was nothing more than his property. What she couldn't understand was why she should be viewed in such a way—as having no more value than a table, a chair, an armoire, or even the mattress on which certain nights she and her husband commingled.

Three days had passed since her husband's departure, and with each passing day, the jealousy eating away inside her grew stronger. On the fourth day, around four o'clock, just as the drum began to sound for the first evening prayers, the Bendoro returned. She heard his carriage stop outside the receiving pavilion. She then heard the creak of wheels and the clopping of hooves as the carriage passed slowly by her room outside. She heard the heavy slap of sandals in the central room. Her heart beat faster. She quickly closed the door to her room but did not lock it. Had he brought a new woman into the house? she asked herself silently. No, he couldn't have.

The girl sat in the chair and laid her head on the dressing table, staring wide-eyed at the door while waiting for her husband to appear. The door opened slowly. First she saw his face, with its pale skin and prominent nose, as he peered into the room. So tall and lean, he moved agilely to her side and leaned his head toward her neck. He whispered softly into her ear: "You're feeling fine, aren't you?" She closed her eyes.

She continued to wait, her body trembling from the pounding of her heart, but the face of the man she was waiting for did not appear again. No hand pushed open the door to her room.

A mysterious force lifted her body from the chair and drove her toward the door. She opened it slightly and strained to hear any words that might be spoken beyond the wooden barrier.

She could hear no female voice—only the sound of sandals shuffling heavily, back and forth, inside the room; the occasional sound of a door, opening and closing; and the scraping of the legs of a chair on the floor.

But then suddenly, she heard the sound of his voice, a call with a strange and threatening tone: "Mardi!"

Knowing immediately what this meant, the girl's heart shrank; the master's carriage was to be ready. He was leaving again.

How many more days must she wait for him to return? Tears suddenly welling in her eyes caught her unaware and she closed the door again, to return to her one and only constant refuge, the mattress and her pillow. If only her servant could provide such comfort! But the more she herself learned and the more clever she became, the less the woman could do to console her. And so she returned again to her protector, embracing the cold pillow with her arms. She began to think of her mother, her father, and her relatives, but then felt ashamed for not thinking of them more often.

God, how she longed for her husband. What kind of jealousy was this that could torture her so? Who was this person who could hold such sway over her husband, the powerful Bendoro? And who had the power to make him leave his house, travel for such a distance, and keep him enthralled for days on end? Oh, where were the answers?

As the time for twilight prayers approached, she still didn't know. And as the drum in the mosque sounded, she could still hear the Bendoro pacing the floor in his slippers. He hadn't left the house.

She rushed from her bedroom to the bathhouse where she ritually purified herself and then went into the prayer room where she sat waiting, and waiting, and waiting for her husband. But the distant door in the opposite wall remained closed. That door. What a door it was, she thought, so solid that it allowed no sound to enter the room, even though a single wall separated the *khalwat* from the main parlor.

When finally the door did begin to open, the girl quickly lowered her eyes, though not before she caught a glimpse of the figure she had longed for these past few days. He was wearing a new sarong, a red one with blue stripes. Without a glance in her direction, he began to pray. He had changed!

Then she, too, prayed. Wrapped in her white prayer gown, she felt safe, much safer than without it, for it concealed her body, her thoughts, even her feelings from prying eyes.

After prayer, she immediately returned to her room. She fixed her clothes and makeup, then went to the dining table to wait for her husband. Surprisingly, he appeared at the table much quicker than usual and he came straight to her.

"There's a guest for dinner tonight," he said softly, then stood in place, watching her.

She rose from her chair, bowed to him, then lowered her body and went back to the bedroom that was her cage.

Following the guest's arrival, she listened from inside her room to the conversation at the dinner table. When she heard the guest speak, she felt somewhat relieved; the person was not a woman. But what were the two men talking about during their meal? Was it about a possible new consort? Every fiber in her body strained to hear their words and to understand their meaning.

"Yes, there was a disturbance," the guest said.

"Those people show absolutely no gratitude, neither to God nor to the government. What hasn't the government done for them to safeguard their welfare? I'd say, sir, that it would be best to wipe them out."

She listened. That was the voice of the man she so longed for. There was no doubt.

"My thoughts exactly. You know, of course, that I was sent here by the Governor."

"What's that, sir?"

It was apparent that the Bendoro was listening intently.

"Yes, the Governor. The East Indies Council has resolved to settle the matter quickly but, before doing so, would like to learn the thoughts of the leaders here in Java about the recent disturbance in Lombok."

"Of course, I understand the reasoning."

"Yet you are the first one to speak frankly, a quality I admire. The other regents that I've visited, I dare say, don't even know where Lombok is."

"I share your admiration for frankness."

The two men then talked about war. The Girl from the Coast spoke softly to herself, as if memorizing a lesson. During the past year, in the time of her residence at the Bendoro's home, she had often heard talk of war, yet had never seen evidence of one. The war she had heard spoken of was far away, taking place in a distant land, the name of which she did not recognize and did not care to know. All she knew was that the place was somewhere across the sea, much farther in distance than her father could possibly sail in a day. The pounding of her heart lessened as she regained her sense of inner peace.

"Would you like to stay overnight, sir?" the Bendoro asked. "There is much we could discuss."

"But haven't you called for the carriage?" the guest responded. "No, I really must leave tonight. Tomorrow morning, I must prepare a report on the views of the Regent of Blora."

"And will you be traveling throughout Java?"

"Not the whole of the island. There are six of us who have been assigned to this task. I was given the northern coastal area to cover—not the entire northern coast, mind you, just that of Central Java."

"Then there won't be time to talk about another matter?" the Bendoro inquired. "There was something I had hoped to discuss."

"I'm afraid not," his guest replied.

The Girl from the Coast liked the sound of the guest's voice. It was strong, manly, a voice of command and knowing authority. With that kind of voice giving orders, she would be willing to carry out his commands, anything at all. With great care, she opened the door slightly and peered outside. Over the back of the Bendoro, she could see a young nobleman. He was small. His headdress, sitting high on his head with the ends of the cloth that protruded from the knot pulled slightly upward, was of a fashion not common among the coastal nobility. He held his neck straight, rarely lowering his head. His eyes sparkled and were much brighter and more interesting than any diamond, pearl, or emerald that she had ever seen. He was fairly dark-skinned and demonstrated great dexterity in the use of Western eating implements—the fork, knife, and spoon. The girl's heart beat differently now—softly and more soothing.

Suddenly conscious of what she was doing, the girl felt a flush of shame and closed the door again. She immediately picked up her knitting basket and began to work on a piece of embroidery.

When she heard the sound of the chairs in the dining room being pushed back, she stopped momentarily. A mysterious force drew her from her chair and to the door. She opened it slightly and looked out again. The young nobleman, now standing straight and tall, turned and began to walk out of the dining room toward the entrance hall.

Putting down her knitting basket on the vanity, she left her room and proceeded directly to the dining table. She sat down on the chair the young man had occupied, taking delight in the man's residual warmth that infused her entire body. She turned toward the kitchen to see her servant coming toward her. She quickly took a spoonful of rice and put it on the plate the guest had used, but before she could top it with a spoonful of vegetables the old servant was at her side. The woman's eyes scoured the girl's features and made her shrink inside.

"It's all right," she mumbled to the servant, "the Bendoro used this plate."

She herself didn't know if the old wives' tale was true—that one way to acquire for oneself the traits of a person one admired is to eat from that person's plate—but she could tell the servant did by her look of surprise when she saw the girl sitting in the chair of her husband's guest. Nonetheless, the servant's voice was calm: "Would you like some vegetables, Young Mistress? Or could I get you anything else?"

"No, thank you, really."

The servant then withdrew to the kitchen.

The girl spooned some vegetables onto the plate and began to eat slowly. She saw in her mind the handsome young nobleman and felt, if only subconsciously, his youthful energy and vitality. Though he had never seen her, his sparkling eyes had completely conquered her heart. A man like that would never leave his wife unattended, she thought. The leftover vegetables, the cooked kernels of rice on his plate tasted wonderful on her tongue. Who was he? What was his name? Where did he live?

The servant returned to the room to collect more dishes.

"Who was the guest?" the girl asked her diffidently.

"I couldn't say, Young Mistress, but I heard he's from Batavia."

"Batavia is such a large city. I'd love to see it."

"Everyone dreams of going there."

"When you're finished in the kitchen, will you come to my room?" the girl then asked.

"Yes, Young Mistress."

The girl rose from the table and went back to her room. Her

heart, which only a few hours previously had been pounding with jealousy, was now filled with something she couldn't quite describe. Was it hope? Surrender? Or possibly devotion to a man whose name she did not even know. Whatever it was, her heart now beat slowly and soothingly.

As it turned out, the guest did not leave the house immediately; instead, he spent several more hours with the Bendoro, talking with him in the front parlor. But the girl, in her room, could hear nothing of their conversation, except for the occasional peal of laughter that penetrated the rumble of the night wind off the sea.

"Are you asleep, Young Mistress?" the servant asked from her mat on the floor.

The girl's mind was still adrift. "What was that you said?"

"Are you tired?"

"Why do you ask?"

"The guest will be leaving soon, so you mustn't fall asleep. The Master was gone for four days. Four whole days, isn't that right?"

"Yes, four days," the girl confirmed.

The older woman spoke slowly, in a deep voice: "When the guest leaves . . ." She paused. Her voice then changed, revealing a much more strident tone: "Well, why is there any need for me to say anything?"

"Tell me a story," the girl said.

"Which one? The one about Solomon, perhaps?"

"No, not that one. Tell me about yourself."

"What's there for me to tell? I know that what most people like to talk about is themselves, but as for me, I wouldn't know where to begin."

"Tell me about your husband, Mbok. Did you love him?"

"What *are* you asking me, Young Mistress? Wherever is a

woman like me going to find love except from her husband? It's only my husband that I could ever love."

"Which one, the first or the second?"

"That doesn't matter, Young Mistress. First or second is not important."

"Did they ever beat you, Mbok?"

The servant didn't answer directly: "Sometimes I think that women were put on this earth just so that men could beat them. So let's not start talking about that, Young Mistress. Besides, what's a beating every once in a while when compared with the beating a husband himself must take in providing for his wife and children? Oh, if only God had granted me a child . . . One, a dozen, however many. What would a beating matter if I had children of my own? Just think of your own father, Young Mistress, and how he has to face death each day."

"I know, Mbok, that's true: every single day, and for what? A plate of rice mixed with corn."

"To talk to me about poverty, Young Mistress, is useless. That is something that's in God's hands."

"I know, Mbok, but there are so few people who *aren't* poor."

"What story do you want me to tell you, Young Mistress?"

"How about one where everyone is rich or everyone is poor?"

"That's impossible, Young Mistress. You shouldn't even think such a thing. It's blasphemy! You do know the meaning of 'blasphemy,' don't you?"

"No, but it sounds awful."

"It's like this: God created the earth and the heavens, the world and nature in its perfection. He created day and night, angels and devils, what is high and what is low. If He had meant for everyone to be rich, or everyone to be poor, what would be the meaning of alms or tithing? Where would be the master and where would be the servant? It would be the end of everything. Indeed, it would probably mean the end of the world, Young Mistress."

The girl harrumphed: "What an awful story you're telling me! Why don't you massage my legs instead?"

The older woman rose from her sleeping mat, pulled back the mosquito curtain, and began to massage the girl's feet.

"I really want you to love me," the girl whispered to the woman.

"Don't you think I do?"

"I want to make you happy," the girl said in reply.

"Don't you think I'm happy serving you?"

And so the two of them talked into the night, without either the girl hearing the words she wanted the older woman to speak—a simple and direct declaration of affection, unfettered by bonds of convention and politesse—or the older woman finding from her mistress an assertion of the appreciation she felt for her obedience and service, the very things through which she herself showed her affection. Though both felt something was missing in their lives, neither quite knew what it was.

At one point, the girl asked the older woman, "What if I were your daughter?"

The older woman paused in her ministrations.

"What's wrong?" the girl asked.

"You say anything that comes to mind," the woman scolded. "How could that ever be, Young Mistress? How could that possibly be?"

"But let's pretend. What would it be like then?"

"Don't do this to me, Young Mistress."

The older woman stopped massaging the girl.

"What is it, Mbok?" she asked while pulling herself into a sitting position. "What's wrong?"

When the older woman tried to turn away, the girl scooted around in front of her. She placed her hands on the woman's shoulders and felt them tremble beneath her touch.

"You're crying. Why?"

"Please permit me to go back to the kitchen, Young Mistress."

"First tell me why you're crying. What did I do wrong?"

"Please let me go, Young Mistress."

"Just tell me why you're crying."

"Because of what you asked, Young Mistress, because of what you asked. Haven't I been hurt enough?"

"Who could ever hurt someone as good as you, Mbok?"

"Who? My master, that's who!"

"You mean, the Bendoro?"

"No, not the Bendoro. Fate!"

The girl nodded silently.

"He took away my child. He stole my husband. And then, when I remarried, he stole that husband from me, too. What's going to happen to me? Where will I go when I can no longer serve the Bendoro? I'm not as young as I used to be, Young Mistress. Did you have to remind me of my age?"

"I'm sorry, Mbok. I didn't mean to hurt you. You still have me, don't you? You can stay with me as long as you like. And when you're too old to look after me, I'll take care of you."

The woman suddenly wanted to warn the girl, to tell her that the Bendoro could replace his principal consort twenty-five times in a day if he so wished without any recrimination on his own social standing, but she found herself unable to speak. Tomorrow, the day after, or at the latest, after she had given birth to her first child, the girl would probably be gone. The Young Mistress, through no fault of her own, could be turned out of the house at any time. And then what would she herself do? For the servant, the answer was clear: She would be forced to continue to make her own way in life and, just as she had done for longer than she wanted to remember, live off the pity of strangers, as a servant. The girl's suffering, she admitted, would of course be all the greater, even greater than her own. She would be forced to leave her child behind and not permitted to set eyes on him again. And if in the future, by chance, she should meet the child she had given birth to, she could never claim him as her own. He would be not her child but that of the Bendoro, whose status obliged her to serve him and to bow down before him.

Suppressing her own feelings, the older woman gently tried to enlighten her mistress as to what kind of life might lie in store for her.

"You mustn't think about me, Young Mistress. I'm nobody, just one of the lowly masses, so when I fall, it might hurt, but not all that much. You must always remember, Young Mistress, that the higher your position in life, the more it hurts when you fall. The higher up you go, the more deadly the fall. A person like me can fall a thousand times in a day but can still get back on her feet. For people like me, that's what life is: the struggle to keep standing on your own two feet."

The girl failed to grasp the woman's intent. "Tell me then, why do people fall? Is it because they're not careful enough?" she asked in complete innocence.

"That's right," the woman affirmed, "people fall because they're not careful, but you also have to remember, Young Mistress, that a person can't spend every moment of her life trying to be careful. There are times when you might start thinking about your mother or father, for instance, and forget that your first duty is to the Bendoro. We are God's creatures, but being weak, we sometimes forget our duties."

"And me? Is that what you're saying about me?"

The older woman hesitated. "Forgive me for saying anything, Young Mistress. I do not mean any harm."

"Please tell me, Mbok, what have I done wrong?"

"You've not done anything wrong, Young Mistress, it's just . . ."

The girl, seated on the mattress, stared at her servant, hoping for her to continue, but she merely bowed her head.

"Won't you tell me what's wrong with me?" she asked plaintively.

Her servant raised her head. "The same thing that's wrong with me. We were born common."

"So, what does that mean, Mbok?"

"That it's our fate to serve those of a higher station. Remember me telling you that without a lower class there would be no upper class?"

"So what am I then, Mbok?"

"Forgive me for saying this, Young Mistress, but you are a person of the lower class who, for the moment at least, has been hitched to the upper class."

"Then what am I supposed to do?"

"How many times have I told you, Young Mistress? You must serve your husband faithfully. You must bow to him and kiss the ground beneath his feet." She sighed. "Now let me tell you a story . . ."

"I don't want to hear a story now," the girl insisted. "I want you to tell me how to serve the Bendoro better. How am I supposed to bow before him?"

"You remember the story I told you about Trunojoyo when he tried to cross the Bengawan River?"

"Oh, I can't remember just now. And what does that have to do with the way I serve the Bendoro? I want to know how to improve."

"It's always possible to improve," the servant agreed. "Constant practice leads toward perfection. But there is one thing you must remember, Young Mistress: The greater the perfection the more obvious the minor flaws. How about the tale of Surapati? Wouldn't you like to hear about Surapati?"

"He was a slave, wasn't he?"

"That he was, Young Mistress, but he ended up becoming a king. He conquered all the other kings of Java and even defeated the Dutch army . . ."

"Tell me what's wrong with me!" the girl now demanded.

"The 'wrong' is neither in you nor me, Young Mistress. The 'wrong' is in what people think us to be." She stopped and held up her hand. "Listen!"

The girl pricked up her ears. From the front of the house came the crack of a whip. The Bendoro's guest was leaving.

"And so . . ." the girl begged for the woman to continue.

"There's no 'and so' about it, Young Mistress. Not tonight, not anytime. It's not proper for us to speak about the Bendoro. And now you must excuse me; the guest has gone, and I must be getting back to the kitchen."

Without waiting for her mistress to grant permission, the woman rolled up her sleeping mat and left the room.

The girl walked to the dressing table and began to straighten her hair. As she looked into the mirror, the tall, slim figure of her husband appeared behind her.

"My bride," she heard him whisper.

The girl turned quickly and dropped to the floor, first kissing his feet and then throwing her arms around his legs. When he lowered his body to sit on the edge of the bed, she raised his legs and pressed her face against the soles of his feet.

"I am yours," she said to him.

"Are you all right?" he asked, somewhat confused.

The girl repeated a line she had previously memorized: "I suffer from a longing I cannot endure."

"Is there something that might cheer you up?" he quizzed. "Gold? Jewelry? A fine piece of batik cloth?"

"Your well-being is all I ask for," the girl pronounced carefully.

Through her mind's eye, the girl watched herself, and in her ears the sound of the waves falling on the shore turned into laughter at her performance. For reasons unbeknown to her, as she pleaded her love to her husband, he took on the image of his guest that evening. The downy hair on her husband's legs became the gentle stroking of the young man's hand.

"Tell me how you are," the Bendoro said. "Do you have everything you need?"

"Now I do, with you here beside me. Your love is all that I need."

The Bendoro smiled. "Who's been teaching you to say these things?"

"No one. My own awareness is all, Bendoro, the realization that I am your servant."

"You are not my servant; you're my companion. Stand up, child. Now stand up next to me."

But the Girl from the Coast remained squatting on the floor. The Bendoro stroked her hair. He then got down off the bed and, with his hands placed beneath her armpits, lifted her up toward him.

"Come to me," he said.

"Yes, Bendoro."

He yawned. "I'm very tired. I want you to give me something to dream about."

"Yes, Master."

"Come up here with me now, on the bed."

"Yes, Master."

The girl climbed onto the bed, where she sat in thought.

"Aren't you tired, too?" he inquired.

"No, Master."

"Well, lie down beside me anyway."

Momentarily, the room was silent, but then the wind from off the sea began to shake the roof tiles overhead. And in this night, absent of human sound, the murmur of the sea as it rose, steadily pressing into the city, suffused the couple's hearts.

"Listen!" the Bendoro said.

"Yes, Bendoro."

"Tell me what you hear."

"The wind."

"Only the wind?"

"And the waves, Bendoro."

"Do you like the sea?"

"The sea, Bendoro, is my home."

"Listen."

"To what, Bendoro?"

"Don't you hear anything else?"

"Your voice, Bendoro."

"But nothing else?"

"No, Bendoro."

"Come closer to me."

"Yes, Bendoro."

"Now what do you hear?"

"The sound of your breathing, Bendoro."

"Come closer."

"Yes, Bendoro."

"And now?"

"What, Bendoro? The beating of your heart?"

"I can hear you breathing, too."

"Yes, Bendoro."

"And I can hear the beating of your heart."

"Yes, Bendoro."

"Tell me what else you hear."

The wind shook the roof tiles more furiously. The ocean waves rushed faster toward the town.

The Bendoro asked the girl, "Do you know the pine trees that line the coast? Did you know that even a wind this strong will not break them or cause them to fall? Do you know where they came from?"

"No, I don't, Bendoro."

"They were grown from the seeds of the pine trees that were brought in by the Dutch Governor-General when the Great Post Road was under construction. That was before I was born, but my father told me about it."

"Yes, Bendoro."

"What do you hear now?"

"The sound of your heart, Bendoro."

The Bendoro laughed. "That's right! The sound of my heart."

"It's beating fast."

"I know."

"What do you hear now?"

The girl didn't answer.

"Listen carefully."

"I'm listening, Bendoro."

"Hear something?"

Neither spoke for a moment. The wind had eased and they could hear, drifting to them from the banyan tree in the city square, an owl's melancholic cry. The waves sounded more threatening.

"Yes, Bendoro."

"What is it?"

"I hear you, Bendoro. I hear love speaking through your heartbeat."

He chuckled. "You are getting to be very clever. Who's been teaching you?"

The girl laughed softly.

"Tell me who."

"Your very own love."

"And how would you treat that love?"

"I would welcome it every time I hear the sound, Bendoro."

"Young Mistress, you still haven't asked if I brought you anything."

"I know, Bendoro." The girl paused. "But what else would I ask from my husband except his longing?"

"You might, for instance, ask me for batik, new pieces from Lasem and Pekalongan that I brought for you. I'm tired of seeing you always dressed in Solonese-patterned batik. You might think of changing your style every now and then. And pearls, Young Mistress. Have you ever seen pearls?"

"Never, Bendoro."

Delighted and surprised, the Bendoro burst into laughter.

"What? You, a girl from the coast, and you've never seen pearls?" He laughed again. "You know what we call them here? We call them 'diamonds of the sea.' Didn't your father ever collect them?"

"He never said anything about them, Bendoro."

The Bendoro continued to laugh. "It takes a great deal of bravery to harvest them, Young Mistress. You must dive to the bottom of the sea and look through the coral to find the oysters that are hidden there."

The girl felt as if a dagger had cut out a piece of her heart. Her heartbeat stopped and she stumbled through her reply:

"Maybe my father isn't brave enough to do that, Bendoro. He doesn't dive. I feel sorry for him, Bendoro. I feel really sorry for him. He doesn't go looking for pearls, but for rice and corn for the family."

"Well, that's wrong," her husband interjected. "You don't look for corn in the sea."

"I know, Bendoro. But maybe that's what fate is for the ignorant and the poor."

"Now I know," the Bendoro announced, "it's your Koran teacher who's been teaching you these things."

"No, Bendoro, it's not."

"Then who is it? Tell me."

"Someone once told me, Bendoro, that people in the lower class are always hungry and that it is for that reason their eyes see everything, their ears hear everything, and their hearts feel everything, even as they give their blood for everything."

"That's it! Starting tomorrow, I won't have that Koran teacher of yours coming here any more. And you, Young Mistress, are to stop this talk about upper and lower classes. We're human, all of us, set down on earth to obey the rules and commands of the Most Powerful. I won't have you talking about it anymore."

The girl said nothing in reply.

Her husband looked at her closely. "You are indeed a very clever girl."

As she lay beside her husband, the stories her maidservant had told her repeated themselves in her head, stories about the fate of commoners and the great deeds of noblemen; about the failure of the common people and the nobility of the upper class; about common people who gave their lives for their superiors; about power and about fate; about God the Almighty and the Dutch military. Her young soul had taken them in, absorbed them all, regardless of whether she understood them either in part or not at all.

She opened her mouth to speak: "Bendoro?"

"Yes?"

"May I ask you something?"

"Yes, but don't tarry; the roosters will be crowing soon."

"Why do you go away so often? You go for days on end and leave me here to suffer."

The Bendoro's attitude suddenly changed. His icy demeanor melted, and he spoke with a new and gentle warmth in his voice: "Why, you're jealous?!"

The girl bowed. "Yes, I am. I am jealous."

"When your father took his boat out, did you ask him where he was going?"

"No, I never did."

"Why not?"

"Because I knew that he was working."

"Then you should know that I am working, too."

"Yes, Bendoro."

"It's so very quiet; time for the roosters to start crowing."

The girl whispered faintly: "Oh, Bendoro, my master, my husband . . ."

At that moment, it was only the dancing wind that ruled the world. Time moved forward, sometimes creeping slowly, sometimes advancing in wild leaps.

The Girl from the Coast entered the second year of her marriage. Now, once a month, she was called by her husband to assist him in the central parlor. There, while he sat in a chair with his back to her, she would remove the leeches from their large apothecary jar on the side table with a pair of bamboo tongs and place them on the nape of his neck, on his temples, forehead, and arms.

The Bendoro would guide her placement of the leeches with his voice: "Yes, that's the spot."

"Here, Bendoro?"

"A little bit lower, about three fingers down. That's where I'm feeling stiff."

Each month it was that way: What started as finger-sized shriveled-looking creatures would—after one minute, five minutes, ten minutes, or even fifteen minutes of wriggling activity as they sucked greedily from the Bendoro's veins—transform into hugely swollen transparent balloons, their stomachs filled with a dark brown fluid. When the leeches could increase their girth no more, the girl would be ready with a sheet of rubberized netting in her hands to catch them as they dropped. She could not allow them to fall on the floor, to burst, or to be hurt in any way. She exercised extra caution when returning them to the apothecary jar. The job demanded great patience and care, but when it was over, the girl could be assured of hearing her husband thanking her and God for the usefulness of those primeval creatures.

The leeches, her husband liked to say, offered proof that even animals had trading skills and that, therefore, engaging in trade was no uncommon feat. He would grow excited even as he spoke to her about them: "Just look at them!" He pointed his finger at the jar. "That one is Kempul. That one is Karti and that one is Kutil. I don't know why I named him that. This one is Gempal and this one is Kunyuk. They're real traders, all of them. They take my blood and give me back my health. Don't you think they're fair-minded and virtuous characters?"

"Very virtuous, Bendoro."

"I don't get rich from what they give to me and they don't get rich from what I give to them. I think that's very fair."

"Yes it is, Bendoro."

"Now that their work is finished, you may go."

After being dismissed, she would sometimes go directly to her room, sometimes to the workroom where she made batik. But whatever her destination, she always felt disappointed when she left. This was now the second year of her marriage to the Bendoro, and still her wish had not been granted.

In hopes of better serving her husband, the girl had suppressed her thoughts about and longing for her parents and relatives in the village. She hoped to provide, in the eyes of her husband, complete and unblemished service and would allow nothing to deter her from that goal. She refrained from ever mentioning her family or village. Her personal servant had successfully taught her the ways of the true nobility, how to play the role of a superior, a member of the upper class.

Several times, her husband had asked if she would like to visit her parents, but she had always answered, "No, I would rather stay and serve you."

Her answer made him laugh contentedly. "But you are their daughter," he reminded her, "not just my wife."

"But now my duty is to serve you," she told him. "My parents can get along without my help."

"Do you ever send them messages?" he would ask.

"No, Bendoro," was her answer.

"Or money or food?"

"No, Bendoro."

"Why not?"

"I wouldn't dare, Bendoro. Not on my own."

And in the several times this conversation had taken place, this is where it would die, without continuation. Naturally, when she returned to her bedroom or her workplace the girl would immediately think of her parents and other family members and it would take an extra effort to expunge from her mind her great longing for them. Personal prayer seemed to be her only consolation. How very much she prayed that the situation would change, and that she would be able to repay the moral debt she owed her parents for all they had done for her, especially her father, who risked his very life to give his family their own.

Now it was the second year of her marriage, and she was almost sixteen, but the situation hadn't changed. She had begun to think matters through on her own. She had come to see that in the future she would have to make her own decisions and act on her own behalf. Increasingly, her personal servant was unable to provide what she needed, and because the answers to her questions were not forthcoming, she now had to think for herself. It was no longer enough for her to accept what she was told, without explanation; she wanted to know the reason why.

On one occasion, her servant had remarked: "For a young woman like yourself, there should be no problem getting along. You're very pretty, and forced labor is a thing of the past."

How that comment had riled her! She knew that the woman was mocking her, but she chose not to reply. She had indeed wanted to reply with equal sarcasm, but awareness of her own reliance on the woman made her hold her tongue.

It was around this same time that the Girl from the Coast asked her husband's relatives, the young men who lived in the house, to help her clean her room. The room's entire contents had duly been trundled outside for airing, and by evening the room had been scoured clean and its air scented with the smell of lime from drying whitewash.

After the furniture had been brought back into the room, she discovered that her wallet, which she usually stored in one of the drawers of her dressing table, was missing. This was a new experience for her; nothing like it had ever happened to her before. She knew her servant would not have taken it; the woman might only be a servant, but she would never, the girl was sure, jeopardize her position or her future in such a way.

When the girl discovered that her wallet was missing, she had never before felt such fear. Without the money in it, which she used to pay house expenses, how were they going to eat?

Immediately, any annoyance she might have felt toward her servant disappeared. Now, she knew very well, she needed the servant's help. The girl immediately called her and held her hands tightly as she explained what had happened.

As the woman listened to the girl, she stared at her mistress with a weary, dispirited look.

"I'm not blaming you," the girl hastened to say when she saw her servant's apparent dismay. "I know you wouldn't do it. You know that if you need anything, all you have to do is ask and I will give it to you. But you've never asked me for anything. It's simply that I don't know what to do. How are we going to eat? How am I going to replace the money?"

"Who do you think did it?" the older woman asked.

"How can I dare to say? It's all my fault," she muttered, "I should have been more careful. Aren't you the one always telling me that carelessness is as bad as dishonesty?"

"Besides the master's nephews, was there anyone else who entered your room?"

"No, no one."

"Sit down and be calm while I look into this."

After the woman left, the girl searched the room again, but without success. Her husband's young relatives were nobility, too. How could they possibly steal? The very thought troubled her immensely. Aristocrats, the nobility—these people were the upper class who, by birth and destiny, ruled the lower classes. It was inconceivable that they might steal. She tried to drive the thought from her mind. It was blasphemy to even think such a thing. Fate would not have it so. I must be wrong, she told herself. I must have forgotten where I put it. I'm the commoner here, one of the masses, a member of the lower class; it's only people like me who steal. None of the kitchen staff would dare enter her room. Why, they wouldn't even dare set foot in the main house. A thief in their midst? Who was the thief?

The girl felt herself trembling all over. She wanted to scream but forced her lips shut and called out silently: "Mama, Papa, forgive this daughter of yours. My beloved parents, forgive me. Where can I place the blame for what has happened? Not on a member of the upper class. No, I couldn't. They were born to rule."

The girl picked up a glass of tea from off the dressing table and gulped down its entire contents. This served to calm her momentarily, but then her servant came back into the room to announce, "I've called together the Master's nephews, Young Mistress. You must examine them."

"What?" the girl shrieked but, when hearing the piercing sound, immediately lowered her voice and spoke in a frightened whisper: "How can I do that? They're my husband's relatives."

"You must examine them," the woman insisted while leading her out the door. "You must ask them."

The servant woman could feel the trembling of the young girl's hand as they faced the Bendoro's relatives who had gathered outside her door. With no hesitation on her part, she immediately began to speak. The accusation in her voice was clear: "You mustn't cause trouble for the Young Mistress. All we want to know is who took her money. That was the shopping money for the house. So if it's not returned by tomorrow, no one here is going to eat. Not the Bendoro, either. That money must be returned."

The Bendoro's young relatives glared defiantly at the two women. The servant woman felt the quiver in the girl's hand and noticed the paleness of her mistress's features. She tightened her grip on the girl's hand to give her strength.

One of the young men, eyes blazing, immediately grew defensive: "Who do you think we are? Village people? Country hicks? Fishermen who don't even know what money is?"

Another joined in: "Yeah, what are you trying to do? Insult us?"

"No insult is intended," the older woman said. "Not at all. But we have a problem here. Who knows, the money might have been misplaced. But if the Bendoro hears of this, we're all going to suffer for it."

"To hell with you!" yet another hissed. "You treat us like starving thieves from some fishing village."

The girl, still unable to speak, now began to cry.

"We're educated. We've been to school."

"And you treat us like bandits!"

"Do you think tears can wipe away this insult?"

Unable to control herself any longer, the girl screamed: "I come from a fishing village. I'm the thief. It's me!" Her voice became a roar: "Yes, it's me! I'm the only one who could have done it. It's me, it's me, it's me," she moaned as she embraced her servant.

Unprepared for the outburst, the Bendoro's nephews looked at one another in fright. The kitchen staff stood in the doorway, their mouths agape as they watched the scene.

The girl's servant patted her mistress on the shoulders, an action that seemed to give herself more strength. She stared back at the young men. "All right, then, I take it that no one is going to confess. Maybe I'm just a villager, a servant here in this house, but at least I know what I must do."

All of the young men paled.

"Return the money now!"

None of the young men spoke.

"No? Well, then, I will straighten this out. You wait here while I call in a person from the village who will know what to do." She then began to lead the girl away toward her room.

"Wait!" one of the young men called. "Why don't we talk about this in a civilized fashion?"

The girl and her servant turned around, facing the young men again. The girl continued to bow her head in fear, but the servant gave the young men a challenging look. She spoke slowly, carefully enunciating her words: "What is there we have to talk about?"

"Are you going to the Bendoro?" the same young man asked.

"We have a duty to right a wrong. Isn't that true?" the older woman sparred.

"Who is this 'we'?" the young man then asked.

Another young man, the angriest-looking of the bunch, added: "I think you should first remember that we are the Bendoro's relatives. The villagers here can be gotten rid of at any time and die of hunger for all we care. We're the ones who live here. This is our place. A thousand villagers can come and go in the space of a day, but at the end, we're still going to be here."

The girl clutched the old woman tightly, whispering between her sobs: "I didn't come here because I was hungry."

"I know that, Young Mistress," she replied before conveying this to her master's nephews: "The Young Mistress did not come here to escape from hunger. The sea is deep and rich with food. It's only the human heart that's shallow and poor. Look at the high walls around this house. Do you expect me to believe the money just disappeared?"

"Are you saying we stole it?" one of the men asked. "Why not come right out and say it?"

"All I'm saying," the woman insisted, "is that the money must be returned. There are rules here, and if they can't be obeyed, then we had best call in someone to determine who's at fault."

"Who do you think you are, calling in someone to judge us? If that happens, it's you who is likely to receive the harshest sentence."

"For village people like me," she said to the young men, "being born into this world is its own sentence. There's nothing worse than the life of a villager. There's nothing more to talk about. Is that money going to be returned?"

The men were not going to back down. "If that's the way you want it, fine. Get your village judge and he can sentence you himself."

"All right, I'll do that," the servant responded. "Come with me," she said to her mistress as she led the girl toward her room.

In the late afternoon of that same day, the Bendoro returned home. After refreshing himself, he retired to the parlor where he reclined on a lounge chair. On the small table beside him was a crystal jar containing imported Dutch cookies. Beside it was a pair of silver tongs. The early-evening sun illuminated the Koranic commentary in his hands.

At that moment, the Girl from the Coast entered the room, her servant beside her, and approached her husband on bended knees. They stopped next to his chair but remained in a crouching position.

"Excuse me, Master," the servant intoned.

The Bendoro closed the commentary, then removed his spectacles and placed them on his lap. He pulled himself into an upright sitting position and looked down at his side to where the two women were crouched. "Yes?"

"I'm sorry to bother you, Master. I know that it's almost time for your evening prayers. I would never do anything to disturb your prayers, but there is a problem, a problem of money, Master, that needs to be addressed."

"Money? Did the Young Mistress lose some money?" he asked.

"I'm sorry . . ." was all the girl could say. She bowed lower and lower until her head touched her hands that were stretched outward on the floor before her.

"I see, you've been careless," her husband said before waiting to hear more. "Money is a gift from God. Even so, it does not fall from the sky."

"I'm sorry," the girl repeated, even more softly.

He looked at the servant. "So the Young Mistress lost some money. What are you making a fuss about?"

"The money, Master, it's gone."

The Bendoro's voice betrayed impatience: "I know it's gone. So what's the fuss?"

The older woman said no more. Her arms, supporting her torso, began to shake, causing her body to sway.

"Mardi!" the Bendoro called.

From a distance came the houseboy's reply. Moments later, the young man appeared at the doorway. Raising his hands to his forehead, he bowed and lowered himself before advancing toward his master in a crouched position.

When Mardi was directly behind the two women, the Bendoro spoke to him: "Call my nephews here."

Mardi bowed again and then removed himself from the room.

Soon afterward, the Bendoro's nephews began to appear, one by one, at the rear doorway of the room. Without bowing, they approached their kinsman and sat down cross-legged on the floor beside the two women. They lowered their eyes toward the floor.

The Bendoro spoke to them in a flat voice. "Some money is missing. Who took it?" he asked, without even looking at them.

No one answered.

"Is there no one who will answer?"

Again, there was no reply.

A soft chuckle emerged from the Bendoro's throat. The girl looked up and watched her husband, whose eyes were on the commentary in his hand. He spoke as he read: "From the time of the prophets, the devil has always had his tools. Thieves!" he snorted. "As long as the devil exists, there will always be thieves. But even thieves need to be shown some respect, especially since they themselves have no self-respect." He then snapped the book shut with a loud plop.

As if wakened by the sound, all of the young men present looked up; but when they saw the Bendoro glaring at them, they lowered their eyes again.

"Who didn't understand what I just said?" the Bendoro asked threateningly.

The young men bowed their heads still lower.

"I see, then you all understand. That's important to know. I'd like to find out who among you can tell me the meaning of 'honor'."

No one answered.

The Bendoro turned his head toward one of the young men: "Abdullah, you tell me."

The young man didn't speak.

"A question is made to be answered, Abdullah," the Bendoro

said softly. "How many years have you been living here? Seven, isn't it? Yet you will not answer my question? I want to hear your answer. That's all; it won't cost you anything."

"I know that, sir."

"Then tell me the meaning of 'honor'."

There was still no answer.

"You know the meaning of 'thief', I presume?"

"Yes, Uncle," Abdullah answered.

"But you don't know the meaning of 'honor'?"

Yet again, there was no reply.

"Then what have you learned from your religious studies? Do you really not know the meaning?"

The youth appeared to be dumbstruck.

"Then you have no honor?"

"No, Uncle, that's not . . ."

The Bendoro cut him off: "Then you are a thief!"

"No, sir, I'm not a thief. I know the meaning of 'thief' and I'm not one."

"Well, if you're not a thief, what does that make you?"

"There is no proof of me being a thief, sir," the young man protested.

"Who is your religious teacher?"

"Haji Masduhak, Uncle."

"And what do the prophets suggest to do if no proof exists?"

"To take an oath, sir."

"Are you willing to take an oath?"

"That is for you to decide."

He looked at one of the other young men. "Karim! Haji Masduhak is your teacher, too, isn't he? Tell me, Karim, what he has to say about hypocrisy."

"I'm sorry, Uncle, but I didn't memorize that."

"How old are you, Karim?"

"Nineteen, Uncle."

"And what class are you in?"

"The sixth form, Uncle."

"Come here and stand in front of me."

Remaining in seated position, Karim edged his way forward until he was in front of the Bendoro, but he did not stand up.

"Didn't you hear me, Karim? Stand up!"

"I'm sorry, Uncle," he said but remained seated.

He then spoke to another nephew. "You, Said, is your religious teacher the same as Abdullah's?"

"Yes, Uncle."

"The same as Karim's?"

"Yes, Uncle, Haji Masduhak."

"Did he ever teach you about the signs of hypocrisy?"

"He did, Uncle."

"And do you remember what they are?"

"Yes, Uncle."

"So, tell me then, since Karim refused to obey me, would that be called hypocrisy?"

"Not according to our teacher, Uncle."

"Then what is hypocrisy?"

"For one to appear to be loyal and virtuous when in fact he's not, Uncle."

The Bendoro now stared at Karim: "Why did you take the money?" he asked forcefully.

Karim studied the floor with his eyes.

The Bendoro now addressed the entire group: "All of you, except for Karim and the two women, may leave."

All of the young men except Karim edged backward toward the door, not standing until they reached it. Thereafter, they turned and left the room.

"Karim!" the Bendoro barked.

"Forgive me, Uncle. Forgive me for my mistake."

"That was no mistake, Karim."

"Forgive me, Uncle."

"Didn't you hear me, Karim? That was not a mistake. Now you listen to me: Your parents sent you here and I opened my house to you. I gave you the best education possible. I brought in the best religious teacher in this city. I gave you the best education in the world. What is not better than the teachings of Allah and His prophets? If that's not enough for you, then go and find a better teacher. Go! Leave! I never want to see your face again as long as I live. Get out of here!"

Without another word, Karim stood and left the room. The two women watched him leave.

When he had left the room, the Bendoro addressed the servant: "Mbok, I can see that you're a person who would fight evil with your bare hands if you had the strength, or with your tongue if you were able. But not having those gifts, you use your heart. You might not win, but at least you can be said to have tried."

"Yes, Master."

"That is very good. Who taught you to do that?"

"Just my feelings, Master; that and years of experience."

"Unfortunately, it appears that feeling and experience are insufficient."

"Of course, Master."

"Do you know your mistake?"

"I believe I do, Master."

"Then I would like to hear what it is."

"My mistake was that in trying to be loyal to you and in doing everything that was required of me, I was brazen enough to accuse your nephews of committing a crime."

"In a nutshell!"

"Yes, Master."

"So you know what your punishment must be."

"For people like me, Master, there is no punishment except life itself."

"That is blasphemy! Are you not grateful to God?"

"Yes, Master."

"You must leave this place. From this day forward, you need never set foot in this house again. I don't want to see you come anywhere near."

"Yes, Master."

"No!" the girl screamed. She clutched her servant's hands. "Forgive her, Bendoro. Please forgive her," she pleaded.

The Bendoro answered curtly: "Don't make a scene! Now go back to your room alone."

From her seated position, the older woman bowed and then backed out of the room. The Girl from the Coast followed suit. Leaving the room, they found, waiting for them outside the parlor door, the Bendoro's nephews, all with the same defiant look on their faces as before.

"What did I tell you?" one of them taunted.

"It's you who got the boot."

The older woman said nothing. The girl quickly pulled the servant away from the group and into her bedroom. There, she held the woman tightly. "You knew this would happen, didn't you? Why did you do it? What am I going to do without you?"

The older woman spoke wistfully: "Let me tell you a story, Young Mistress, probably the last story I'll tell you. You remember the one I told you about my grandfather who followed Prince Diponegoro in his war against the Dutch? You remember that one, don't you? Well, the junior district chief at that time gave my grandfather a very valuable piece of advice. He told him, 'You must not pledge your service to me. If I should die before you, who then would you serve? Another overlord? And if he were to die, what would you do then? You must pledge your service to the land.' That's what the man advised. He said, 'It is the land that provides you sustenance and drink. Sadly, the kings and princes and regents of Java have sold this sacred land to the Dutch. And now, to regain it, you must fight them, but that is not a job that can be easily done, and it will take more than just one generation to complete. Only then, after you have defeated the feudal rulers, can you face the Dutch. Imagine how many generations it will take to defeat them! Even so, the job must begin.' "

The girl held the woman's hand tightly. "I don't know what you're trying to tell me, Mbok. All I know is that I don't want you to go. And if you go, I want to go with you."

"No, Young Mistress, that is one thing you cannot do. You'll soon come to understand the advice that was given to my grandfather. My father passed it on to me and now I pass it on to you. You might not understand now, but experience will soon teach you. I pray that God will always watch over you." That said, she quickly left the room.

Now alone in her room, the girl felt completely bereft of strength and energy. Her breath came in gasps as she curled up in her chair, her chest rising and falling while her arms lay listlessly on the table. Through her swollen and bloodshot eyes she could barely see the mirror in front of her. In her mind, she turned over and over the servant's final words to her as if they were a mantra, but she could not grasp their intent. Her father had always uttered a mantra before going out to sea. She hadn't known its meaning, either.

After the Girl from the Coast's personal servant was dismissed, the days crept by sluggishly for her in the high-walled, fenced-in building she now called home. While previously she had rarely spoken because she was not permitted to speak, now she was silent because she had lost her desire to talk. She couldn't understand why her servant had been dismissed. "A person as good as that . . ." she kept repeating in her mind.

To soothe the irritation of the slow-moving days, the girl immersed herself in her batik work. She wanted to give a length of batik to the servant, but no one in the house even knew her real name, much less where she lived or where she might have gone. Unless they were relatives, the people who left the Bendoro's house were like ghosts, it seemed, able to vanish without a trace. Maybe she was the only person there who still thought about the older woman.

That year, the rainy season began earlier than usual, heralded by the arrival of brisk winds which, suddenly and unexpectedly sweeping into town from the northeast, carried with them light debris: sand from the beach and topsoil from the city square that now, after the months of dry weather, was almost barren of grass. The sand bore into the house, through doors and windows, to be deposited, a fine layer of grit, in her room, in her armoire, and even on the food. In the village, the girl remembered, this time of year would be a time of intense prayer. This practice was something she herself had never taken seriously before, but now, at the Bendoro's house, she felt an intense and almost incessant urge to beseech God to keep the wind from blowing too fast, to prevent the waves from rising too high, to tame the sea's fish, and to protect all sailors and fishermen from danger.

One morning, a group of four women came to the house. Drenched from the pouring rain outside, they were immediately taken to the kitchen to dry themselves. Afterward, Mardi brought one of the women to the workroom where the Girl from the Coast was making batik.

"Young Mistress," he said as a way of introduction, "this young woman is to be your new servant."

Not responding to the houseboy, the girl put down the small brass wax writer in her hand and loosely rolled the half-finished cloth on which she'd been working. After hanging it on the drying stand, she turned to the young woman.

"What is your name? What should I call you?"

"My name is Mardinah, Young Mistress."

"That doesn't sound like a village name."

"I was born in the city, Young Mistress, in Semarang."

"How old are you?"

"I'm fourteen, Young Mistress."

"Are you married?"

"I'm divorced, Young Mistress."

The girl was momentarily stunned. She looked at her new servant. Mardinah was taller than she was and had a bright and carefree look on her face. She exuded a certain confidence that was apparent in her movements.

"Where did you work before coming here?"

"At the Regent's house in Demak, Young Mistress."

"Why did you leave there to come here?"

"The Regent's daughter ordered me to come here, to work in this house, Young Mistress."

"What does the Regent's daughter have to do with me or this house?" the girl asked.

"How would I know, Young Mistress?" she said with a pout. "I'm just following orders."

"You're much too pretty to be my servant, and far too young."

The girl was startled by her own words and surmised immediately that this young and carefree servant standing before her was well aware of her own attributes. Why was she here? the girl asked herself. She had come to be suspicious, a trait alien to her life in the village. She thought of the older woman, her former servant. What would she have done in such a situation? No! Now she had to think for herself, to act without anyone else's assistance.

Why had this fourteen-year-old girl been sent to her? she asked herself. Her former servant's advice echoed in her mind: "You might not understand now, but experience will soon teach you."

Yes, she could see that she was now beginning to understand, and because of that, to grow suspicious.

No more than two days after Mardinah's appearance at the house, something precipitous took place. It happened in the evening, when the Girl from the Coast, not feeling well, was resting in her room. Mardinah came into the room and sat down in the chair between the vanity and the bed.

The girl gave her new servant a look of annoyance and surprise. "Come here a second," she said, and motioned for Mardinah to come closer.

Mardinah rose from the chair then sat down on the edge of the girl's bed.

"Didn't your former employer get angry with you for sitting in a chair?"

"She never saw me," Mardinah stated flatly.

"Did she ever get angry with you for sitting on her bed in this way?"

"She never saw me do that, either."

"I'm not angry with you . . ."

Before the girl could finish her sentence, Mardinah interrupted: "Well, of course not. Why should you be?"

The girl's boldness was astounding, so unlike the behavior of any other servant in the house.

"Why do you say that?"

Mardinah looked at the girl without bothering to lower her eyes. "Because you're not my employer."

"Then who is your employer?"

"The Bendoro, to be sure."

"Then what am I?"

"You're a villager, aren't you?"

The girl's heart began to race. She immediately rose from her reclining position and stared at Mardinah, who stared directly back, not looking away at all. The girl, upon seeing the gleam in her new servant's eyes, became frightened and anxious. Nonetheless, she tried to keep her voice even: "You're right, I am a villager and I have no regrets about coming from a village. But now tell me who you are."

"Well, I'm not a villager. At least that should be obvious." Mardinah seemed to find the very possibility upsetting.

"What, is there something wrong with being a villager?" the girl asked her.

"Why, they're all coolies."

For the second time, the girl felt her pulse race. As fear spread through her, she tried to muster the strength to calm herself.

"Well, tell me then, why did you come here?"

"Clearly not just to wait on you," Mardinah stated.

"Then what are you doing in my room?"

Mardinah opened her eyes and smiled but did not answer the girl's question. Her teeth were straight and even, a brilliant white not the least stained by betel nut.

"I can read and write," she said instead, before looking directly at the girl. "Can you?"

Yet again, the girl felt a shock run through her.

"What does your father do?" Mardinah asked the girl. "He's a fisherman, isn't he? My father's a retired scribe."

Mardinah laughed when she said this, causing another tremor to run through the girl, who then proceeded to get out of bed and inspect the armoire and the drawers of her dressing table. After making sure they were all locked, she left her room with Mardinah still in it and went to the back garden.

Because of an earlier rain, the soil of the garden was deep brown; chips of coral, embedded in the coastal earth, made it shimmer in the sun. Steam rising from the sun-warmed soil had made the air heavy, which made it difficult for the girl to breathe. She sat down on the garden bench, beneath the mango tree, where she had sat with the Bendoro shortly after her arrival at the house.

Once again, the girl recalled her former servant's final words to her. This was a new beginning for her, or so it seemed, and she didn't know what to think or who to turn to for advice. She wasn't prepared for this kind of confrontation—first with the Bendoro's nephews and now with the new servant girl. Such a thing would never have happened in her village. One by one, the members of her family appeared before her eyes: her father raising his net and jumping from his boat onto the shore; her mother pounding dried shrimp; her older brothers patching the rear of the boat while her younger brother retouched the paint on the carved sections of the ship's bow and stern. And she saw herself, too, cooking a meal of corn and rice. Corn and rice! That was two years ago. In this place, in the Bendoro's house, she never cooked, never had to grind chili peppers for *sambal* sauce, never had to wash the plates or scour the mortar and pestle. The fishing village had disappeared from her life and, along with it, the boundless sea. Her world was now her bedroom, a space just a few square yards in which she might move about.

Out of the blue, the image of Mardi, the Bendoro's majordomo, came to mind. Perhaps she could ask him to convey her feelings to the Bendoro. But then, just as suddenly, she discarded the notion. "No! I must settle the problem myself," she resolved. "I will not upset the household. I will not have the Bendoro burdened with my complaints. No! I will settle the problem myself," she again swore, "and any other problem that arises—all by myself!"

The girl rose to her feet, huffing as she did, walked briskly up the steps off the back of the house, and headed directly to her room. There she found Mardinah resting lazily on her bed. Not breaking her stride, she went directly to her. "Get up, city girl!" she demanded. "At least in the village, where I come from, it's impolite to sleep in someone else's bed without their permission!"

Mardinah giggled and rose with a shrug.

"I suppose you think you can lie down or put your body anywhere you please."

Apparently immune to the girl's criticism, Mardinah simply laughed. She then raised her hand and pointed at her own chest. "This is my body, Young Mistress, and nobody else's, and it's up to me to do with it whatever I please."

The girl was shocked. "No, it's not up to you, not completely. I want you to leave this room and never come in here again!"

The smile vanished from Mardinah's face. Fire was in her eyes. "No villager is going to give orders to me!"

The girl jabbed her index finger between Mardinah's eyes and pushed. "Get out!"

Mardinah slapped aside the girl's arm, but she then raised her other hand, placing her other index finger on Mardinah's forehead. Bucking her head back, she shot a gob of spittle directly on Mardinah's nose.

In the week that followed this incident, Mardinah kept out of the girl's room and the girl's way. She spent her time in the kitchen, but because she was not part of the kitchen staff, she did nothing but sit around and talk to the workers there.

Every morning, the girl would leave her room and go to the kitchen to watch over the preparation of her husband's meals. She would taste each dish to make sure that it was to his liking, help to set the table, and then retire to the workroom and her batik. During that week, she watched the servants' every move but spoke not a single word.

Then one morning, when going into the kitchen, the girl found Mardinah waiting for her behind the door. Mardinah wanted to speak to her, that she could tell for sure, but the girl gave her no mind and went straight to the hearth. After she had finished her business and was ready to return to the main house, she noticed Mardinah, still standing, waiting for her, by the door. This time Mardinah attempted to stop her as she passed—"Young Mistress, I . . ."—but she did not bother to turn her head.

As the girl made her way into the house, Mardinah raced ahead and blocked her way.

"Young Mistress," she began anew, "I need you . . ."

The girl looked blankly at her. "What? Am I your servant?"

"No, of course not, but I am not your servant, either."

"Then leave, get out of here. What I need is a servant, nothing more."

"I could help you, Young Mistress."

"I don't need your help. I know why you're here and will talk to the Bendoro about it myself."

Mardinah was silent now, confused, it seemed, and not knowing what to do. The girl used the opportunity to brush past Mardinah and walk on to her workroom.

No sooner had she positioned herself on her low stool, where she sat when making batik, than Mardinah came into the room, carrying a set of batiking implements and materials of her own. She, too, readied herself to work. After blowing through the fine spout of the wax writer to clear it of any dust, she turned toward the girl. "Young Mistress," she whispered.

"What are you doing here?" the girl asked her.

"Making a batik cloth, Young Mistress."

"Who's paying you to be here?"

Mardinah paused as if studying the question before dipping the small bowl of her wax writer into a pot of melted beeswax. After carefully positioning the writer over a piece of white cloth, she began to draw an eagle's beak. Only then did she speak, this time not waiting for the girl to cut her off: "Young Mistress, you can read, can't you?"

Well aware of her disadvantage in this respect, the girl said nothing.

"I have a letter for you."

"I don't need a letter, from you or anyone."

"But this letter is very important."

"There's nothing important for me except one thing."

"Nothing? Not even love?"

"No. I serve the Bendoro, nothing more."

"Then you're stupid," Mardinah retorted. "All the wives of important men have their own pastimes. Some like to play cards, others take lovers, but all you do is stay at home, like you're sick or something."

The girl paused in her work. Unexpectedly, the image of the

young man who had visited her husband that one time came to her mind. She smiled briefly to herself, then refilled her writer in the wax pot. But then, just as she was moving her arm toward her cloth, Mardinah announced: "I was once married to an important man."

The girl's movement was suddenly arrested, causing her writer to slip from her fingers and fall to the floor. The hot wax inside the receptacle spilled out and onto the floor where it immediately began to congeal.

"If you drop your writer when making batik," her former servant had once told her, "you must stop work immediately. It means the devil is trying your mind. Stop and turn your thoughts to the Bendoro."

The girl emptied the writer of its contents and put the tool inside a cigar box. Glancing at Mardinah, the girl noticed that she was smiling. After hanging the cloth on the drying rack, she rose to her feet and looked again at Mardinah; the smile was still on her face.

"Who are you thinking about?" Mardinah asked the girl.

The girl was startled and confused. Could Mardinah read her mind? Had she seen the image that appeared before her? She turned away, avoiding Mardinah's eyes, and walked out of the workroom to her bedroom. Sitting in her chair, she thought about what had happened. She brushed her face with her hand—once, twice, three times. She wanted to talk, to share her thoughts with someone, but there was no one in the house for her to talk to except for Mardinah, and speaking with her was out of the question. For the past few nights, the Bendoro had not come to her room, and she herself had been so tired, she hadn't had time to think through the matter at hand before she fell asleep.

She wanted to see her former servant, to put her questions to her and to learn what the woman was now doing. But the only person available to her for discussion in this house was Mardinah.

"Mardinah," the girl called loudly.

"Yes, Young Mistress," came the sound of Mardinah's reply. A moment later, she entered the girl's bedroom and stood somewhat distant from her side.

"Tell me what you had wanted to say," the girl began.

"I know of a young and handsome man who would like to meet you."

"Is that all?"

"I have a letter for you from him. Do you want me to read it for you?"

"No. I don't want or need the letter, much less have it read for me," the girl stated forcefully. "Is there anything else you wanted to say?"

Mardinah was surprised by the girl's response. "Don't you want to know what it says? Don't you want to answer it, Young Mistress?"

"No, I do not. Is there anything else?"

Mardinah was tongue-tied.

"When will you be leaving this house?" the girl then asked.

"You can't order me out of here. This isn't your house."

The girl was astounded by Mardinah's abrasiveness. "Then what am I? Who do you think I am?"

"Well, you're a concubine."

"Oh, a concubine is it? And yourself? What are you?"

"A servant."

"I don't need a servant like you. When can I expect you to leave?"

"I'll speak to the Bendoro myself."

"Oh, will you? When are you planning to do that?"

"I don't know, sometime."

The girl grew more self-assured. "I see no need to put it off. Let me take you to see him now."

"That won't be necessary."

"But I must accompany you. The Bendoro hasn't ever been introduced to you, has he?"

"No, there's no need," Mardinah protested. "I'll go, but not right now."

"Fine. Then I'll take you to see him at two o'clock this afternoon."

The girl was growing angry. She looked over at Mardinah, who remained standing facing her at a distance. "Who is paying your salary here?" the girl then asked.

"You are, Young Mistress?"

"If you think that, you're wrong. If you want to be paid for being here, you can ask for it from the Regent's daughter, your real boss. I know who you are and why you came here. You were sent here to make trouble."

"That's not true. I was sent here to help the Bendoro."

"What do you mean by that?"

"Because it's not right for him to keep on taking village girls for wives," Mardinah sputtered.

The girl paled as she tried to catch her breath. She knew she lacked the strength to rise, to hold herself erect among the nobility. She grasped the edge of the dressing table with her hands, but its hard marble top would not infuse her with the strength she so desperately needed.

Recognizing the girl's plight, Mardinah pressed her advantage: "So, now you know why I'm here, Young Mistress, and I don't care. I was sent here by a person of higher status than your Bendoro. It's been decided that it's time for him to marry a woman of royal blood. In Demak, where I come from, there are many such women available. He would have his choice. Even four, if that is what he wanted."

The girl's breath became stuck in her throat and she whispered weakly: "Stop, stop. Go away. Don't come near me again."

Mardinah shrugged. "Thank you, Young Mistress. I believe I'll go to the kitchen."

The girl didn't bother to watch Mardinah leave and could barely hear the sound of Mardinah's footsteps as she walked away. She sensed that Mardinah had stopped at the doorway to look at her, but she didn't move.

"The only thing that's permanent here is the Bendoro himself," her old servant had once told her. "He and the gods, that is. Everything else is temporary, with no steady base. My own birth was punishment."

The sound of her servant's voice resounded in the girl's ears. Was it a sin to have been born a commoner? the girl silently raged. And if so, why was it a sin? What was wrong with it? Without realizing it, she had begun to cry. She wept for all common people, but especially those who had been born in a fishing village.

I must think this through myself, the girl reminded herself. "You might not understand now," the older woman had said, "but experience will teach you well!"

But then, the woman had gone, and now, at the age of just sixteen, she, this girl from the coast, had to think for herself.

She thought of her home, her fishing village so far away, and of former days that were filled with laughter; of sweat flowing freely from labor gladly given; of muscled arms, dark from the sun; and of hands, both gentle and strong, lending needed assistance.

Here, in this house, all she could do was cry. Here, in this place, there was only struggle. And for what? In this house, everyone was a beggar, forced to ask for both respect and rice. In the fishing village, one had to work and sweat, but that alone did not ensure a person respect. It didn't even ensure steady meals of rice. A small plot of ground was the only thing one could realistically hope for. Respect? Rice? What a high price one had to pay for those things in this place. And she was only sixteen.

In the end, the girl decided to talk to her husband. It was a Sunday. The next time he stayed overnight in her room, she decided, she would pour out her feelings to him. She would ask him about both Mardinah and her own position.

Several nights passed with the girl lying awake, waiting for her husband to come. But during that time, after taking his evening meal, he retired to the parlor, sometimes without even acknowledging her. The next day was Thursday and she knew that he would not visit her room that night, not with the week's day of prayer starting in the evening. So, when Friday passed, she waited for Saturday, but still he didn't come. The next Sunday came, then went. So, too, Monday, and so on until another week had passed. Then finally, one night, a full fifteen days after her conversation with Mardinah, she heard the distinctive sound of his gentle knock on her door.

The girl rose and opened the door for her husband, who went directly to the bed. After relocking the door, the girl sat down in her chair. She appeared to be dazed. She had lost the courage to speak.

The Bendoro looked at her questioningly. "Are you sick?"

"No, Bendoro."

"It's late. Come to bed." He motioned for her to join him on the bed.

The girl rose but then sat back down again, her head bowed.

Her husband then got out of the bed and went to her. "You're pale."

"Yes, Bendoro."

"Are you sure you're not sick?"

The girl shook her head and looked at her husband momentarily, but then lowered her eyes again.

"Are you missing your parents?" the Bendoro coaxed.

The girl released a mournful sigh. She still didn't have the courage to tell him what she felt.

The Bendoro placed one hand on the girl's shoulder and with his other hand gently stroked her hair.

"I know you want to speak. Tell me what it is."

The girl felt a little braver, but her tongue felt numb and a knot of fear locked her jaw in place.

"Speak to me, I'm listening."

"Bendoro?"

"Yes?"

"Why was Mardinah sent here?"

"To help you."

"Who is she?"

"A distant niece, Young Mistress."

A relative of her husband? The girl could not continue. She had no right to complain. She stood and listlessly made her way to the bed.

When the Bendoro lay down beside her and held her in his arms, warm tears flooded the girl's cheeks. The Bendoro caressed the girl, using his hand to wipe away her tears. Suddenly he stopped and sat up. Light from the lamp overhead, filtered by the mosquito net, allowed him to study the girl's face.

"Why are you crying?" he asked.

The girl tried to speak but could not.

"What is it?"

"It doesn't matter, Bendoro. Forgive me."

"But I don't understand."

"Forgive me, Bendoro, but may I, may I ask you something? Just don't be angry with me."

"I won't be. Just tell me what it is."

"I want to see my parents," the girl confessed.

"Is that why you were crying?"

"I just want to be allowed to go home to see my parents, Bendoro. I was afraid that you'd be angry."

"Of course you may go. When do you want to leave?"

"With your permission, tomorrow."

"Tomorrow would be fine. Mardinah will go with you."

"Please, Bendoro, no."

"What, did Mardinah do something to you?"

"No, Bendoro. I'd just like to go alone."

"Hush, that wouldn't be right. Someone must accompany you."

"Of course, Bendoro, but not Mardinah. I'm sorry, Bendoro, but please . . ."

"Then whom should I send?"

"Anyone but her."

"Has this Mardinah been making trouble for you?"

"Of course not, Bendoro, but she's a relative of yours. It wouldn't be right for her to go home with me."

"You can't go by yourself."

"Of course not, Bendoro, but . . ."

"You belong to me, and I will determine what you can and cannot do and also what you must do. But now be quiet, it's getting late." As if an afterthought, he then added: "But you're not prepared to go, are you?"

"What do I have to prepare, Bendoro?"

"Hush. You mustn't forget who I am. You must remember

never to do anything to diminish the respect people hold toward me. Take with you a gunnysack of rice," he ordered.

"Yes, Bendoro."

"Tomorrow morning go to the market and buy a bolt of fabric, a few sarongs, sealing resin, sandals, and some tins of cookies." He paused to think. "And some good rosaries, too, the ones with the black and shiny beads. Make sure they're not chipped and that you count the number of beads before buying them to make sure they have the proper number. And as a personal gift from me, take with you a basket of scented rolling tobacco."

"But that's too much to carry, Bendoro."

"I'll rent a carriage to take you straight to your door."

The girl wanted to tell the Bendoro that her village couldn't be reached by carriage; one had to walk from the nearest road post, which was a couple miles away, but she refrained from saying anything. Few people used the path, and she imagined herself having to struggle along it, weighed down by a pile of goods on her head, just like any other woman from the fishing village who could not afford to buy one of the broad straps of cloth that better-off women used to carry goods on their back. If she were to arrive in the morning, the village would be quiet, with only the women milling about; the men would be out to sea, asleep in their huts, or shivering from malaria. There would be only women there to greet her.

For the girl, the hours of the night passed slowly.

Beside the girl, her husband lay spent, snoring loudly as he slept in weary contentment, with his mouth agape and his eyes slightly open. Carefully, the girl got out of bed and made her way to the bathhouse.

The night was completely black, and when passing through the garden, she stopped to stare at the stars that lay scattered across the darkened sky. Her lips moved silently in a prayer of gratitude.

In her mind, she saw the faces of the people she loved—people who had nothing to give except labor, love, and fish. "Oh, Papa," she whispered, and then remembered the words her father had spoken to her the night before she left for the city: "We here in this village could live out our lives twelve times over and never be able to buy all the things that you can find in just one room of a person's house in the city. The ocean is big, that's true, with riches we could never ever drain, but there's no value to our work. Tomorrow, you're going to the city, to be the wife of an important man. All you'll have to do is open your mouth, and whatever you ask for will be brought to you. You choose which kind of world you want."

"Oh, Papa," the girl said again. She spoke as if her father were at her side. "Here I am in that world you offered me. Yes, it is a world of ease, where all one does is pick and choose, but it's also a world where my heart can never be free. Papa, I don't need all these things in life. All I need is the people I love, whose hearts are open, who can laugh and smile; a world without fear and sorrow, Papa. What a waste it was for you to send your daughter to the city, to be nothing more than a nobleman's practice wife."

After leaving the bathhouse, the girl walked toward the kitchen. Outside the kitchen door, she stopped. Through that door her former servant had passed tens of times a day. But where was she now? She had been rude to the woman when her own feelings had been hurt, that was true, but now the pain was forgotten and all she felt was regret for ever having acted that way toward the servant.

When suddenly the thought of Mardinah came to mind, the girl hurriedly left the area. Mardinah was there, in the kitchen.

"What a fool I am," she scolded herself. "What am I doing standing outside the kitchen, thinking about such a hateful person, when that very person is inside?" She scampered up the back steps and quickly proceeded through the back room to her bedroom. Closing the door behind her, she locked it from the inside. Sitting down on her chair, she heard her husband's voice calling softly to her: "Go to sleep, Young Mistress."

"Yes, Bendoro," she replied but made no attempt to move.

"It's late. Go to sleep. If you don't get some sleep, you won't be able to go tomorrow morning. You're going to catch a chill."

"Yes, Bendoro," the girl acquiesced and got into the bed where she lay, facing the door.

"Why do you have your back to me?" the Bendoro asked. "I don't like it when you sleep that way."

The girl turned around to face her husband.

"When you reach the village," the Bendoro told her in a sleepy voice, "convey my regards to your parents."

"Thank you, Bendoro."

"And don't act like a villager. You're a nobleman's wife."

"Yes, Bendoro."

"Now, go to sleep."

Moments later, the entire world was sleeping soundly, with only the stars, the waves, and the wind still awake to carry out their appointed tasks.

PART THREE

Heavily laden with gifts and provisions, the horse cart carrying the Girl from the Coast back home to her village stuttered along the Postal Road. The mangrove swamp that lined the shore was a deep green and very cool in color, but the horse pulling the cart labored unwillingly, bucking and starting, in the midday heat. The scent of tobacco aroma, wafting from one of the baskets in the cart, mingled with the smell of the sea.

The girl sighed and glanced toward Mardinah, seated at her side. That she-devil would sooner escort her to hell than be on this ride, the girl thought. Why had the Bendoro insisted that she go along? Could it be that he felt he could trust a relative more than his own wife?

"You should have answered that letter, Young Mistress," Mardinah said to her.

The girl ignored the comment, focusing her attention on the driver instead: "Have you ever been to a fishing village?"

"Yes, Ma'am, I was born on the coast."

"So, I guess you don't like going out to sea."

"If everyone went to sea, Ma'am, who would be left on the land? Other people can earn their food from fishing; I'm happy with my horse. He earns me all I need."

The open air breathed new life into the girl, and feeling truly free for the first time in two years, she suddenly laughed.

Mardinah sneered at her mistress. "I don't see what there is to laugh about; it's not fitting for the wife of a nobleman."

Immediately, the girl's laughter ceased.

A strong headwind had prevented the driver from hearing Mardinah's reprimand. He continued speaking, as if oblivious to the companion of the Bendoro's wife: "Yes, I like the land better, Ma'am. At least when you die, people know where to find your body."

"Whose body are you talking about?" the girl asked. "Yours or your horse's?"

Afraid that he had somehow offended the Bendoro's wife, the driver was suddenly flustered. "No, Ma'am, not my horse's. I meant my own. I just . . ."

"I guess you really care about your body!" the girl declared with another laugh. She now ignored Mardinah's glare and then changed the subject of conversation: "Where do you live in the city?"

The driver kept his eyes on the road ahead while answering: "Not too far from the sea, that part of town where other people from the coast live."

"What's it like there? Can people laugh there?"

The man raised his eyebrows. "What in the world . . . Where can't people laugh?"

The girl fell silent. I might be young, she thought, but even at my age I know better how this world works. "How old are you?" she asked the driver.

"I'm forty, Ma'am."

Mardinah needled her mistress again: "You'd be better off reading that letter I have for you than flirting with the driver."

The girl ignored Mardinah's comment.

"Forty? Then you must have lots of grandchildren."

"Not just 'lots.' I got more than twenty, Ma'am!"

"You must stop talking to that man," Mardinah told the girl. "I'll have to tell the Bendoro about this."

"And do you love them?"

"Of course, Ma'am, I love them all."

"Did you ever have to do forced labor?" the girl then inquired.

"Certainly did, Ma'am, and it took off a good part of my life. A religion teacher once told me that God the Almighty gives everyone the gift of life. But I didn't seem to get much of a chance to enjoy that gift. Most of it was taken from me on the plantation where I was forced to work. What you see now is all that's left of me."

"Why didn't you run away?"

"Where to? The Dutch military were there. They were everywhere. My father, now he lived to be a hundred and twenty, or at least that's what we reckoned. But here I am, only forty, and I am already worn out. My father spent his whole life on the move, Ma'am. He wasn't going to do forced labor. He was a big guy, you see, with lots of pluck. Any sign of ruckus at all and you just knew he'd be there, right in the middle of it. But that's not me. Never had the nerve, was always afraid of dying. Scared of the sea, scared of the big fish in it. About the only thing I ain't scared of is my horse, my horse and my grandkids."

The girl laughed contentedly. She found in the driver's way of talking the kind of language she missed so much: words honestly spoken, words that rang straight and true.

"If you had the chance, would you like to be a government official or somebody big and important?"

"If I had the chance, huh? Well, I'll tell you, Ma'am, right now my horse is tired; it's a pretty heavy load he's pulling. So if it's all right with you, Ma'am, I think we should slow down and take our time. Poor thing. If he's loaded down with tobacco, he never gets a quid. If it's limes he's carting around, no one gives him some juice to drink. So you tell me, Ma'am, why did God make this creature a horse and not a government official?"

The girl guffawed.

Mardinah was aghast. "Young Mistress, this really is too much. What if the driver starts talking about the Bendoro? What will he have to say then? Your laughter is unbecoming."

"Well, if your horse were a government official . . ."

"Eeyah, well I thank my heavens he's not, Ma'am. I'd never be able to feed him enough. It's because of this poor horse's fate that I can put food on my table, that I got married and have all those grandkids I talked about. He keeps me from having to be a horse myself. But just look at him. Eeyah!"

"What is this, 'Eeyah'?"

"It just feels good to say, Ma'am. Makes your chest feel light, helps you clear your throat."

"Wherever did that word come from?"

"I once had this passenger, a Chinese guy just off the boat. Hardly knew how to speak the language, but that sure didn't stop him from talking; talked nonstop, he did, all the way from Rembang to Lasem. Told me that he'd been a human horse once, back when he was in Hong Kong, that he had to pull this cart that people rode in. So it was, Ma'am, every time he said something, he always starting by saying 'eeyah.' He just loved saying that word. Try saying it yourself, Ma'am. Feels good."

"Eeyah!"

"Nice?"

The girl laughed again. "That was great!"

Mardinah was becoming more and more irritated. "Really, Young Mistress, this mustn't go on. I will have to tell the Bendoro."

The girl ignored her and continued her conversation with the driver: "Do you have a boss?"

"Eeyah! Don't I though? Everybody's my boss. That's the problem with my life, Ma'am. That's why I pray for my horse every day: 'Please, God, don't let him get sick.' "

The girl clapped her hands in delight. "If that's what you pray for your horse, then what do you pray for your kids and grandkids?"

"Oh, they can pray for themselves. The problem with being a horse, Ma'am, is that they can't pray. Eeyah! Or maybe they pray in their own language: horse talk. Or maybe they just don't pray out loud. It's such a shame . . ."

"What's a shame?"

"That God never answers my horse's prayers. Maybe right now he's praying that he weren't a horse but a driver, like me. Meanwhile, I'm praying that I stay as healthy as a horse. So if fate were to take a turn, I could be the horse and he could be the driver. Think then what that would do to this old body of mine."

"That's disgusting," Mardinah spat.

The girl looked at Mardinah and then back at the driver. "Do you think it's disgusting, what fate holds for horses?"

"Doesn't matter what I think. That's the way it is."

The carriage rolled ever more slowly forward until finally, when going up a rise, the weary horse balked and stopped in its tracks, forcing the driver to jump down to the ground and place stones behind the carriage wheels to keep it from rolling backward.

"Why don't you let him rest?" the girl suggested.

"Thank you, Ma'am; I'll do that."

"But it will be dark before we get home," Mardinah protested.

The girl stepped down from the cart and stood beside the road, staring across the mangrove-studded coast, toward the open sea.

"Two years and I could only hear the sound of the sea from inside my room," she remarked as if to herself.

The driver looked at her curiously. "What? You spent two years inside your room? Were you sick?"

"Was I sick?" the girl mused.

"You must have been really sick!" the driver commented.

"At night, the wind would blow through the roof tiles and into my room, carrying the sound of the waves. The later it got, the louder their roar became. The sea seemed to be calling me. 'Come here, come to me. Why did you run away? I raised your ancestors—rocked them on my lap, calmed them when they were frightened . . .' "

"And then buried them," the driver said with finality. "That's what all those fishermen's tales are like, Ma'am. They make me never want to go out to sea."

The girl bent down and scooped a handful of sand. Finely ground bits of coral shell made it glitter in the sun. She let the sand sift slowly through her fingers; pushed by the wind, the stream fell at an angle toward the ground. The girl, with a sudden feeling of despondence, scattered the small mound of sand with her foot.

The driver's voice distracted the girl from her thoughts: "Just look at him, Ma'am." He was pointing at his horse.

The girl looked up and walked to where the driver was standing, directly in front of the horse. The horse's eyes were covered by a broad leather strap that was hitched to its bridle.

"What's the use of having eyes, if they're covered like this?" the girl asked.

"When he's doing this kind of work, Ma'am, his eyes aren't much use. If you were to open the blinders, he could see what he's pulling—tobacco!—and then he might not want to work."

The driver's comment reminded the girl of the gifts she was carrying for the people of the village.

"Do you smoke?" she asked the driver.

"Nah, and neither does my horse, Ma'am, but I chew it sometimes."

"Then I'll give you some."

The driver patted the horse's back, which was now lathered with sweat. "Come on, Gombak, say thank you to the nice lady."

"But you're the one I'm giving it to," the girl said, "not the horse."

"That's right, Ma'am, but when I get some chew, he gets some molasses." The horse lifted its head. "He's asking if we can rest a little while longer, Ma'am. Is that all right with you?"

Without replying, the girl walked away from the cart. She stepped off the Postal Road and headed into the shrub land toward the sea.

"Young Mistress!" Mardinah shouted and jumped down from the horse cart. She ran in pursuit of her mistress. "Where are you going? Those are mangroves. There must be snakes out there."

The girl didn't bother to turn around. "And wouldn't you like that?" she muttered.

"Come sit in the carriage," Mardinah pleaded.

The girl stared at her servant. "If I were bitten by a snake, wouldn't that make you pleased? Then you could replace me as the Bendoro's consort."

Mardinah shook her head. "No, that could never be."

"Why not?"

"I'm divorced."

"You're still a woman, aren't you?"

Mardinah shook her head again: "Young Mistress, how long have you been at the Bendoro's house? By this time, you should know that the Bendoro and other men like him will only take for a wife a woman who has come directly to them from God."

The girl was puzzled. "So what does that mean?"

"I've already been with another man."

The girl's curiosity mounted: "So then why do you keep trying to force that letter on me?"

"Please, Young Mistress, come back to the carriage."

"You get back in; I like talking to the driver."

"The Bendoro will be angry."

"That would be all the better for you, wouldn't it?"

Again Mardinah ignored the rebuke. "It doesn't feel right for me to be up there when you are down below."

"Do you often write letters for other people?"

"Who am I going to write letters for? No, but I can write."

"Are all nobility like that?"

"Like what, Young Mistress?"

"Like devils."

"I'm going to have to tell the Bendoro about this."

"Go ahead. Do it now. I'll have the driver take you and all the cargo back to the city. I can walk to my village from here."

The girl turned and walked back toward the horse cart, Mardinah close behind.

"How is the horse doing now?" she asked the driver. "Is he rested?"

"Step up, Ma'am. He's smart and rests up real quick when he knows that I'm going to get some tobacco."

"I won't forget the tobacco for you," the girl assured him—"but I don't think your horse will need any," she joked.

"Maybe not, Ma'am, but his driver sure does. Please, step up," he said again, "the wind is picking up."

After the two women had settled themselves on their seat, the carriage rolled forward again.

The girl looked across the coastline at the sea and then back at the driver. "Just look at the sea!" she remarked with newfound marvel. "It's so big and wide, absolutely endless."

"You got that right, Ma'am," the driver affirmed. He pulled on the horse's bridle. "Come on, Gombak, got to get a move on! We don't want to get caught out on the road at night."

Mardinah pouted. "I just know that's what's going to happen."

"It must already be night somewhere," the girl said, as if to herself.

"In all my life, Ma'am, I've never seen a day go by without a night. I don't suppose it's going to be any different today. Ee-yah!" He snapped his whip in the air. "Giddyap, Gombak, giddyap!"

The girl winced at the sound of the whip. "Do you ever whip him?" she asked the driver.

"It's only stupid people and stupid animals who deserve to get whipped, Ma'am."

"What about the bad ones?"

"It's best to hobble them, tie their feet together."

The girl raised her eyebrows. "Are you talking about people or animals? What if the person is noble born?"

"That's a problem, Ma'am—which is why it's hard being born a horse or a man like me. It's people like me, just like Gombak here, who get put under the whip. But nobody can stay under the whip forever; there's only so much you can put up with. No matter how tired he is, even a sick tiger is going to fight if you keep on prodding him. Eeyah!"

The driver cracked his whip again, its snapping sound a counterpoint to the sound of the waves. The cart rolled slowly along.

Two hours into their trip and the three travelers had yet to meet another vehicle, even an oxcart. When was it market day? the girl wondered. What with the road so quiet, it couldn't be the next day.

As if remembering something, she turned to the driver: "If it gets too late, do you still want to go back to the city?"

"This isn't my first trip, Ma'am, and it won't be my last. I've made this kind of trip lots of times, sometimes even when the tide's been so high—around three in the morning, that would be—that it's come up as far as the edge of the road."

"Weren't you afraid?"

"Who wouldn't be?" the man said modestly.

"But you must be brave, too."

"Have to be, Ma'am. Wouldn't want my horse to put me to shame. He's afraid of nothing—not pirates, not even the devil. Says something for wearing blinders, I guess!"

The girl laughed and, when she heard the sound of her own voice, realized that her laugh had changed. Her laughter had once been compared to the sound produced by a brass pan being struck against a rock. She laughed again. Now what did her laughter sound like? She shook her head, unable to find a comparison.

Glancing to her side and seeing Mardinah, sound asleep, her head resting against the basket of tobacco, the girl stopped laughing and began to study the young woman's face. She soon concluded that only a fool of a man would show her servant no interest. Her lips were small but full, resembling a pair of red shallots. Her eyebrows were dark and full, almost touching each other at the cleft of her nose. Her chin was rounded and smooth, cleaving perfectly to her face. Such a beautiful face, her servant had. But what was in her heart?

The girl found herself starting to tire. She looked again at Mardinah's face. How many men had this young woman given pleasure to? she wondered, but then immediately rebuked herself. What was she doing, thinking such thoughts?

She listened to the pounding of the waves, louder now as the tide crept up the shore. The sun, now lower in the west, made the waves appear all the higher. What would her father be doing now? And her mother?

The sea breeze became a lullaby, as soothing to the girl's senses as the one her mother used to sing to her younger brother, when putting him to sleep. Leaning against the basket of tobacco, the girl smiled contentedly, as the memory of the song pulled her, too, toward sleep.

The next thing the girl was conscious of was the voice of the driver, calling to her: "Is this the place, Ma'am? Is this where we stop?"

Both the girl and Mardinah pulled themselves erect and looked around. The girl turned her head to study the scene beyond the cart. Three giant teak trees clustered beside the road. Yes, she knew the place. She couldn't see the coast, or even hear the sound of the waves, for the sea was now three miles away, but she and everyone else from her fishing village knew this location well. She stepped down from the carriage and walked directly to the cluster, her eyes climbing upward, following the straight and mighty trunks of the three trees that towered over everything else. She put her hands on one of the trunks and tried to shake it, but the tree stood rock-still. She then tried the next, and then the third, but none would be moved.

"The ancestors' final gift," the driver said bluntly.

"So you know the story of these three trees?" the girl asked him.

The driver chortled with recognition: "I've been here before, Ma'am, at least ten times."

Mardinah remained in her seat in the carriage, watching her mistress and the driver as they spoke.

"When the Dutch Governor-General ordered all the men and women of the villages here to work on this road, their babies died of hunger at home."

"I thought that only the people in the fishing village knew that story."

"Lots of people know it, Ma'am. There's even a song about it."

"Young Mistress," Mardinah called, "it's getting very late."

The girl pointed toward a smaller road that verged off to the right. "Can you drive the carriage that way?" she asked the driver.

"It's awfully sandy, Ma'am, the wheels might sink. It would be hard on the horse, but we can give it a try. Just have to take it slow."

The girl looked back at the heavily laden cart. "If we could make it at least as far as the footpath . . ."

"We can try," the driver told her, "but I know from experience you can't make it any farther than that. Will there be anyone there to meet you?"

The girl shook her head. She then returned to the carriage, followed by the driver, who steered his horse to the right, onto the smaller road. As the carriage advanced, its wheels sank an inch or two into the sand, making it far more difficult for the horse to pull.

The driver began to sing:

Pity, oh pity, the babies who died
when the big road was built,
their mas and pas, they had no choice,
'twas slave labor or be killed.

When the road reached Rembang,
only then could they go home;
pity, oh pity, the babies who died,
nothing left of them but bones.

All the village was in mourning,
they gathered with torches so bright,
as an eternal marker for the memory,
three trees they planted that night.

The girl remembered her former servant and the hardships she had suffered. "And not all of them returned home . . ."

"No, Ma'am, they didn't. More than half of them were buried along the road. My father was one of the lucky ones. He ran away and fought the Dutch instead."

Was that a coincidence? the girl wondered. Her former servant's grandfather had also joined the resistance against the Dutch. For the time at least, she did not want to inquire further. She was trying to concentrate on the problem that lay ahead: Who would she be able to ask for help to carry all the things she'd brought? And then she thought of her mother and father, and all her relatives. How would they receive her?

The carriage rolled slowly forward.

"Come on, Gombak," the driver called out. "Only two more to go, then you can get some sleep!"

When the sandy road finally petered out, ending at the start of a footpath, the carriage stopped beside a tiny shack, the watch post for a field. The sun had almost set. Light was fading fast.

"If the Bendoro hadn't ordered me, I never would have come here," Mardinah grumbled.

"Well, I don't need you here," the girl snapped. "You can go back tonight."

Mardinah said nothing, but the driver, having heard the women's raised voices, turned to study the women's faces. His cheerfulness disappeared. It's always the little animals that get trampled when two elephants get in a rout, he thought to himself. He sauntered away from the women, closed his ears to their discussion, and sat down on the bench in the farmer's hut. He stuck a wad of tobacco in his mouth and made a cud, forming it with his tongue between his lower lip and gums.

"Driver!" the girl called.

The driver jumped up from his seat and went to see what the girl wanted, but before he reached the girl's side, he heard the other woman hiss: "You're acting like a hick!"

"Well, that's what I am," the girl hissed back. "This is my village, my home, and if you don't want me to put a curse on you, you can remove your pretty little feet from this sandy ground."

Seeing the driver approach, Mardinah held her tongue.

"Take her back to the city," the girl said to the driver.

Mardinah spoke up first: "The Bendoro ordered me to accompany you, Young Mistress. I could not possibly go back alone."

"You don't belong in a fishing village, so just go back home!"

"I'm serious, Young Mistress. I can't go back alone."

The girl redirected her attention to the driver. "Whatever we do, we have to take care of these things. What do you think you could carry?" she asked him.

"Well, not that bag of rice, for sure. I'm not strong enough for that."

The girl looked at Mardinah, who replied in a huff: "What do you think I am?"

"I suppose Gombak here is strong enough," the girl suggested, "but then he's a draft horse, not a pack horse."

"Exactly, Ma'am."

"Then tether him and go ahead to the village to fetch some help."

"I'd get there faster by riding, Ma'am."

The driver swiftly removed the blinder from the horse's eyes and jumped onto its back. Soon the horse and rider were moving away, heading down the footpath; a moment later they disappeared behind a wall of shrubs and brush.

The girl walked away from the carriage to the small shack, where she sat down on the bench. Mardinah surveyed her surroundings then hurried to follow suit.

The girl looked her servant up and down. "What are you doing here?"

"I'm afraid," Mardinah replied.

"You, afraid? I guess I'm the only thing you're not afraid of."

Mardinah looked out at the growing darkness. "I hate villages, all of them!"

The girl sneered at her. "Then leave, get out of here!"

"How can I?"

"You're not from the village. You're much better than the people here. I'm sure you can figure out a way."

"I am better," Mardinah insisted. "My father was a clerk and I'm related to nobility."

"Well, then go find your nobles now. If you dare set foot in my village, the spirits of my ancestors are likely to strike you down. You have insulted my village and the people in it—fishermen and sailors who risk their lives every day." She pointed upward at the sky. "It's getting dark. You'd better be careful. The lightning here has a way of striking ungrateful city people." She then pointed her finger at Mardinah's chest. "It won't be good for you in my village. Go home, go back to the city before it gets too dark."

As if the girl herself had magical powers, a pair of lightning bolts suddenly flashed behind the darkening clouds.

"Forgive me, Young Mistress."

"Did you see that? Those were the eyes of the great spirit. When they flash, they send out fire. The great spirit has twelve arms, and when she sees an enemy, she sticks her hands out from behind the clouds to torture them, mincing them with the small dull knives she holds in her hands. She might spend a whole week just finishing the job."

Mardinah seemed to grow smaller as her mistress spoke. She looked bewildered, like a cat who had lost its prey.

"Forgive me, Young Mistress. I was just ordered to accompany you here."

"Are you really from Demak?"

"Yes, Young Mistress."

"And what orders do you have from there?"

Mardinah shivered from anxiety but forced herself to speak: "It's a long story, Young Mistress. All I'm doing is following my orders."

"What are they? To get rid of me?"

"The Bendoro's family and his relatives in Demak are very embarrassed, Young Mistress, because he is still unmarried."

"What do you mean? What do you think I am?"

"What can I say? A nobleman is not considered married until he marries a woman of the noble class."

"You're noble, aren't you? Would you like the Bendoro to marry you?"

"To be frank, Young Mistress, I would."

"Even though you're related?"

"Yes, Young Mistress, but what I wish doesn't matter; he would never marry me because I am a divorcée."

The girl rephrased her earlier question: "What you're saying then is that I'm not the Bendoro's wife."

Mardinah appeared more hesitant to speak. "Well, in a way you are, Young Mistress, but you're thought of as a practice wife."

"And you were ordered to get rid of me, so that the Bendoro could marry a noble woman. Is that it? I'm sure it is. Well, I can stay here, in my village. You can go home. Just don't set foot in my village."

"But I'm afraid, Young Mistress."

"Afraid of what? You're from the city, related to nobility. Where's your superiority now? I'm from the village and I'm not afraid."

"Just don't leave me here, Young Mistress."

"Listen to me, Mardinah. I lived in the city for two years before you came along, but it's only now that I realize what city people, people of the noble class, fear the most—it is to not be respected. And yet, you're all so afraid of showing even a little respect toward people from the village."

The Girl from the Coast looked, through the murky light, at her servant beside her. She was sitting motionless on the bench, unable to do anything but to bury her face in her two hands.

Minutes seemed to pass before Mardinah was able to gather her wits together and raise her head from her hands. "But what about you, Young Mistress?" she then asked. "Going back to the village like this, aren't you afraid of losing what you had?"

The girl's tone softened. "People like me, Mardinah, people from the village, that is, have nothing to lose. All we can do is dream. So what do we have to lose? Our dreams?"

"What do you dream about, Young Mistress?"

"About all the things I've never had."

"What about the things you do have? Don't you think about them?"

The girl stared at her servant, momentarily wondering if she would ever be able to understand her feelings, those of a person from the village. "What do I have?" she then asked. "After more than two years at the Bendoro's house, I know that all a villager can hope for from city people is poverty, insults, and fear. In the village, we're paid two and a half cents for shrimp meal, even though we know the real price should be four cents. It's not right; it's not fair. Now take a look at me: I'm not shrimp meal; I'm a person. You can't just take a person like me out of the village and put her in a big house in the city. What do city people know about people from the village?"

When Mardinah did not reply, the girl continued: "There was an older woman at the house when I first came and she looked out for me, but then she was sent away for accusing the Bendoro's nephews of stealing my money."

"Well, of course, she should have been," Mardinah stated.

"But why?"

"She was there to work, not to criticize."

"But one of the Bendoro's nephews stole my money."

"But she was a servant. She had forgotten the meaning of service."

"That kind of service is ridiculous," the girl spat. "My ancestors never had to serve anyone and they survived. The sea is richer than everything." Her voice flattened: "You must go back to the city. I can stay here alone."

"What will I tell the Bendoro?"

"You will beg his forgiveness and then offer yourself to him. I don't care if he's your uncle or even your father; you have my blessing—you can be his practice wife. Wouldn't you like that?" She scanned the path with her eyes, hoping the driver would appear. Seeing no one, she turned back to Mardinah. "Why don't you say something?"

"I don't know what to say, Young Mistress. I don't know what to do."

"What's wrong? Is it because you spit on my village? Think about it: For two years, I've been away from my village, living in a big house, surrounded by strangers, while you have been here just a few minutes and you're already going on like an old woman who's lost her wits."

"I could go crazy in this place."

"I'm planning on staying for a while."

"That's impossible, Young Mistress. I couldn't bear to stay here that long."

"Which is why I'm telling you to go home now. Really, I have no objection."

"How long will you stay?"

"A week, maybe a month."

"The Bendoro never said anything like that."

"If you have any sense at all, you should start to realize, right now, that I am your boss, your Bendoro, and not my husband."

"But that's impossible, Young Mistress! I'm related to nobility. My title might not be much, but I have one, Young Mistress."

As the wind picked up and began to blow wildly through the trees and brush, they stopped to listen to the sounds of the night.

Mardinah shivered. "It's cold, Young Mistress."

"You're cold? Think of the fishermen who go out to sea bare-chested."

"Why do they do that?"

"Because they don't have enough clothes," the girl answered simply.

"Oh . . ." Mardinah mumbled.

"Oh? Is that all you have to say?" The girl shook her head. "Who do you think you are, anyway? If I want to laugh, you tell me to stop. I can do this, but I can't do that, and all you can say now is 'Oh'? The people here are poor; that's a fact of life, but I guess, for city people, even being poor is a crime. I remember not too long after I arrived at the Bendoro's house, he told me that people from the village are dirty, that they aren't religious, and that that's why they are poor. Is that what you think? Do you understand religion?"

"Are you asking if I have learned to recite the Koran? If you're asking that, no, Young Mistress, I've not."

"Well, I haven't, either."

Their attention was drawn to the sound of the driver, who suddenly appeared on his horse. "I got four men, Young Mistress, all of them with carrying poles."

"You can help them organize the loads," she told the driver. "Are you going back to the city?" she then asked.

"Not tonight, Ma'am. Gombak is still tired; he needs to rest, and it's an awfully long way back to town."

"And your tobacco? Take one of the bundles from the basket."

"I appreciate it, Ma'am. It means Gombak will be having molasses for a couple weeks."

When the four villagers appeared, the girl stood by and watched the driver divide the cargo among them. After he had finished, he returned to her.

"Are there enough men to carry all the stuff?" the girl asked.

"Not by a long shot, Ma'am, but they're the only ones who weren't planning on going out to sea tonight. No other way, I guess. I'll have to help out, too."

The girl listened to the bearers talking among themselves: "Boy, there's a lot of stuff here," one of them said. "Whose things are these, anyway?" another one added.

"They're mine," the girl then told them.

"Where do you want us to take them?" one of the men asked.

"The fishing village."

The men looked at one another then silently began to adjust the balance of items on their poles.

"Don't forget your tobacco," the girl reminded the driver.

After the men had formed a line, they returned to the darkness from which they had emerged.

"I'm afraid," Mardinah whispered.

The girl looked at the provisions the men had been unable to carry, then began to arrange her own load. "Those bottles there," she said to Mardinah, "you'll have to carry those. I don't think I can carry any more."

"But, Young Mistress . . ."

The girl stopped her abruptly: "I know, I know, this kind of work is beneath you, but would it be so wrong to give me a hand?"

Reluctantly, Mardinah picked up in each hand a pair of bottles that had been laced together with split bamboo.

The two women then set off on the footpath, following the driver. The pole bearers were already far ahead. Their feet sank into the soft, warm sand. Branches and twigs tugged at the women's clothing as they passed.

Mardinah had trouble keeping up with her mistress. "You're going so fast," she complained. "Can't you go a little slower?"

Without reducing her speed, the girl looked up at the sky. "You'd better pray that we get there before it starts to rain."

Their journey continued, and after a time, Mardinah raised her voice again: "Is it still far, Young Mistress?"

"Do you want us to leave you here alone?" was all the girl had to say.

And so the trio walked on and on.

Exhausted, Mardinah commented, "Young Mistress, you must be tired, too."

"We're all tired," the girl replied, even as she maintained her same hurried pace, "but we have a place to go and we're not going to stop until we get there."

Perhaps worried about not finding a place to stay in the village, the driver asked, "What do you think, Ma'am, should I go back tonight?"

"Yes," she answered, "I think it would be best if you went back tonight. And take this one with you," she then added, nodding her head toward Mardinah.

"But I can't go back, Young Mistress," Mardinah retorted. "I was ordered to accompany you, so that's what I must do."

The girl almost stopped in her tracks. "Listen to me," she warned. "My husband, the Bendoro, is not here with me, so I am your boss now. I've told you to go back to the city. If you don't want to go, that's up to you, but then you'll have to stay overnight, whether you like it or not. It's your choice."

"I'm sorry, Young Mistress, but for me to stay here overnight . . ."

The girl cut her off: "Don't worry, we'll see to it that your needs are taken care of."

They continued on ahead. In the gloomy distance, lanterns flickered. As they breached a small rise, a brisk wind suddenly struck them. Mardinah scampered as close to the girl as possible and tried to take hold of her hand.

"Young Mistress . . ." she pleaded, but the girl would not stop or slow down.

The driver turned his head around, raising his voice to be heard above the wind. "Those are the houses of two of the men helping us, Ma'am."

The houses were the farthest ones from the shore, sitting outside the village limits. The girl recalled that their owners had never had their own boats. Suli and Kardi—yes, those were their names—had always been forced to live off their brawn and to find work from other fishermen. She had never spoken to the men—after all, she had been little more than a child when she left—but she knew their children. There had always been a great number of them, it seemed, and all of them were very young. They spent their days looking for firewood for their mothers and playing on the beach.

Outside of the two men's houses, the trio found the two bearers, Suli and Kardi, standing, waiting for them. The other two bearers squatted on the ground between the two huts.

As the trio neared the bearers' huts, the driver asked, "Where do we go now, Ma'am?"

The bearers waited silently, not moving from their places when the girl, her servant, and the driver appeared. As the girl approached, light from the lanterns inside the huts illuminated her features. The villagers studied her face then looked at each other. They had no words to speak, but their eyes spoke for them.

The girl immediately approached the two men. "*Pak* Suli, *Pak* Kardi, don't you remember me?"

"You look familiar, Ma'am," Suli offered.

" 'Ma'am,' why are you calling me 'Ma'am'? I'm from here, too."

"Of course, Ma'am."

"Ma'am?" the girl said again with a trace of dismay.

"We should get a move on, Suli," Kardi interjected, a sign of his own discomfort.

As they were speaking, the men's wives and children came outside and gathered around. One of the children pointed at the girl and was about to speak, but her mother immediately pulled her away and ordered her back inside, but not before the little girl had cried, "Ma, it's her!"

The woman pushed the child toward the door. "Shush, be quiet, and don't talk that way."

"How come?" the child asked.

The girl stepped toward the woman. "It's all right, you can let her stay."

The woman picked up her daughter and placed her on her hip. "These kids, Ma'am, they'll never learn."

"Please don't call me 'Ma'am,' " the girl insisted. "Why, you've known me since I was little."

The woman had clamped her hand over her daughter's mouth. "But that was then and this is now; you're a different person."

The girl sounded like she wanted to cry: "But I'm not. Please don't think that."

The woman turned her eyes toward the load in the girl's hands. "My kids can carry those for you."

The girl smiled at the offer. "Well sure, if they want to."

The children immediately rushed to the girl's side, fighting among themselves for the girl's parcels.

"That's all right, you can all help!" she said, trying to calm the children. "Won't you come along, too?" she asked the woman.

"I'll wait here at the house, Ma'am. The children can go with you."

All the children of both households, even the smallest, wanted to go, and they soon set off behind their fathers and the other two bearers, who had gone on ahead to the girl's former home.

With a trail of children following the girl, the sight was a festive one, like a wedding procession.

The children gossiped among themselves: "She didn't use to be called 'Ma'am,' " one stated matter-of-factly. "She's so pretty," another girl enthused.

"Oh, these kids!" the driver said in mock irritation.

"Let's sing!" the girl suddenly suggested with renewed spirit.

"What should we sing?" the children demanded to know.

The girl remembered a song from her childhood. "How about 'Blow the Wind Blow'?"

The clear voices of the children soon began to cut through the dark and stillness of the night:

Twisting and turning,
blow the wind blow;
down and around,
then up the mountain you go.

Speed away, fly away,
to the jungle you flee;
all the animals there,
are waiting for thee.

Tears dropped from the girl's eyes as she thought of her father casting his net in the dark with a wicked wind howling at his back. The sky was pitch-black and his net had become snagged on an outcropping of coral. He and her brothers were forced to jump into the cold water and dive far down, beneath the surface, to free the net. How many times had he come home telling such a story?

"Sing something else," the driver suggested.

The girl didn't hear the driver's voice; her mind was on her father. Because of you, I am safe today, Papa. And then she thought of her mother. What would she be doing now?

By this time, the bearers were far ahead of the trio and their escort of chattering children. Suddenly, in the distance, a line of flickering torches appeared and began to move toward them. Sparks from the flaming bundles of coconut husks rose in the sky and danced in the air.

"Who's that?" Mardinah asked, with some fear in her voice.

"My parents, my neighbors, my friends."

Suddenly, the children in the group broke free and ran ahead, shouting as they ran: "It's her! The Girl from the Coast! The one in the song!"

The girl stared after the children. What had they just called her? What were they talking about?

Torches and lanterns multiplied in the dark, lighting up the glistening, perspiring faces of the welcoming party.

"It's her! It's her!" the children shouted again.

"Be quiet, children," snapped one of the adults in the welcoming party. "Don't be so rude!"

The voice roused the girl from her reverie. She felt a shiver run down her spine. The way her fellow villagers were now acting—no one had ever treated her that way before. She felt like a complete stranger. Then she saw, coming toward her in the distance, her father, walking at the head of the band with a torch of dried coconut leaves in his raised hand. Bare-chested, his muscled torso gleamed in the light of his torch.

The girl suddenly ran toward him, the sand on the path scattering from beneath her feet. Among the many people coming to welcome her, she could see one person only.

"Papa!" she screamed, over and over, as she fell to her knees at his feet and threw her arms around his legs.

Her father stood motionless in place while stroking her hair. "Are you all right?" he asked softly.

The welcoming party surrounded the father and daughter. Their torches, held in lowered arms, illuminated the scene.

"Papa, Papa. Give me your blessing."

No one spoke; the entire party stood statue-like.

"Stand up," the girl's father said.

As the girl began to rise, she looked around herself at the faces of the people present. All eyes were upon her, but each time she looked into a person's eyes, that person bowed his or her head quickly, as if nervous because of her presence. The girl winced. She couldn't remember her fellow villagers ever having acted that way toward her. No, of that she was sure, and now she felt even more strange than before, separated from her kinspeople, like a monkey in a cage. She let her father's strong arms help lift her to her feet.

"Let's go home," he said to her. "Your mother is there waiting for you."

She looked into her father's eyes, but even he looked away.

No, not you, too, the girl thought dejectedly. Why are you afraid of looking at me, your own daughter? She felt the earth sway beneath her feet. The fishing village, her home and final refuge, had lost its protective sheath. Behind her, she could feel the eyes of the Bendoro on her, watching her every move. She could not free herself from that feeling. She knew very well all the people in the welcoming party; they were her former neighbors. This one had pulled her ear when she was naughty; that one had told her stories; another had picked her up and comforted her when she had fallen out of a rose-apple tree; yet another had often helped her tend the fire in the kitchen hearth. And all the small children, why she herself had taken care of them and carried them around on her hip. But now they were acting strangely and treating her differently than before. She kept hearing the words "Bendoro Putri"—"Mrs. Bendoro," the Bendoro's wife. The words stung her. Here, in her own village, she was now someone else. All the eyes, fixed upon her, but respectfully lowered whenever she looked their way, seemed to be mocking her. Hypocrisy . . . All of this was hypocrisy!

With her father now leading the way, the girl walked slowly, hesitantly, behind him. It was true, she thought, the fishing village had changed; it was not the village it once had been. Even the darkness, into which the coconut-leaf torches cast their light, was not the same. And the pounding waves, the foamy crests of which turned white in the torchlight, were not the same waves that had for centuries lapped the shore. And the voices of the people, her former neighbors, no matter how softly they spoke, sounded hesitant, reluctant, even mocking to her ear.

Mardinah hadn't spoken a single word. Even the driver seemed reluctant to open his mouth. Children skipped about and scampered around her, ogling her as if she were a mermaid that had floundered onto shore. From both in front of her and at her back they watched her every move and studied every item on her body. When one of the children took hold of her left hand to study the ring she was wearing, the others screamed and ran ahead.

The girl could hardly feel the pull of the child on her hand. Her eyes were trained on her parents' house, where she thought she could see her mother standing, waiting for her, in the doorway. But as she grew closer, she saw the doorway was empty, and her heart shrank from sudden fear.

All of the adults in the crowd were now walking behind her. Only her father could be said to be apace, though even he was a step or two behind her.

She turned his way. "What are you doing there, Papa? Why don't you walk beside me?"

He coughed in reply.

"Where's Ma?" she asked.

"Where else would she be," he retorted, "if not in the kitchen?"

The girl screamed "Ma!" and went running into the house, her sandals flapping so hard one of them came loose and was thrown behind her.

Inside the house she called again—"Ma! Ma!"—but again found no reply, though in the hearth, flames were licking the bottom of a large cauldron that was used only in times of village feasts. She stopped directly before the fire, listening, and then heard a sound—the wind from off the sea—and after that, another: a woman humming to herself.

Turning her head, she saw her mother kneeling in the corner of the room. "Mama, oh, Mama!"

But still, her mother didn't speak. Her only answer was silent sobs. Wordlessly, the girl dropped to her knees and also began to weep.

As they knelt embracing each other, the other villagers entered the house, but upon sight of the scene before them, they made no move to come closer. The girl's father turned away and quickly left the house, vanishing into the darkness looming over the shore.

"Are you all right?" the girl's mother finally managed to say.

"Give me your blessings, Ma," the girl entreated, just as she had with her father.

"It's been so long," the mother whispered between her sighs.

"You and Papa never called me to come home."

The girl's mother shook her head sadly. "How could we? You're married, the wife of a *bendoro*."

"Forgive me, Ma," the girl pleaded.

One by one, following the example the girl's father had set, the older villagers moved away from the house, leaving only the village children as witnesses to the small drama being enacted by the mother and her daughter in the corner of the fisherman's hut.

The girl, with her head lowered, spoke into her mother's breast. "Why are you crying, Ma?"

Her mother answered with a hesitant question: "Can't I cry for my own daughter even if she's married to a nobleman?"

"Don't you want me here, Ma?"

The mother suddenly wailed loudly, then the girl cried, too. "Oh, Mama, oh, Mama . . ."

The women of the village now began to enter the house but stopped behind the children who were clustered by the doorway.

"Why are you here?" the mother stuttered. "Doesn't the Bendoro want you anymore?"

"I did everything you and Papa wanted me to do," the girl insisted, "as well as I knew how."

"It wasn't what your Pa and I wanted. It was God's will."

The girl attempted to calm her voice. "Are you all right, Ma?"

"All I ever do is think of you," she said with a sigh before looking into her daughter's eyes. "Why did you come home?"

The girl smiled faintly. "I'm still your daughter, Ma."

"Is the Bendoro angry with you?" the mother quizzed.

"No."

"He's not returning you to us?"

"No."

"You mean you came on your own?"

"Yes."

"With your husband's permission?"

"Of course, Ma."

The girl's mother brushed away her tears, then stood up so that she was looking down at her daughter. Suddenly, her tension had eased. "You're so pretty."

"Just like an angel," one of the neighbor women affirmed.

Not moving from her place, the girl looked around. She sensed that her fellow villagers were trying as best they could to behave with city ways and manners, but this only served to distance them from her. She felt like a leper.

Whenever she looked at them, they would smile momentarily then bow their heads, with their hands hanging uselessly at their sides. Those same hands that could grind hard kernels of corn into meal, those same hands that could deftly wield an ax and turn a trunk of wood into kindling for the kitchen fire.

The girl took a deep breath, then attempted to lighten the atmosphere by saying, "Well, let's start cooking!"

All the women moved silently into the kitchen area, saying nothing among themselves until an older crone finally shrieked, "Okay, where are the men? Get your butts moving and start to work!"

The children gave a loud cheer.

In no time at all, the sack of rice the girl had brought had been carried into the kitchen. Bottles of soy sauce and other provisions soon followed. Her gifts were set out for people to see on the sleeping platform. The men of the village gathered around to look. The girl took two plaid sarongs from the display and handed one to the village elder and the other to the village chief.

The elder felt the cloth in his hand, then looked around at the other men. "As for the rest of you," he snorted, "your gift is a good meal."

"There's more than enough rice here for everyone," the girl told them.

"Thank you, my lady," the men answered as one.

"My lady?" the girl asked. "The only real lady here is that one there," she added while pointing with her thumb toward Mardinah.

Only then did the villagers' attention turn to Mardinah. When they stared at her, studying intently her smooth round face and small rose-colored lips, she did not look away but returned their gaze in kind.

That night, the fishing village was bathed in torchlight. Inside the girl's home, women of the village kept having to tell the girl they did not need her help. Outside, the men were singing, and even as dawn approached, none of them set out to sea. The girl's driver joined in the festivities, completely forgetting about Gombak standing, tethered and alone, at the end of the footpath.

For the fishing village, such festivity and gaiety usually came but once a year, on the day of Pilgrim's Homecoming, the tenth day of the twelfth month on the Moslem calendar, when the families of the fishermen gathered on the shore to offer packets of cooked rice to the gods of the sea and to pray for their blessings in return and that they not be bothered by the gods when doing their work.

All of the villagers were proud that a girl from their village, one of their own as it were, had joined the nobility and now lived in the city. They were also pleased to have Mardinah, a hereditary noblewoman, paying a visit to their village.

As the villagers fussed and fawned over the girl, Dul, the village storyteller, provided musical entertainment. With his tambourine in hand, he sang out the story of Governor-General Daendels, who had built the great Postal Road that traversed the area's southern border.

No god in heaven was ever so cruel,
the least defiance meant death,
for regents, overseers, noblemen, too,
the commoners were their tools.

From his left hip hung a shining blade,
but his tongue was even sharper,
his words like lightning, striking a ship at sea,
no less than a command, impossible to evade.

All men quaked at the sound of his name,
mountains, rivers, and swamps bowed to him,
the road followed the coast, as far as the eye could see,
and all the village chiefs his agents became.

And when work on the road was done,
fine carriages passed that way,
lords and ladies and princes, too,
the Governor-General, his aides, and everyone.

"Sing something else!" someone called out.

"Yeah!" another shouted in agreement. "Tell us the one about the Girl from the Coast."

The tale-singer stopped for a moment. He drew a deep breath and exhaled. He took a gulp of coffee then began the new tale:

The sea was calm, the wind at peace . . .

"Call Mrs. Bendoro out here," someone said. "She should hear this, too."

"Sing louder," another suggested instead. "That way, she won't have to be called."

The tale-singer struck his tambourine and began to sing louder:

The sea was calm, the wind at peace,
the fishermen came home to quench their thirst,
'twas no one so lovely as the Girl from the Coast,
a goddess come down to earth.

"Mrs. Bendoro!" someone shouted. "Come out and listen to this."

The tale-singer struck his tambourine more spiritedly.

The prettiest lass in the fishing village,
every girl's idol, every man's dream,
for both old and young, men and women,
the Girl from the Coast, her beauty supreme.

A flower had bloomed by the sea,
and all the people in the city were amazed,
in no time the Bendoro *sent his envoy out,*
with a marriage bid to be appraised.

Bathed in rosewater, covered with jewels,
she was a flower any man would boast,
but she never forgot her parents and friends
such was the way of the Girl from the Coast.

As the tale-singer struck his tambourine, its tiny cymbals jingled. As the night progressed and the pounding of the waves grew louder with the rising of the tide, the man's singing grew more lively.

The climax of the night's festivities finally came when the meal was served, a veritable cornucopia, fragrant with spices from the city. As the villagers ate their fill, the revelry of the party began to die. Torches began to flicker and dim.

Some of the men, drunk on palm wine, lay sprawled beneath the trees in the sand. Empty bamboo containers were everywhere. Exhausted children were stretched out on the front decks of the houses; some had even curled up beneath the steps. Finally, the entire village seemed to fall asleep. That night, even the watchmen forgot their duties.

Inside the girl's house, the girl's servant, Mardinah, looked around herself perplexed. "Young Mistress, where am I to sleep?"

"You can sleep here with me," the girl answered as she made herself comfortable on the mat in the open room.

"Isn't there a bedroom?"

"No, there's not," the girl whispered. "You can lie down here, like the rest of us."

"But, Young Mistress . . ." she started to complain, but the girl had fallen asleep.

At daybreak, with no one in the village conscious enough to notice, the sun climbed quickly into the sky. Only when one of the children who was sleeping outside started to scream—a chicken was pecking at one of his many scabs—did people inside the house begin to open their eyes. Soon, a cluster of them were yawning and coughing and then walking outside to find a place to relieve themselves. The tide was out, far from the high tide mark, and the boats that had been made ready for sea the previous evening lay tilted and stranded on the shore.

In no time at all, the sound of children could be heard fighting in the kitchen of the girl's home for scraps from last night's meal. The village was returning to life.

Sitting up in the place where she had slept, Mardinah spoke softly to her mistress: "How am I supposed to bathe, Young Mistress?"

The girl looked at her in wonder. "With a washbasin, of course."

"But the water is briny. It will be hard to get the soap out."

"Don't use soap then."

"But after the trip yesterday? And not bathing last night?"

Mardinah clearly did not know what to do.

"We're all poor villagers here," her mistress reminded her. "Sometimes we don't have fresh water and have to bathe in the sea or even in our own sweat."

Mardinah didn't know if the girl was serious. "One week here will be enough to turn me into a dried fish," she grumbled.

"Driver! Driver!" the girl suddenly called out, ignoring Mardinah's mutterings.

The driver came running, still trying to hitch his sarong around his waist. He spoke first, not giving the girl a chance to speak: "You'll never guess, Ma'am. I forgot all about my horse last night."

"Don't worry," she told him, "I'm sure there were no thieves last night."

"Maybe not," the driver countered, "but what if a snake bit him in the leg?"

"Well then, you'll just have to become a sailor," the girl said with a smile.

"Nope, Ma'am, there's nothing better than having a horse. All it needs for food is some oats and grass, but in return it gives me and my wife and kids everything we need. Better yet, I don't have to go looking for him, not like you do for fish."

"Did you remember to take your tobacco?" the girl inquired.

"Yes, Ma'am, I did; in fact, I used my bundle for a pillow last night. Wouldn't want to see it turn to smoke without going through my own nose first."

"Now that you're awake, I want you to get ready to take this young woman back to the city." She nodded her head toward Mardinah.

"Yes, Ma'am."

"But, Young Mistress, you have to go back, too," Mardinah interrupted to say.

The girl glared at Mardinah. "Since when did you get the right to tell me what to do?" She looked at the driver again. "Be quick about it, Driver. I want you to do it now!"

"But where am I supposed to bathe?" he whispered.

"I guess you'll have to ask your horse," she replied.

So it was that same morning Mardinah returned to the city, but her departure did not provide the girl with the relief she expected. To her dismay, her fellow villagers continued to ogle and stare at her and to act toward her in a feigned and, for her, most annoying and disconcerting manner. It was her parents, however, that caused her the most distress, acting so distant, making her feel like a coral atoll, separated from the motherland, with only the lonely sea around her.

When she entered her home, it wasn't her loving and ever

protective mother whom she would find but instead a neighbor woman eager to do whatever pleased her. And her father seemed reluctant, almost afraid, to come inside the house, except when she was not there. Several times that morning she had called out for him, asking him to come in from out of doors, but he had advanced only as far as the threshold, where he looked at her, bowed, and then went outside again.

She was not allowed to work. Everyone kept watch on her, closely following her each and every move and motion. Not even a thief caught in the sunlight of midday could suffer a fate worse than this, she thought. Her childhood home was no longer the haven it once had been.

"I'll try one more time," she thought before calling out "Papa, Papa!" as she had several times earlier that morning. Again her father appeared at the door. "Why won't you come in, Papa?" she asked him.

"It's nicer out here. It's too hot inside."

"That's not it," she stated flatly. "It's because I'm here, isn't it, that you won't come in?"

"That's not true," he told her. "What is it? Is there something I can do for you?"

"Just come here," she pleaded.

"It's hot inside."

"You won't even say my name anymore."

He shook his head. "That wouldn't be right, not for someone of your standing."

"Please come in."

"I'd rather stay here."

The girl walked to the door, toward her father, but he turned away and descended the steps to the landing of the front deck where he stood facing the beach.

The girl stood beside the doorway talking to his back: "I want it to be like it used to be, Papa, when people weren't watching me all the time."

He turned his head slightly toward her. "Nobody is watching you."

She lifted her right hand toward him. "Let's go for a walk, Papa, along the shore."

"What do you want to see there?" he asked with a dismissive tone.

"I've been gone two years, Papa. I want to feel the sand beneath my feet."

"You should stay in the house," he advised. "You're still tired from the journey."

The girl walked past her father and went slowly toward the beach. Almost immediately, a pack of children gathered to trail noisily at her heels. Neighbors stepped out of doorways and followed her with their eyes. Her father finally took after her but followed several steps behind.

She looked back toward him. "Papa, why are you walking behind me like that? You're still my father."

The pack of children scrambled around the girl, overturning driftwood, picking up shells, hooting and screaming with each new discovery, but the girl's attention was on the coastline, her eyes taking in the once familiar sights, as she walked farther down the shore. Her eyes opened wide and her nostrils expanded as if to ingest the sights and smells of her former home. She could feel the ocean's pull.

"I want to go in the water."

Her father raised his eyebrows. "That wouldn't be proper."

"Maybe not, but I want to anyway."

"You can't."

"I know," the girl said sadly.

With the children still clamoring around them, the girl's father fixed a mean stare on the biggest of the bunch. "Break it up and settle down! Squirming 'round like bait in a bucket. Get out of here!"

The children immediately retreated, falling back to a distance from which they could more safely watch the girl and her father as they continued their way down the shore.

"Why can't it be like it was before I was married? The village is still the same. Why have the people changed?"

"Maybe because we're all getting older," the father posed.

The girl pointed toward the sea. "But look, the sea hasn't changed." She turned and pointed toward the village. "And the village hasn't changed, either. I don't see any new roofs. I don't see any new coconut trees. Has anyone died since I left?"

"No."

"I guess it's only the children, then," the girl mused, "they're bigger and there's lots more of them."

The girl's father cleared his throat.

"I guess not much has changed."

"Not much at all," he voiced in agreement.

"But, Papa, the people have changed. They have, at least toward me. Even you, Papa. It's like everybody is pointing at me and telling me to go back to the city."

"That's not true," her father insisted. "That's not true at all." A scream was stifled in his throat.

"Nobody went out to sea last night," the girl observed.

"You've been gone two years," her father pointed out. "We had no word of you. Is it so bad for the men to be happy, for them to want to stay on shore with me?"

"It's been two years and a little more, Papa, but you don't look happy to see me."

He parried the comment with a question: "What's an old man supposed to do? Jump up and down like a little boy?"

The girl smiled slightly. "I'd never expect you to do that, Papa." She then pointed toward the sea. "That boat, Papa. It doesn't look like one from our village."

Her father looked in the direction she was pointing, then shook his head.

"I brought some string for nets," she added.

"That's a nice gift."

"And some rosaries."

"You mean, prayer beads?"

"Yes, they're from the Bendoro, for you. They're black, hardwood beads from Mecca."

"What am I going to do with them?"

"The Bendoro sends his greetings, and he asked me to tell you that if there is no prayer house in the village, he would be willing to pay for one to be built."

"Very noble of him," the father commented.

"But I'm sure nobody here has time for that kind of thing," the girl rushed to say. "Everybody is busy, going out to sea—and it's not easy catching fish."

"Don't mock me." There was a touch of anger in the man's voice.

"Oh, Papa, I'm not mocking you. I know how hard it is here. When you can hardly find the strength to put corn on the plate, there's not going to be time for building prayer houses or studying the Koran."

"Do you remember what the elder said last night?"

The girl shook her head.

"No matter how hard you try, you don't have much of a

chance for anything here—not money, not heaven, not even what you need to get by. And all we can expect from death is hell."

"That's the fisherman's life."

"When Dul started his tale last night," the father continued, "he said if the elder thinks that he's going to hell, it's pretty certain we're all going to go with him. He is the wisest man here, after all."

"The Bendoro said he would send a religious teacher."

"How would we pay him?"

"The Bendoro would pay."

"I suppose that'll make the fish easier to catch."

"Who knows, it might."

"I guess we can ask the old man about it. He's the only one with answers."

"The Bendoro also said to rebuild our house with wood. I brought money from him to do it."

"Lot of good that will do," her father commented. "There's nothing to buy here. Besides, our house is the same as everybody else's, and we're not going to be different from the others."

"You could use the money to buy a new boat," the girl suggested.

"We make our own boats here, just like we always have."

"Then what should I say to the Bendoro?"

"Just tell him that the sea is rich, that it gives you everything you need, from food to pearls."

The girl remembered her conversation with the Bendoro. She looked at her father, wondering why he had mentioned pearls.

"You've never talked about pearls before."

"Why should I? They don't make our work more valuable."

"The Bendoro bought me a set."

"Pearls are valuable, even if our labor is not. Only the chosen can wear pearls. Those who dive for them do not."

"Papa . . ."

"Now what?" her father asked.

"Why don't you say my name?"

"It's enough that I say it to myself," he told her.

"Oh, Papa, with you that way, it's like this isn't my home anymore."

"Let me tell you a story. Look around you. Up and down the coast, there's almost no mangrove trees left because they've all been cut down for firewood. But not here. This place is almost untouched, full of young trees, too. Remember that foreigner who we rescued and who we took care of until he was well enough to go back to the city? Before he left, he told us to leave the trees alone. He said that when he got rich, he would come back here to repay his debt to us, that the trees would tell him that he was in the right spot. Now that foreign man never did come back, but the trees are still standing and we leave them alone.

"What I'm trying to say is that anyone who's ever been here, any man who's drunk the briny water here, will never forget this place. And anyone who was ever born here will always be a child of this village."

The girl still persisted. "But look, Papa. None of my older brothers will speak to me."

"They're busy working on the boat. You know that."

"And the younger kids? What did you do? Tell them not to come near me?"

"They're just being taught to show respect for their older sister from the city."

"Oh, Papa, I don't feel any different now from the day you took me to the Bendoro's house."

The father bowed his head, his eyes glistening.

"Maybe I should just go back to the city."

"Well, I'm sure you find this place disappointing; it's a miserable place to live."

"That's not what I'm saying, Papa. I just want to be treated like before. Give me a slap if I'm wrong, but don't hurt me this way. Living in the city is hard for me, but I'm doing it because that's what you wanted for me. Isn't that enough? I'm a nobleman's wife, but so what? What can I do to make you and Mama happy? After all these years, Papa, why are you suddenly acting this way? Ma won't hardly talk to me. What did I do wrong?"

Her father looked up. "Do you think I ever would have given you away if I thought that you'd have to suffer?" He then stopped, suddenly unable to talk. Taking a deep breath to collect himself, he then turned away, but when he began to speak again, his voice was so soft, the girl could hardly hear his words over the sound of the wind: "I know I haven't been the best father. There were times I had to hit you kids . . ."

The girl looked back to see her father, with his head down and his eyes boring into the sandy shore. How was it, she wondered, when seeing him this way, that such a courageous man, who could go out fishing every day and face the storms and the sea, could become so fainthearted when merely in the presence of his daughter, a nobleman's wife?

"What am I doing feeling sorry for myself?" her father finally muttered. He then looked at his daughter and asked, "When will I be granted a grandchild?"

"That only God can say, Papa."

"I'd like to have some grandkids around the house."

"And if you had them, Papa, what would you wish for them?"

"Safety, prosperity, not living like us."

"Like what then? A nobleman?"

"If you have a boy, he'll be a true nobleman."

"If it were up to you, Papa, would you like to be a nobleman?"

"Isn't that what everybody wishes?"

"But if only people knew how the nobility lived their lives . . ."

"At least they don't have to put them at risk every day. At least they're not always covered with mud."

"You have such strange ideas, Papa."

"Both strange and useless," he sighed. "We live, we work, and that's all we do till we can't do anything more, except maybe sit around and give advice to others like the village elder."

"Let's go watch the men fix their nets."

The girl's father looked briefly at the sun. "This time of day, they'd be resting."

"Then how about going to the fishpond?" was the girl's next suggestion.

"It's too far, you'd wear yourself out. Besides, we only just planted the pond eight weeks ago."

The girl encouraged her father to say more: "Have there been lots of people coming to buy hatchlings this year?"

"We've been lucky there. The boys are getting older now and can catch all the more. You should have seen the younger kids; they caught more than a thousand in just one week!"

And then the girl thought of herself, just a few years ago—naked as on the day she was born and armed only with an oyster shell, scouring the shoreline, scooping up milkfish hatchlings and placing them in a small pot of brackish water and mangrove leaves.

"I haven't seen anyone making fish paste," the girl observed.

"No one's buying. Almost nobody comes here looking for fish paste anymore."

"Why is that?" the girl asked. "In the city, most people seem to buy the fish paste from Lasem."

"It's not our fault," her father said knowledgeably. "We heard the buyers who came here were mixing our fish paste with clay before they sold it."

"Not just ours!" the girl emphasized. "A lot of the fish paste in the city is like that."

"Well, we didn't do it. We're not made of swindler stock."

"Of course we're not, Papa, but I did hear about one trader in the city who was doing that. He calls himself a *haji*—says he's been to Mecca and all that—and has three wives: one in the city and two in fishing villages not far away. I heard he was the one mixing clay with ours so that the fish paste from his wives' villages would sell better."

"And we hardly make anything off the hatchlings we sell . . ."

"But do you make enough?"

"Well, we're still alive and we're healthy and not in too bad shape."

They continued their walk back toward home, but the girl's father remained taciturn, speaking only when spoken to.

"Just once, Papa," the girl finally said, "I'd like to hear you call me by my name." She could sense the discomfort that her request caused in her father, but then she herself felt uncomfortable. Why couldn't the two of them be at ease?

The tide was gradually going out, retreating from the village, revealing a sandy, chocolate-colored strand, flat and empty, devoid of motion, that stretched far into the distance. The sea was a narrow ribbon of azure, with a blurred white band as a fringe on top. No boat could be seen on the ribbon. No gusting wind roiled the waves. The mangrove trunks that dotted the shore were black and stiff, utterly lifeless, exuding an air of death. Seagulls, usually hovering over the shore, like kites in the sky, were not to be seen at all. Overhead was only whiteness, a blanket of cotton wool, with no trace of color at all.

"Your mother's making chicken satay for dinner," the girl's father finally said.

Far from cheering the girl, her father's words made her feel empty inside. Never in her life had her mother prepared satay especially for her. The family had only a few chickens, layer hens mostly, for the eggs that were needed to give her father additional strength. Of these hens, how many would have to be sacrificed to prove that she, a young woman born in that fishing village, was different from the town's other inhabitants?

On unsteady legs and with a restless heart, the girl returned to her family home. At the doorway, she looked around to say something to her father, but he had somehow disappeared. Oh, Papa, she screamed silently.

Inside the house, a number of neighbor women were busy helping her mother cook. When they saw the girl, they bowed their heads, eyes fixed on the floor, and stepped aside to give her room to pass. Maybe it's my jewelry, the way I'm dressed, the girl thought. She decided that she would remove her jewelry that evening.

She went to her mother, who was busy grinding chilies for dipping sauce. Her mother immediately stopped working. "Don't come too close; you'll get dirty."

Dirty? The girl suddenly remembered the verdict her husband had laid on the people from this fishing village: They were dirty people and of little faith, which is why they were so poor. She smirked, remembering her own naivete and the question she had asked him at that time: "But if everything and everybody is supposed to be clean at all times, who will do the cleaning up?"

"Dirty!" "Poor!" "Heathens!" "Hell!"—she had rarely heard

such words before she went to live in the city. And it was their frequent use that caused her such confusion. How are you going to salt and dry fish if you're not prepared to gut and clean them first? The fish would rot, and the heroic effort on the part of her father and brothers to catch the fish in the first place would all be in vain. And the distinctive fishlike smell of nets and of the sea, for that matter—what could one do about that? Imported perfume might smell good, but it's certainly not going to make the fish volunteer to come to one's home.

"So what if I get dirty?" the girl finally asked.

"For city people, it's not right. It's different here; we're used to it. Why don't you rest?" her mother suggested. "I'm sure you're still tired from your journey. If you want, I can ask Mak Pin to give you a massage."

"A massage?" The idea of a massage suddenly seemed wonderful. "Yes, I would like that," the girl said, and so one of the neighbors went off to call the masseuse.

Not long afterward, the neighbor returned with Mak Pin, who after positioning herself and the girl on the sleeping platform, began to exercise her skills. For the girl, the expert touch of the woman's hands on her shoulders and back was an entirely new sensation. She marveled at how the woman's fingers were able to relieve the tension in her muscles.

"Have you been doing this long?" she asked the masseuse.

The woman nodded her head.

"Have you ever lived in the city, Mak Pin?" she asked to start a conversation.

After a struggle, the woman finally uttered the word, "Yes."

"Why do you live here then?"

"Yes," she again said with difficulty.

"What did you say?" the girl inquired.

"Yes," Mak Pin said yet again.

The girl smiled to herself. What was the point in asking the woman questions when she apparently couldn't hear? She had never seen the woman before. She lifted her head and turned toward the kitchen.

"Where is Mak Pin from?" she asked no one in particular.

"Don't know," one of the women answered. "She just appeared here one day."

"Where does she live?" the girl then asked.

"Wherever she can," came the answer.

The girl smiled. In the two years that she had lived in the city, she had become of the mind that every person must have a place of his or her own to occupy. She had grown accustomed to thinking that a person was safe only when she was locked inside her house, sleeping peacefully with the knowledge that no stranger would dare to disturb her. But now, back in the fishing village, her birthplace and home, she had begun to rediscover the ways of the world that she had once known. She smiled again, then scolded herself silently for being so forgetful. No one locked their doors in the village, neither during the day nor at night. Doors were meant to block the wind, to keep the sand from coming in the house, not to keep people out. Day or night, the sleeping platform in a person's home was a place shared by everyone, even strangers and guests, without thought of their origins. She sighed again. In the city, a new person would always be asked, "What's your name? Where are you from?" and a host of other questions. Here, no one cared where Mak Pin was from. She could have been born in hell, the girl suspected, for all the attention the villagers paid to her origins. That she could not speak was simply accepted, and no one paid her undue attention because of it.

"Then how do you know her name is Mak Pin?"

"Look at her leg," one woman said, while pointing at the woman with her nose.

"What's wrong with it?"

"She's *pincang.* She walks with a limp."

"*Pincang,* of course!" The girl saw the origins of her name now; the kids in the village must have made it up: first shortening *pincang* to "pin" and then adding "Mak"—meaning "Mrs." or "older woman"—as an honorific. She laughed with delight, not only because of the children's impertinence, but because of the tone of the woman's reply. There was no trace in it of her setting the girl apart from the others. The woman's voice was a true villager's voice, not the voice of a servant addressing her mistress.

Mak Pin then tried to say something, which to the girl's ear was an unintelligible roll of sounds.

"What did she say?"

The clutch of women burst into spontaneous laughter. The girl sighed. The laughter of her fellow villagers—what music that was to her ears, completely free and unrestrained, not in the least like the titter of a servant in front of her *bendoro.*

"That Mak Pin! She'll say anything!" one of the women exclaimed.

"Well, what did she say?"

"She said you don't have a child"—the girl stared at the woman, waiting for more information—"and then she asked if you wanted to have one soon."

Mak Pin released another series of strange growl-like sounds, her voice more beastlike than human. The women broke into laughter again.

For the life of her, the girl couldn't understand what Mak Pin had said. "Now what did she say?"

Another woman volunteered to explain: "She said you have a really small waist—I mean hips," she said, correcting herself before breaking into further laughter.

The girl raised her head and turned to watch Mak Pin speak.

Apparently, she was able to clarify her strange prattle through a descriptive use of her hands.

"What does it matter if I have a small waist and hips?"

At that moment, one of the women pinched Mak Pin on her backside, causing the masseuse to jump up with a shriek and break into a fit of giggles. The woman who had pinched Mak Pin attempted to speak to her in sign language, but the masseuse could not stop laughing. The girl stared at the sight, completely perplexed. Mak Pin then shook her head and began to gesticulate with her hands.

The girl still couldn't discern the meaning. "What's she saying?"

"Such a joker!" a woman chuckled with an embarrassed smile, while stirring a pot of curry.

"She really is too much," another woman boomed.

"Why's that?" the girl asked.

The woman held her sides to keep from laughing as she spoke: "Well, she said, if the Bendoro did . . . If he did that, hmm, and you did this, then this would happen . . ." She couldn't go on.

"Now you're making no sense at all!"

One of the women flipped her hand. "She's just speaking nonsense is all. Nothing to worry about."

The girl felt immensely frustrated. "But I really don't understand what she's saying."

"What she's saying," the woman offered to explain, "is that if you do that thing that married people do you could already have children."

The girl suddenly jumped up from the mattress on which she was lying. She stared into Mak Pin's eyes and studied her features. A sudden look of knowing spread over the girl's face. She looked around at the other women. "Is Mak Pin really not able to speak? She said yes, didn't she?"

"That's all we've ever heard her say. Just imagine how long it took her to learn that. She probably learned it after being beaten in the head by her boss a hundred times or so."

Mak Pin nodded encouragingly and said, "Yes!"

The girl turned back toward Mak Pin, who was motioning for her to lie down, but something was bothering her and she did not know what it was, at least not until she looked into Mak Pin's eyes again. Suddenly, the girl felt a surge of fear that completely drained the color in her face. The laughter in the house died as all her mother's helpers looked back and forth between the girl and Mak Pin.

The girl stepped down from the sleeping platform, her eyes still on Mak Pin. She began to walk slowly backward and away from the woman. The atmosphere in the room had suddenly changed; tension filled its every corner.

At the doorway, the girl screamed, "Papa!" with a wild and frantic look gleaming in her eyes.

The girl's scream brought a number of men running into the house, her father among them. He went to his daughter, whose back was now toward him. Without turning, the girl stretched her one arm behind her until her father had taken her hand.

With her other arm, she pointed at Mak Pin. "Who is she?"

"She's Mak Pin; that's all," the girl's father said, attempting to reassure her.

"She's not Mak Pin," the girl shrieked. "She's a man!"

"A man?" everyone gasped.

Mak Pin suddenly found herself encircled. She turned her head, this way and that, trying to speak to the crowd with her eyes, but no words were forthcoming. Meanwhile, all eyes were searching her face for an answer.

The girl's father suddenly took hold of Mak Pin's arm, causing the masseuse to tremble. "Are you a man or a woman?" He looked around the room. "How long has she been here? What is it now, a couple weeks?" He looked back at Mak Pin. "How long have you been here?"

"How's she going to answer you?" a calmer voice asked. "She can't speak."

"Yes, she can," the girl shouted. "She said yes to me before."

"Say it!" the girl's father roared.

"Yyyeeesss," Mak Pin stuttered.

"She's not dumb," the girl's father said to the crowd. "Come on, are you a man or a woman?" he then asked Mak Pin.

Mak Pin began to gesture with her hands, but the girl's father slapped her across the cheek with his hand.

"Are you listening to me? I'm asking you, are you a man or a woman?" Still receiving no answer, he roared: "Okay, off with the clothes!"

Arms reached out to strip Mak Pin of her clothes, but she struggled and then broke free, finally escaping from the circle. As she ran from the house, several of the men took off after her.

"Catch her!" screamed the girl's father, but Mak Pin had already disappeared from sight.

The rest of the men then took off after her as well. "Grab a rope!" one of them called.

Only the women were now left in the house, all of them staring at the open doorway.

"Never would have thought," an old woman whispered.

"Who would have?" another asked.

The women's comments then came faster, the conversation traveling around the room: "It was yesterday she slept at my house. No, not yesterday, the day before."

"And before that?"

"At my house, but I swear, I really didn't know."

"And last night? Where did she sleep last night?" the girl asked, but no one had an answer.

"Was she at the party?"

The women weren't able to answer that question, either.

"What about during the day?" the girl then asked. "Where was she then?"

"I didn't see her, Bendoro Putri," one woman answered.

"Who did see her?" the girl now demanded, but all the women could do was stare. They didn't know what to say.

"It's such a surprise," one finally said. "None of us had the faintest idea."

She posed another question: "If she really is a man, what do you think she wanted?"

"I suppose what all men want," one said airily, but her answer did not lift the tension in the room.

The girl thought more about the questions that Mak Pin's presence raised. "So, if she wasn't mute . . ." she began to say to herself.

"She was pretending, I suppose."

"But why would she pretend?"

Unable to answer the question, the girl walked to the doorway and looked outside, but there was nothing to be seen. The women hastened to gather around her.

"Maybe he was a thief or a pirate. That's it!" one woman decided.

"Oh, please no," another moaned, as if remembering something.

Just hearing the word "pirate" was enough for the women to immediately close and bar the door.

"What would a pirate want here?" the girl asked. "There's nothing here worth stealing."

Suddenly, all heads turned toward the girl. The women

studied the girl with their eyes, traversing her body from the top of her head to her toes, stopping now and then to study the precious items that adorned her neck, her ears, her fingers, her chest, and her waist. They all then bowed and looked down at the floor.

When one of the women slipped the girl's hand into her own, she discovered the girl was shaking. "Get her something to drink, fast!" she immediately called out. "Sit down," she said to the girl. "The men will take care of it. Don't worry, they're sure to catch him."

The girl suddenly looked around, searching the room with her eyes. "Ma, where are you, Ma?"

"Here I am."

She was standing right beside her.

"How long has Mak Pin been here? Two weeks?"

"No, not that long," her mother told her.

"The men found her on the beach one day when they were going to go out to sea," another added.

"She was shivering from the cold."

"They took her to the chief's house and gave her some coffee."

"She slept right away. Everybody thought she didn't want to speak."

"But it wasn't till the next day we learned that she couldn't speak."

One of the women suddenly slapped herself on the forehead. "Why didn't I remember? When she slept at my house, she talked in her sleep. She really talked. She wasn't dumb."

"What did she say?" the girl asked her.

The woman shook her head. "I don't know. It was too soft for me to understand, but I could tell that she was speaking."

"Where does she keep her things?"

"Doesn't have any that I know of; didn't bring a thing."

"Let's eat," the girl's mother suggested, trying to divert attention from Mak Pin, but none of the women felt hungry.

"Has anything gone missing here?" the girl then inquired.

"What's there to go missing, except maybe some fish bones?"

"That's right," another woman confirmed. "It's been a long time since there's been a robbery here."

"There's nothing for anyone to steal."

"Nobody would come here, no robbers, that is. It's city people who are rich. That's where the money is."

"Yeah, there's nothing here."

"In the city, everyone has gold and jewels." The woman speaking looked at the girl for confirmation. "Isn't that right?"

"Hush. Enough of that," the girl's mother said with finality. "You're just talking nonsense."

The women in the room could not keep from staring at the girl. Meanwhile, skewers of grilled chicken lay cold, uncooked, on the hearth.

Toward sunset, the men of the village returned. The girl's father, along with several other men, came directly to his home. An unhappy look was on his face as he approached his daughter, who was seated on the sleeping platform. The older women in the house immediately gathered around.

The girl raised her head and looked into her father's eyes. "Was Mak Pin a man or a woman, Papa?"

"Mak Pin wasn't a woman, that's for sure," he answered.

"Where is Mak Pin now, Papa?" the girl asked.

"Mak Pin won't be coming back," was his answer.

"Where is he?"

He answered obtusely: "He should have confessed right away. That was his mistake."

"But where is he now?"

The father ignored the question. "He said he was from Demak."

"Demak?"

"Yes, he said Demak, but who's going to believe that? You don't find pirates coming from there. Stubborn, he was; wouldn't confess to being a pirate spy, wouldn't tell us when they were planning their raid. In the end, we had to put him on trial."

The girl remembered something from the past. "You mean you asked him to swim?"

"We took off his clothes and chased him out to sea with six of our boats."

The girl imagined the sight. In the past, whenever a pirate was caught, the men of the village would drive him out to sea with their boats until he could not swim anymore and drowned, that is, if he wasn't attacked by sharks first.

"How far did he swim?"

"Not very far," the girl's father answered.

"What, a few hundred, a few thousand strokes?"

"Not even a dozen. He sank as soon as he was thrown overboard."

"What, he couldn't swim? Then he couldn't have been a pirate," the girl concluded.

"Whatever he was, he shouldn't have been dressed up like a woman."

"That was wrong, Papa. He might have been innocent."

The girl's father shrugged and stared at the floor.

The girl's mother stepped in to defend her husband: "Then why did he pretend he couldn't speak?"

"And why did he pretend to be a woman?" another woman asked.

Yet another villager jumped into the conversation: "And

where was he last night? Nobody saw him eat. He probably was a spy, just one who lives on land."

Anger shone in the father's eyes. He looked at the person speaking, then bowed his head again, shaking it back and forth.

"Then who was he?" the person asked. "What was his name?"

"He called himself 'Mardikun.' "

The girl was startled and immediately thought of Mardinah. Most people didn't have family names, but the names of children within a family were frequently similar. Could Mardikun have been Mardinah's brother? Or was it simply a coincidence that both their names started with 'Mardi'? She tried to picture the man's face more clearly but was unable to draw a clear enough image; he had always bowed his head when she spoke to him.

"Mardikun . . ." she whispered to herself, then looked around to ask the crowd: "Do you remember the young woman who came with me, Mardinah?"

"Mardinah?" they repeated as one.

The girl's father looked at his wife and then at the other women. Something seemed to dawn on him. "There was a resemblance between the two."

The girl asked, "Did Mardikun have a round face? I can't remember clearly."

"It was pretty round, almost like Mardinah's."

"And Mardinah comes from Demak . . ." The girl thought this over. Maybe he was Mardinah's brother or, possibly, her father. But what would he be doing here in her village? "Does the elder know what's happened?" she then asked.

"He's still asleep," one of the men said.

"But that's a good idea," her father continued. "He'll know what this is about."

One of the men immediately broke away from the group to

call the elder to the house. When the old man arrived, his eyes were bright, and he showed no trace of being drowsy or having just woken up. He had already been told of what had happened.

Everyone looked at him, waiting for an explanation, as he raised the mangrove wood cane that he used to help support himself and pointed it at the girl's mother. His voice was gruff and edged with disappointment: "How many times must I tell you? It's gold! Gold is the root of all evil."

The father spoke up defensively: "What does this have to do with gold?"

"What does it have to do with it? How many times have I told you it's gold that runs boats aground and leaves them buried in mud? It's gold, gold, gold!" His eyes jumped from the father to his daughter and the jewelry she was wearing. "That's what makes your daughter here different from all the rest. Tell me what the difference is between us here. What's the difference between you and me? All of us here live off the sea."

The girl's sense of estrangement from her village immediately reemerged. She spoke softly to the old man: "Are you saying, then, that you don't want me to stay here?"

"That's not what I said," he answered gruffly. "You said it."

His words shook the girl. It had finally dawned on her why her fellow villagers' attitudes had changed, why they viewed her as an oddity. It was because of her jewelry; because of that, she was no longer seen as one of the village members.

The father begged for further clarification: "So what's the connection between gold, my daughter, and this Mardikun who was pretending to be Mak Pin?"

The old man could hardly restrain his anger with the girl's father: "You still don't understand? Answer me this, then, where does a civet cat go if not in search of prey?"

Before her father could answer, the girl cried: "Who's the prey? Me? Is it me? And who's the civet cat?"

With the passing of time, the house had grown darker, and more and more villagers had crowded around the open door to see what was happening inside. None of the children dared to stay inside; they were so frightened by the men's raised voices that they had run off to hide in their own homes close to their mothers.

"Shut up!" the old man screamed at the girl.

Now it was the father's turn to be angry. "Hey, we didn't call you here to have you start screaming like a rabid monkey. We want an explanation for what happened."

"How would I know?" he said simply.

"Well, if you don't know, then why are you screaming like the devil's got into you?"

The old man tapped his cane on the hard earthen floor. Calming himself, he spoke in a lower voice: "I ask again, how many times have I told you that on land it's gold that is the root of all evil, just as in the sea it's pearls? The more gold you find in this village, the more often pirates are going to come here."

"Mardikun wasn't a pirate."

"Well, then he was a thief," the old man quipped. "And just wait, there's never a pirate or a thief who works alone. In time his mates are going to show. Just wait," he repeated with marked finality, "whether the gold you have is yours or not, it's not going to matter. They'll cut off your head to get it if need be."

The girl whimpered at the thought.

The old man glared at her. "Makes you scared, doesn't it?" He looked around the room, as if to seek agreement. "There's no point putting the whole village at risk, is there? Not just to protect some gold." In a flash, his anger emerged again: "You're fools, all of you! And so are the police. They're paid to protect the gold of the nobility, the Chinese shopkeepers, the Dutch and the rich *haji*. Idiots, fools, all of you! Even a buffalo can see that."

"You've never been to the city," one of the younger men said accusingly.

"And how old are you, boy? I was going back and forth between Kedah, Trengganu, and Macassar even before your mother could wipe her nose."

"You were a sailor?" someone asked.

"No, I wasn't a sailor. I was a pirate," the old man stated proudly.

The crowd's attitude toward the old man suddenly changed.

"Why are you surprised? What's so strange? When a sailor has had it because he can't make a living from his job, what other choice does he have?" The old man waved his cane at the crowd. "What do you know about how it used to be? Things are a lot better these days."

"I suppose you raided this village, too," one of the men said half-jokingly.

"Hey, you brat," the old man shot back, "if you don't know it already, I'll tell you now that forty years ago I saved this place from pirates. That was before you were a gleam in your father's eyes. You don't know nothing."

"So what are you going on about?" another asked.

"I want to keep this village safe is all, out of harm's reach. The older ones here know about the Dutch military police. But the rest of you? You've never seen them come into a village and slaughter every man and woman present, even babies born just yesterday. If they find out how you killed a man, thinking he was a pirate when he couldn't even swim, what are you going to say to them when they come here looking for him?" At that moment, the old man was racked by a fit of coughing.

"The man is dead; so what do we do now?"

He pointed at the girl with his cane. "Go back, go back to the city!" he yelled at her.

"She just wanted to see her family," her father said. "It's been two years."

"And throw that jewelry you're wearing into the sea!"

"But they're not mine," the girl protested.

"You can say that! Because the fact is, you don't own a thing. They're all the Bendoro's, so return them to him."

"Don't be so hard on her," one of the villagers advised. "She's one of us. She came to visit her folks. Don't tell me you weren't happy when she gave you that Buginese sarong."

This comment caused the old man to pause.

"So why'd you take it?" the person asked.

"She gave it to me. Why shouldn't I take it?" he said defensively. "Do you think it's right a man my age should have to die of cold? Is that too much to ask?"

"Everybody would like to have a nice sarong, not just you, old man."

And so it was, that day the village came to know the meaning of turmoil. For the people there, suspicion and resentment toward their neighbors were unfamiliar sensations. The village's former peace and tranquility seemed to have vanished.

That night, none of the fishermen prepared to go to sea. There was no moon, only the stars in the firmament, blinking meaninglessly. Even the wind refused to blow. And in the darkness of that night, between the howls of feral dogs, the villagers listened to Dul, the tale-singer, singing a new story for them. The boom of his tambourine, the jingle of its bells, accompanied his melancholy song.

No boat went out to sea that night,
no fish were delivered to the shore,
all the fishermen were in misery,
for the many troubles they bore.

A deadly calm bestilled the sea,
nary a ripple ran up the strand,
on each fisherman's face was a frown,
for the curse the gods had put on their land.

The next day, the men of the village gathered again to discuss the problem. Most of what they had to say was cautionary in tone.

"Nobody is to say a word about Mardikun."

"The military police must not find out."

"Or the regular police, either."

"And not the Bendoro."

"Or Mardinah! There has to be something there: She's from Demak and so was Mardikun. Both of them use 'Mardi' in their names."

Perhaps because the old man hadn't been asked to join in the discussion, the atmosphere was not as heated as it had been the day before. Uninvited, the old man had gone for a walk alone down the beach, among the mangrove trees.

At one point, one of the men noticed that Dul, the tale-singer, wasn't present, either.

"Call him here!" another suggested. "We have to be together on this, so we need everyone's opinion."

After he had been called, Dul came, carrying his tambourine with him. After receiving an initial explanation, he was asked what he thought. As if automatically, he slapped his tambourine and began to sing:

When jealousy reigns in one's heart . . .

One of the men immediately held up his hand. "Put that tambourine down, Dul. We don't want to hear a song; we want to know your opinion about what has happened here and your suggestion of what to do."

Another man pulled the tambourine from the tale-singer's hands and carefully placed it on the sleeping platform where the girl was seated. Dul looked around at the circle of men. His mouth hung wide open, and his eyes kept darting toward the tambourine.

"Come on, say something," one of the men cajoled, but Dul's odd behavior continued. His mouth remained agape, his eyes stayed fixed on the tambourine.

"What's with him?" someone muttered.

"What's wrong with you?" another put it to Dul directly.

"He's just being weird," yet another man answered.

Dul could do nothing, it seemed, but stare at the tambourine. He was completely tongue-tied.

"Give him back the tambourine," someone finally suggested.

The singer's face brightened as soon as the tambourine was returned to him.

The girl was the only one in the room really paying attention to the tale-singer. She was fond of him and had known him ever since she was a child. People said he was mad and often called him Crazy Dul, in addition to his more common moniker, Dul the Storyteller, which he had earned because he never did anything but tell stories. In the girl's village, where everyone worked and the word "lazy" was not in the normal vocabulary, Dul was a lazy man. Strangely enough, though, he was also fit and strong.

Word had it that Dul had been so afraid of going out to sea when he was small that during the day his father had let him wander about wherever he wanted to. At night, after the sun was down, his parents would find him asleep outside the door. And in the early morning, when his father was ready to set off to sea, he always took great care when opening the door in order not to disturb his son.

Dul was now thirty or older, but no woman would have him for a husband. Though he was not an unattractive man, his indolence was incurable. "*I'd even take a granny for a wife, if she would only have me,*" he sometimes sang at night as part of his evening repertoire. Be that as it may, not even the oldest women in the village wanted to be the wife of a lazy man.

As the rest of the room tried to come up with a solution, Dul suddenly beat his tambourine and began to sing, even amid the cries for him to stop.

Go back, young lady, go back,
to the city where riches are found,
don't bring your gold and diamonds here,
the village will be razed to the ground.

"Tell that good-for-nothing madman to shut his mouth!" a man shouted. "Put a plug in his mouth."

"But we called him here to help solve this problem."

"Maybe so, but not to tell us stories."

"That's all he can do," came the rejoinder, "and then only if he has his tambourine."

The conversation began to wander.

"Why can't he use a drum?"

"You don't find drums anywhere except in rich people's homes."

"He's been to the city, hasn't he?"

"Where else does he go when he disappears if not to the city?"

"Come on, Dul, tell us: Do you go to the city a lot?"

"Nobody's ever asked him where he got the tambourine."

One of the men tried to steer the conversation back to the matter at hand: "Enough of this; we're here to discuss things, not talk about him."

"So what's there really to discuss?"

No one had an answer.

Dul suddenly struck his tambourine and began singing again:

Go back, go back to the city,
take your gold and diamonds, too,
happiness awaits you there,
the village is no place for you.

The girl herself finally raised her voice in protest. "Why do I have to go back to the city? I was born here. My parents are here."

When darkness comes to the village,
the lamps are filled with oil,
if all one thinks of is money and gain,
there's no getting 'round trouble or toil.

"Don't preach to us," someone hooted at Dul. "Keep your advice to yourself, and go find yourself a job!"

"How could he? Couldn't catch himself a turtle if he tried!"

The tambourine immediately resounded in response to the man's critical remark:

Catching a turtle is no great effort,
for a man with air in his head,
since eating fish is all he's known,
his brain is pickled, his stomach is lead.

"I'm going to kick the shit out of you!" the man screamed, but Dul kept banging on his tambourine, nearly drowning out the man's voice.

"You're just pretending to be crazy 'cause you got the brain of a spiny fish."

"Not a spiny fish, a mullet!" someone interjected.

"More like a shrimp," another corrected.

"A dead anchovy!" another had to say.

With the storyteller now becoming the butt of everyone's jokes, the atmosphere grew lively. Everyone was laughing.

"You know what he has inside that head of his? A jellyfish!"

Not finished with his commentary, it was the storyteller's turn to respond:

When the soldiers come, their guns aroar,
they'll turn the village upside down,
all the blowhards, guess where they'll be,
at sea, for sure, all safe and sound.

A sudden pounding on the door threw a hush over everyone except for Dul the tale-singer, who continued to tap his tambourine. All eyes turned toward the door, where the village elder was standing, fiercely upright, with his cane pointed directly at Dul.

"So that's what people who have been to the city are like?" Anger was in his eyes. "You crazy, good-for-nothing. You can't even show respect toward a fisherman's work. That tambourine of yours doesn't give us food. It's the fish from the sea that keep us alive. But all you can do is make fun of us here, just like a city man!"

"He's never said he's been to the city," came a voice in the singer's defense.

"Well, where did he get that tambourine then?" the old man

asked. "He used to use a tin can." He looked back at Dul. "Come on, where did you get the tambourine? I'll tell you," he said to the crowd. "He got it from begging. In the city, you see, you can't go to the mosque shaking a can for alms; they'll throw you out as soon as they look at you. But with a tambourine, he could go right in and plop himself down beside the preacher at the pulpit. Begging is easier with a tambourine. And he is a beggar, nothing but a beggar and an ungrateful one at that!"

The drum at the mosque is big and grand,
with a fine sound, there is no doubt,
but have you heard of the pious preacher,
who is in fact a dirty lout?

"Go peddle your songs in town," the old man advised. "We can get by without them here."

But now the crowd was curious. Who was Dul referring to?

"Come on, Dul, tell us who this lout is who pretends to be devout?"

Dul's hands moved more rapidly over the tambourine, creating a story of sound, at once inviting, protesting, rebellious.

"Sounds like he's mad," someone said.

"Are you mad, Dul?" another asked the tale-singer, but Dul kept on playing the tambourine.

"If you spend your time talking to crazy people, you'll end up crazy yourself," was what one man had to say.

"Get him out of here!" another ordered.

At once, one of the men gave Dul a well-aimed kick and sent him sprawling on the floor. His tambourine, knocked from his hand, rolled away from him and out the door. As though half-paralyzed, the singer stared at his tambourine for the longest time before he crawled across the floor and out the doorway.

"Look at him; he's acting even crazier than before," a man remarked. "How'd he get that way?"

"Cursed from birth is what I heard," the first man answered. "When his mother was pregnant with him, she pulled the legs off a live crab—which is why he can't use his arms and legs for work."

"Come on, what are we talking about here?" a third man asked, causing the crowd to fall silent.

"There's nothing really to talk about," the girl's father said. "Yesterday, we asked the elder's opinion and he went off the handle, like he had the devil inside him, and then he got everybody else riled up. What is there to fight about?"

No one in the room seemed to have an answer. Into the room's silence came the sound of Dul's voice and another melancholy song.

One of the men held up his hand. "Listen! He might be crazy, but he does know how to sing. It sounds to me like he's trying to tell us something."

The crowd now listened more carefully.

Waves curl and break on the shore,
as fisher boats race toward light,
in the village no greed is found,
people work hard, both day and night.

Like a school of tuna, out at sea,
where one swims, the others go,
supporting a family demands hard work,
but with the sweat, grace, too, shall flow.

A strong wind strikes the brow,
the shrimp are dry and ready to pound,

both men and women might be afraid,
but as one can stand their ground.

"He is trying to tell us something!" one of the men announced before sticking his head out the door and motioning for Dul to come back inside.

This time the singer refused to come in and began to play his tambourine all the louder.

Woe be the fate of the fisherman,
no wealth will he ever hold,
forget the thought of gold and gems,
when a spoonful of rice is wealth untold.

Let the young lady decide for herself,
the choice is only her own,
two years of living in the city, she says
is like tens of years of living at home.

The tale-singer now stood up and began to walk away, singing his song as he went. Inside the room, everyone looked furtively at the girl to see her reaction.

All eyes on her, she finally announced, "I'll make my own decision."

The sound of Dul's tambourine grew fainter until finally it faded away.

"I suppose he's going to the city," someone commented.

"We can't let him do that!" another announced. "If we don't stop him, it could be the end for us."

"What, do you think he'd go to the military? Or the police?"

"We can't take the chance. We have to catch him."

The girl suddenly grew worried about Dul's fate. "Don't do anything to him," she pleaded.

"Nothing's going to happen to Dul," one of the men told her. "We'll just tie him up for a while, so that he doesn't go talking to the authorities in town."

And that is exactly what they did.

The day passed quickly, the night came fast, and before the villagers could digest all the events that had happened the previous day, the village was roused again, this time by the return of Mardinah, who had come with a retinue of men.

Upon arriving at the village, Mardinah went directly to the girl's house and there delivered her news: "The Bendoro has ordered you to come home, Young Mistress, this very same night."

"He gave you his written orders?" the girl asked. "Do you have them with you?"

From inside her chemise, Mardinah withdrew an envelope and handed it to her mistress. The girl looked suspiciously at her servant. The girl's parents and siblings were there in the house with her, but they all remained standing, watching the scene unfold, without bothering to ask their uninvited guest to be seated. By this time, the other villagers had once again gathered outside the door to the house.

"Since you can't read, Young Mistress, I can read it for you," Mardinah offered.

The girl turned to her father. "Who in the village can read, Papa?"

"Here? No one," he stated flatly.

"I might be able to," came a voice from the crowd, "but it has been a long time since I read anything."

"Here, let me read it," Mardinah insisted as she took the envelope from the girl's hand, then tore it open and removed the letter from inside. She then read out, "Young Mistress, please come home." That said, she stood silently in place.

"Is that all?" the girl asked.

"Yes, that's all," Mardinah affirmed.

"There's a lot of writing there."

"But that's all it says," Mardinah insisted.

The villager who had spoken early spoke up again: "Here, let me give it a try,"

"That won't be necessary," Mardinah snapped.

"Fine then, if it's not necessary—but if the Young Mistress has to go back to the city tonight, then we'll all go with her."

Mardinah rejected the idea immediately: "That's impossible. There are only two carriages."

"Then I guess we'll just have to walk."

"Walk? You mean on foot?"

"It's either that or squeeze into the carriages."

The onlookers watched the girl, waiting for her to speak.

Finally, she turned to her father and asked, "Must I go back, Papa?"

"If you ask your mother," he told her, "I'm sure that she would tell you to go."

Mardinah's four escorts silently stood in attendance. When one of them coughed, all heads turned toward him. To them, there seemed to be a strange light in the man's eyes, one that could only excite distrust and unease.

"Give me the letter," the girl's father said to Mardinah.

"What's the use? You can't read," she said with a frown.

"The letter is for my daughter, not for you."

"Yes, give him the letter," the onlookers said in unison.

Sensing that she was being threatened, Mardinah's four escorts drew closer to her, forming a protective circle.

"No, I'm not going to," Mardinah stated as she began to slip the letter back inside her chemise.

The girl's father was just as insistent: "Then my daughter is not going to leave. You can go back to the city without her."

"That's impossible," Mardinah argued. "She must go back home tonight."

"There's no proof of that."

Mardinah patted her breast. "This letter is the proof."

One of Mardinah's escorts attempted to break the standoff: "If the Bendoro says she has to go, then she has to go."

"It's you who can go," the father announced. "I can take her back to the city myself, tonight if need be."

"There's no place in the carriage for you," another escort remarked.

"And there's no place in this house for you," the father shouted. "Now get out of here."

Suddenly, the girl's mother was at her daughter's side, telling her, "Don't go." And then the clatter of bamboo alarm gongs suddenly was heard, spreading throughout the town. In an instant, all the men of the village were at the girl's house, attempting to push their way inside. In their hands they carried an assortment of weapons: machetes, axes, clubs, even oars. Those men who were unable to fit inside the house took up positions around the hut.

"My daughter will go if there is proof. Give me the letter," the father repeated.

"Yeah, give it to him," the crowd repeated.

In the face of so many armed men, Mardinah's escorts drew back in fear. Mardinah had no choice but to hand the letter to the girl's father.

The father looked around the room. "Who said he could read?"

An older man spoke up. "I did, but that was twenty years ago."

The man took the letter from the girl's father and held it close to the lantern. He stared at the sheet of paper and the words it contained.

"What does it say?" someone asked, beginning a round of comments.

"You're taking an awfully long time."

"I said it's been twenty years."

"We know that. Just tell us what it says."

"But this isn't written in Javanese."

"What is it then?"

"The devil's tongue for all I can tell."

Mardinah huffed sarcastically. "I already read it for you, but you don't believe me."

"Count the number of lines," the girl's father requested.

"One, two, three . . . Twenty!" the older man announced.

"But you read only one line," the father said to Mardinah. "Why not the other ones, too?"

"Why should I?" She pointed at the sheet of paper. "Those lines are the Bendoro's address, and those are the address of the Young Mistress here."

"And what is our address?"

Never before had the two young women—the Girl from the Coast and Mardinah—stared at each other so intently. As they looked at each other, Mardinah's escorts kept a careful eye on the girl's father.

Mardinah didn't ask for the letter back and made no attempt to read it.

The girl pointed her hand accusingly at Mardinah. "I'm ordering you to read the entire letter."

"That's not necessary," she retorted, then flicked her hands at the villagers around her, trying to chase them away. "What are you doing in here anyway? Go on, get out of here."

Then there came a sudden shouting at the doorway—"What's this? What's happening?"—and the village elder made his way into the house. Looking around, he raised his cane and pointed it at Mardinah and her retinue. "City people! Wherever city people go, trouble is sure to follow."

Mardinah turned toward her escort, giving a sign for them to leave. "Fine, we'll go, but when we come back, it will be with the police," she warned.

"The police?" the crowd murmured.

"Yes, the police!" Mardinah threatened. "I'm sure they'll have a lot to ask you."

As this was happening, the girl's father whispered something to the man beside him, who immediately left the house. Then, as if attempting to distill the mounting tension, he turned to Mardinah and spoke to her in a patient voice: "There will be no need to bring the police here. Let's sit down and talk about this. Really, there's no need to be upset."

Mardinah had no patience left and pounced angrily: "There's nothing to talk about! The Young Mistress must go back to the city now!"

"Of course," the father assented, "but you must give her time to get ready."

As if an agreement had been reached, the tension suddenly diminished, and from the look on their faces, even Mardinah's escorts had regained some of their former self-assurance. But just then, all the bamboo alarm gongs in the village began to ring at once. Everyone looked around, wondering what the danger was, until they heard someone shout: "Pirates! They've landed and are going to attack. Run!"

Immediately, all the men ran out of the house brandishing their weapons.

"They're coming this way!" another person shouted.

Mardinah turned pale. Her escort was frantic, not knowing what to do.

"Where can we hide?" she cried weakly.

"Follow the others," she was told.

"But where to?"

"To defend the village!"

"No, we'd best go back to the city fast."

"It won't be safe on the roads."

"I'll get my things," the girl decided.

"They'll be here soon," her father warned.

"We should blow out the candle," she whispered.

"No, not just yet," he said under his breath.

Suddenly, they heard a clamor of voices outside: "We got two of their spies!"

"Bring them in here!" the girl's father shouted.

Thereupon, two men were pushed inside the room, their faces black and blue. The men staggered as they were dragged closer to the light.

"Oh my God!" Mardinah cried. "Those men are our drivers."

"Yes, they're our drivers," one of her escorts confirmed.

"Your drivers, are they?" the father asked.

"No, they're not," one of the men's accosters shouted. "They're pirate spies!"

"No, we're not!" one of the drivers yelped. "We're only drivers. A band of pirates attacked our carriage. We managed to get away, but when they saw the carriages were empty, they took our horses."

"What happened to the horses?"

"They're dead," one of the villagers announced. "We found them near the brush line; they'd been axed in the head and their legs."

"What about you?"

"They followed us, but we got here first."

"Blow out that candle!" the father screamed.

In an instant, the house was pitch-dark.

"Everybody outside!" he then barked, and everyone ran outside. A baby could be heard, wailing in the distance.

"They're getting close," someone whispered.

Suddenly, the darkness seemed even darker.

"Come on," the father said, "we have to go out to sea." He began to herd the people toward the shore. "Hurry up."

In their scrambling toward the shore, one of the drivers asked the girl: "Who's going to get us new horses?"

"Shut up!" she snapped. "You two are lucky you didn't have your throats slit."

The entire village had left their homes and all the inhabitants were making their way along the shore toward the river's estuary where the fishermen moored their boats.

"Save the girl!" someone called. "Take her out to sea!"

"Both of them," another person shouted. "Take them both out to sea."

"They can go in one boat. The escort can go in two other boats."

"That's good. We've got to break up. We don't want to get caught."

Mardinah was still very nervous. "But aren't there pirates out there, too?"

"Even if there are, it will be easier to get away by sea than by land."

The fishermen untethered their boats, ready to receive their passengers.

"Get in, fast!"

The darkness was filled with the sound of feet splashing through the water.

"Don't worry, city folks," a villager commented. "There aren't many crocodiles here."

"That's right," another man added. "There aren't no crocodiles here. They like to swim in the rivers closer to town."

One of Mardinah's escorts looked at the man in surprise and asked him, "Why is it none of you seem very scared?"

"We're used to it," the man answered. "Happens at least twice a year around here."

"Where do the pirates come from?"

"I don't know. The city, I suppose."

"Stop your talking," the girl's father warned. "And get in those boats now!"

Soon after, the three boats carrying the girl, Mardinah, and her bodyguard were racing through darkness toward the open sea.

As the sun rose, it looked like another normal day in the village. Chickens were pecking in the lanes. The villagers were tending to their customary tasks.

At the house of the Girl from the Coast, friends of the girl's father had gathered and were speaking to him. Their conversation was quick and guarded.

"So, what do you think?" the father asked.

"Seems to have gone off all right," one of the men answered.

"What about the horses? Were they really killed?"

"No, just moved somewhere else."

"But the drivers said they were killed."

"Nah, just had to hit 'em a little hard is all."

"Where are the horses now?"

"We took them into the jungle and left them there."

"And the carriages . . ."

"Cut through the spokes is all. They'll be easy enough to repair."

"And my daughter? Is she back to shore?"

"Yes, but we're holding her for the time being."

"And Mardinah's bodyguard?"

"Since they were armed we had to beat them in the dark with our oars."

"Did they confess to anything?"

"Sure did. Said they were supposed to kill your daughter on the way home."

"What for?"

"They didn't know. All they were doing, they said, was carrying out orders from Demak."

"What did you do with them? Throw them overboard?"

"We had to."

"And were they like Mardikun?"

"Just like him. Couldn't even swim."

"And the two in the other boat?"

"I suppose the same."

"And Mardinah? Did you find out why she's here?"

"She came to find her brother."

"Who told you that? Those men?"

"None other."

"But they didn't know who in Demak was giving the orders?"

"No."

"So, Mardinah was their only contact?"

"Looks like it."

"I guess, then, it's Mardinah who knows what's going on."

"We'll have to keep her here."

"What was in it for her? Who was behind it?"

"I'm sure we'll find out."

"It's too bad nobody can read."

"What about Dul? We forgot about him. He might have learned how to read."

"Is he still tied up?"

"Yeah, he's in the shed where we keep the fish traps."

"He didn't catch sight of the drivers, did he?"

"Couldn't have."

"Then release him and bring him here."

When Dul appeared at the house, tambourine in hand, all eyes turned toward him. As he looked around the room, he patted the sides of his tambourine, trying to figure out what was happening.

"Can you read?" the girl's father asked him with a shout.

Startled, the storyteller automatically began beating the tambourine while shouting at the same time, "No, no, no!"

The girl's father looked at the other men. "Then tie him up again."

Once more the tambourine rang in protest, causing the men to wait before seizing the tale-singer and to give him a chance to speak. Dul's beating on the tambourine slowed, and he began to sing in a firm voice:

Wherever it is the little one goes,
impostors hold reception,
villagers are such an innocent bunch,
an easy target for deception.

Who would have thought, who could have known . . .

"Who would have known what?" the listeners cried as the tambourine changed its tone.

Since even' time with sails unfurled,
boats have gathered fish into their nets,
oh, pity the villagers of today,
deceit is a hobby, the game to play.

"Is he calling us cheats?" one of the men asked angrily.

"Don't go making things up," another warned.

Dul kept on singing, ignoring the comments around him.

What pirate would call at this village,
when dried shrimp is all he'd find,
what pirate would come here to commit his crime,
when all he'd find is girls covered with grime.

There is no wealth, there are no goods
even the jellyfish stay away . . .

He wasn't given the chance to finish his song. "Get the hell out of here," one of the men yelled, before pushing him unceremoniously out the door.

The tale-singer's song had had an unsettling effect on the men; the very thought of it made them angry. What were they to do, they all wondered, about this man who would not stop singing his crazy but telling songs?

As they listened to the sound of Dul's tambourine, now growing fainter as the singer walked away, the conversation resumed.

"He's never acted that strange before," one of the men said.

"The old man was right," another commented. "The city ruins everything. Dul really is crazy."

"I'm not sure about that," the girl's father said. "I think he just acts crazy. He's got a watchful look in his eyes, and you can tell his mind is always turning, thinking."

"Then he's dangerous," one of the men surmised. "What are we going to do with him?"

"It's that mouth of his that's going to get us all into trouble. We'll have to tie him up again." He motioned for two of the men to apprehend Dul. "And take away his tambourine!" he told them. "Put it away somewhere, anywhere, as long as it's out of reach."

Although the sound of the tambourine could no longer be heard, uneasiness still reigned in the room. The air was stifling and the wind, as if averse to blowing, had died and provided no relief. The leaves of the sago palm that grew beside the hut were motionless. The labored breathing of the men and the waves of heat from off the sand were the only signs of motion and life.

"What are we going to do now?" someone asked.

"What do you think the chief would say?"

"What more is there to say?"

"His life is on the line, too."

"Not just him, all of us."

"It's only the old man who doesn't seem too worried."

"What's he got to be worried about except where he's going to be buried?"

"That old devil; he only thinks about himself."

"That's not true. He's thinking about our safety, too."

"I just don't understand how all of this happened."

"It's too late to worry about that now. We've gotten ourselves into a fix and we have to find a way out of it. There's no other choice. What happened to the two bodyguards in the other boat?"

"You, Timin, go find out what happened."

The man named Timin immediately left the house. The rest of the men waited for him to return. Most sat silently, thinking about the events of the past few days, musing over how slowly time seemed to have passed, as if their lives were suddenly being enacted in slow motion. No one had gone fishing the night before; their fresh food stores had been depleted. The men's nerves were taut; they were exhausted; almost none of them had slept. Their provisions of kerosene had been exhausted, forcing them to use coconut oil to light their lamps, whose wavering soot-filled flames served only to increase the gloomy atmosphere.

Eventually, Timin returned, bringing news that the other two guards were dead. They, too, he reported, had been carrying weapons. And then, finally, the Girl from the Coast and Mardinah appeared, both of them looking exhausted and pale.

"I'm afraid you won't be able to go home," the girl's father told them. "The pirates destroyed the carriages, both of them."

He looked at Mardinah, who seemed to be only half-listening to him.

"And that's not the worst of it. They killed some of our people and three of your bodyguards, too. Doesn't look like the other one is going to make it either. He has a spear going straight through his shoulder."

Mardinah's face flushed. Her eyes flashed, and her hands and lips began to quiver.

"We found their bodies this morning. The pirates must have surrounded them at sea. There were knife wounds all over their bodies."

The father stared at Mardinah.

"Didn't you hear anything? You must have heard them scream."

Mardinah shook her head.

"I heard some screams," his daughter whispered, "but they were very faint. It was completely dark. We didn't have lanterns and our boats got separated."

"You're lucky they didn't catch you, too. Those people don't show mercy on anyone. Thank God you're safe," he said to his daughter. "And you, too," he nodded toward Mardinah.

The father looked at the other villagers, who simultaneously expressed their thanks for the young women's safe return.

"We were worried about you," one of them said.

"But you won't be able to go back to the city, Young Mistress," another confirmed.

The girl's mother then came into the house, along with the girl's siblings and some of her other relatives.

After they had said their greetings, the girl looked toward the kitchen hearth. She was famished. "Ma, is there anything to eat?" she asked.

"I just got here," her mother answered apologetically.

"Then we'll have to cook something," the girl announced. "Is there any of the rice I brought from the city?"

"Yes, there is," her mother answered, "but not much of anything else." She looked at the other women in the room. "Well, let's get to it!"

Weary as they were, the women began preparing food.

As the women busied themselves in the kitchen, Mardinah collapsed on the sleeping platform and, a moment later, was fast asleep, showing no sign of movement except the rise and fall of her chest. Soon afterward, the girl lay down beside her and fell asleep, too.

Although the men were also tired, they were intent on continuing their discussion, and together, in a long and whispered discussion, they tried to work out what they were going to do. Gradually, however, they began to drift away until only the girl's father was left. And then even he went away.

When the food was ready, the two young women were awoken, but the meal proceeded slowly; as hungry as everyone was, no one seemed to have an appetite. After the dishes had been cleared away, Mardinah returned to the sleeping platform, intending to rest again. The girl sat down beside her.

Almost as if he had timed his return, the girl's father appeared in the doorway at that moment and walked straight to the sleeping platform.

"I'm afraid that you'll both have to stay here," he said to the two young women. "We can't call for another carriage, at least not for now." He then looked directly at Mardinah. "We're willing to help you, but you're going to have to help us, too. We're poor people who don't eat unmixed rice but once a year. Usually, we eat corn. We don't have anything more to give you, except this one meal. Starting tomorrow, you're going to have to work for your meals—help fish, mend nets, or whatever you're good at."

Mardinah looked incredulous. "Me, do that kind of work? Do you know who I am?"

"Of course I do," the father said sympathetically. "That's why I'm telling you this now. Starting tomorrow, we won't be able to provide your food. And you'll have to find your own place to sleep. Where is up to you."

"But you were able to help before. Why can't you anymore?"

"You were our guest then. Now you're not," the father explained.

"I can't do it," Mardinah stated. "I just can't do that kind of work."

"Then I guess you'd best go home," the father said.

Mardinah shook her head. "But there's no carriage."

"You can walk."

"I'd be too afraid."

"Then you're going to have to stay here."

"I can pay. Just tell someone to take me."

"There's nobody here who would. You'll have to go home alone."

Mardinah tried to reason with him: "I'm afraid, and I don't know how to work, but I do have some money. I can pay my way. I can pay for my food, for a bed, a place to bathe, something to drink . . ."

"How much money do you have?" the father asked.

"Not that much, but probably enough for a few days, at least until a carriage can come for us."

"But no carriage is going to come here, not unless we call one."

Mardinah was getting angry: "Well, then, call one!"

"That's not possible. We haven't been fishing for days. And what with all the ruckus around here, everybody's plain worn out."

"Let me think about this tomorrow."

"I'm sorry, but in the morning, you'll have to find your own food and your own place to stay. You'd best make your decision right now."

Now she looked offended. "You don't have to speak that way to me."

"I'm sorry," the man apologized, "but I can't speak any other way."

"Really," Mardinah insisted, "I'll pay for everything."

"So, you don't want to work, but you do want to pay?"

Mardinah huffed: "That's what I said, isn't it? How much do you want?"

The girl's father cocked his head, stood up, and walked toward the door. There he coughed and cleared his throat, then turned around and came back to the sleeping platform. Mardinah no longer looked drowsy at all.

"It'll cost a lot," he said.

"What, a *ringgit,* two and a half rupiah?"

The father laughed.

"Three?"

He laughed again.

"Five, six, ten? Just tell me!"

"Where'd you ever get that much money?" he asked Mardinah.

The girl rose from the sleeping platform. "In the city, she's my servant, Papa," the girl explained.

He looked at his daughter. "A servant, is she? Then maybe you can tell me where she got that much money."

Mardinah bowed slightly to gather the hem of her batik wraparound in her fingers. She then glared at the girl. "You do know who my father is, don't you, Young Mistress?"

"You said he was a scribe," the girl answered.

"What, don't you think scribes make any money?"

"Well, is he rich? What does he own?" the girl asked.

"He owns rice fields, lots of them. Houses, too, and dozens of rental carriages."

The father interrupted: "Even so, you cannot leave this village."

"I can pay however much is asked."

"Then you can pay with those fields and houses and carriages of yours," he suggested. "I could have the village chief go to the city tomorrow. Give him five rupiah so that he can go take a look at those fields, houses, and carriages of yours. He can deal with your family and have it all put down in writing that you're turning those things over to us. When that's done, we'll take you back to the city. How's that for a plan?"

"Impossible! How could I hand over rice fields to you?"

"I'm sorry," he apologized again, "it was only a suggestion.

If you don't want to do that, that's all right, too, but then maybe you'd better find a new place to sleep tonight. No need for you to wait until tomorrow."

Mardinah bowed her head.

The girl's father pricked up his ears. "Listen to that!"

Mardinah raised her head and listened. She could hear the howling of feral dogs.

"Go," the man told her. "Please go. I'm sure you can find some place to sleep among the mangroves."

The dogs howled plaintively.

Mardinah clenched her hands to her breast. Her face was so pale, her lips appeared blue. With the light of the lamp shining behind her, her hair seemed higher, as if it were standing on end.

"Please go," the father repeated. "If you don't want to go on your own, I guess I'll have to drag you out myself."

"Oh please, please don't," Mardinah moaned.

"I don't have a choice. But first tell me how much money you have on you. Now!" he yelled at her.

Mardinah cringed with fright. All the villagers, crowding into the house with various implements in hand, made the room seem all the more threatening.

"These people have come to help you prepare a place to sleep in the mangroves," he told her.

"Please, no, don't make me sleep out there."

"Then tell me, how much money do you have here with you?"

"Fifty rupiah," she answered weakly.

"Where did you get all that money?"

"My father is rich," Mardinah repeated.

"Liar!" several people said in unison.

The circle of villagers around Mardinah converged on her

with menacing looks. The young woman covered her eyes with her hands and began to cry.

"Your tears aren't going to do you any good here," the father warned. "Out there, in the mangroves, you can cry as much as you want to."

"Stop!" Mardinah screamed in fright.

"Where did the money come from?"

"Nooooo," she moaned.

The father looked at his fellow villagers. "Take her away!"

Even as the girl pleaded, the father continued to bark out his orders: "What are you waiting for? Take her away!"

Mardinah's hands clutched the mat on the sleeping platform. "Have mercy," she pleaded.

"There's no need for mercy. Just tell me where you got the money."

Mardinah began to tremble uncontrollably.

"Tell me, now!"

"From the Bendoro in Demak," she whimpered.

"Which Bendoro?" the father asked.

"I can't tell you."

"Was it your master or mistress who ordered you here?"

"No."

"Then who ordered you?"

"It was me, nobody else!"

"Why did you want to kill my daughter?"

"I didn't, I really didn't."

He shouted an order at the crowd: "That bodyguard of hers, the one with the spear in his shoulder . . . Bring him here!" He looked back at Mardinah. "We'll have him give his confession here, right in front of you. Do you want that, young lady?"

Mardinah couldn't speak.

"He swore that if you didn't own up, he'd slit your throat

himself." He spoke again to the villagers: "Tie her legs together. We can do the job ourselves. There's nobody who knows she's here. Even her Bendoro in the city doesn't know."

Mardinah rolled onto her stomach and, with both arms outstretched, clung tightly to the edges of the sleeping platform.

"You're wasting your time," the father told her. "If we cut off your hands, what are you going to hold on with then?"

Mardinah screamed in panic and fear.

"And stop that screaming! There's no one from the city to hear you. And nobody here is going to help."

The Girl from the Coast sobbed as Mardinah wailed.

"Confess!" the father screamed again.

Mardinah hugged the platform more tightly. "The Regent promised that I, that I could be . . ."

The villagers moved in closer to be able to hear.

"His wife, his fifth wife, if I . . ."

"If you what?"

"If I could help, if I could help . . ."

"Say it!"

"If I could help his daughter become the Bendoro's wife."

"And how much was your boss paying you to get rid of my daughter?"

"One hundred rupiah."

"Where is it now?"

"There were a lot of expenses. There's only half of it left."

"And if you succeeded, how much more when it was over?"

"Mercy! Have mercy!" she pleaded again.

"What are you going to do with a woman like this?" the father asked.

The question caused everyone to stop and think until one of the villagers announced: "I got it! We can give her to Dul!"

The suggestion caused everyone to cheer.

"Just think of how happy he's going to be!" someone said.

The crowd laughed again, even as Mardinah softly wept.

"Have you met Dul?" the girl's father asked Mardinah. "He's got a good voice. At night, you can listen to him sing."

As he began to play an imaginary tambourine, some of the villagers whistled. Their cheer helped Mardinah stifle her sobs.

The father now addressed Mardinah: "So, how about it? Do you want to sleep in the mangroves or spend the night with Dul?"

Mardinah had stopped crying; now she was staring at the floor.

"So what's it going to be?" the girl's father repeated. "You're not married, are you?"

His daughter supplied the answer: "She's divorced."

Because Mardinah said nothing, the girl's father spoke again to the crowd around him: "As you can see, the young lady here isn't saying anything. That being the case, I'm going to take her silence to mean that she agrees."

The crowd waited for Mardinah to speak, to protest, to do something, but she remained sitting in silence on the edge of the platform.

"What are you waiting for?" he then asked the crowd. "Stand up," he said to Mardinah, "they're going to take you to Dul's place."

Mardinah rose wearily to her feet.

"Be gentle with her," the father advised. "Take her to the fish trap shack and don't leave until she's safe inside."

Mardinah walked slowly toward the door, her head bowed deeply. The Girl from the Coast ran ahead of her, and stood in her path.

"I didn't want this to happen, Mardinah," the girl whispered.

"I know, Young Mistress."

"If only you'd thought about what your actions might do . . ."

She stepped aside, permitting Mardinah to move forward, and then asked, "Do you object to being given to Dul?"

Mardinah shrugged her shoulders and walked outside, disappearing into the darkness, with the crowd of villagers around her.

"Timin!" the father called, whereupon the young man immediately strode to his side. "I want you to stay outside of the fish trap shack and keep an eye on Dul and Mardinah. Make sure they don't try to escape. You can untie Dul and give him back his tambourine but don't go far away."

With a simple nod, the young man turned and left the house, then ran to catch up with the cheering crowd of people who were leading Mardinah to the fish trap shack.

Inside the house, the Girl from the Coast was crying. Her father looked at her momentarily, then turned and went outside.

The girl's mother came over to her and sat beside her. "Why are you crying?"

"I feel sorry for her," her daughter said.

"None of the women here will have Dul. It'll be good to have a woman looking after him," her mother reasoned.

"But they're villagers, Ma. Mardinah is from the city. She wouldn't want a man like him."

"Considering the crime, the punishment isn't so harsh."

"What? Having to marry a man who can't even look after himself? That's not harsh?" The girl thought of the recent events that had caused such an uproar. "Tell me, Ma, were Mardinah's bodyguards really killed by pirates?"

"You'll have to ask your father that," her mother said. "Now you should get some sleep. I'm going to talk to your father," she added, while leaving the house.

As dawn approached, roosters began to crow. The girl listened silently to them and also to the sound of the waves throwing themselves down and running up the shore.

"Another night and no one has gone out to sea," the girl whispered to herself. "What's going to happen to everyone?"

She moved about on the sleeping platform, trying to find a more comfortable position. She stared blank-eyed overhead as she recalled all that had happened. Her breath rose and fell until, finally, she was asleep.

By the time the girl's parents had returned to their hut, the girl was lost in dreams. The couple looked at their sleeping child.

"Poor thing," the father said.

"You shouldn't have married her to the Bendoro," the mother ventured.

"Be quiet!" was all the father could say.

And then, the two of them lay down as well. The girl's older brothers were not at home. Her younger siblings soon followed their parents in sleep. The village, too, swathed in a layer of dew, was hushed.

By nine o'clock in the morning, the house was busy again. First, the two carriage drivers appeared, but they were soon taken to the home of the village chief, where they were to eat and where he would listen sympathetically to their story. Then Timin, the young man who had been assigned to watch over Dul and Mardinah, came to the house. He immediately went to the girl's father and drew him aside.

"It was something, really something," he reported, his eyes bulging with delight and surprise. "Dul was smiling and laughing. He was even talking, too!"

"What about?" the father asked. "Not about Mardikun, was he?"

"No, I don't think so anyway."

The father looked relieved. "How about Mardinah?"

"Not her either. The two of them were too busy doing other stuff."

The older man suddenly coughed and then let fly a gob of spittle at the bamboo wall.

"You didn't give Dul his tambourine, did you?"

"Didn't have to. He didn't want it."

"Did you untie him?"

"In the end I did because he was acting pretty normal. And after that he just sat there, not making a move to go anywhere, while the three of us talked. At one point, I asked Dul if he wouldn't mind sharing the shack with a pretty young girl from the city. And later, when I left, they were already getting into . . ."

"Getting into what?" The father was incredulous.

"You know," Timin answered with a wink.

"The devil with you!" the father swore. "I told you to make sure they didn't escape; I didn't tell you to peep."

"Didn't have much choice," Timin defended himself. "It was happening right in front of me."

"Well if they're going to be doing that kind of thing, then they've got to get married properly . . ."

Timin ran out of the house and toward the beach. The other villagers in the house immediately began to talk about Dul and Mardinah, laughing almost every time the tale-singer's name was mentioned.

The Girl from the Coast watched her fellow villagers with a wistful look. Hearing their banter made her think not of Mardinah but of herself and how she, a young girl from the village, had been dragged away from home and offered in marriage to a nobleman in the city. From what she had heard, Mardinah seemed to have accepted her fate. But how could she? The girl listened to the people's laughter. Had they also laughed at her when she was taken away? Suddenly feeling a piercing pain in her chest, she rose from the sleeping platform, walked into the kitchen, and left the house through the back door.

Steeling herself to face the open air and the free world, she made her way toward the beach. The tide was out, revealing a golden white strand of sand that made her heart feel right.

She saw in the distance a boat with a blue stripe moored on the shore. Next to it were two small humanlike shapes, moving slowly away. Mardinah and Dul, that she knew. And then she saw another shape running after them. That would be Timin.

Never in the past two years had she walked as fast as she did now. Her feet, not hobbled by sandals, felt massaged by the warm, wet sand.

The faster she walked, the larger the shapes ahead of her became, until she could make out their human form. She watched as the one shape, Timin, caught up with the other two. The three shapes stopped momentarily then turned and headed in her direction, back toward the village. Soon she could make out their individual features, and finally they arrived where she was standing.

Mardinah and Dul were walking ahead with Timin behind them. The intense morning sun illuminated their features. In the tale-singer's eyes, she could see happiness; in Mardinah's, a complementary acceptance. She saw no conflict between the two.

There seemed to be no reason for regrets, or so she thought to herself. She went to Mardinah and took her hand. Mardinah did not push her away, and together they began to walk back toward the village.

"How are you?" the girl asked softly, but received no reply.

A crowd of people had gathered at the upper tide line, watching the four as they approached.

"It looks like they're planning a party," Timin said while pointing at the crowd.

"Well, there's certainly something to celebrate!" Dul enthused, apparently now able to speak without the aid of his tambourine.

"But you, Mardinah? How do you feel?" the girl asked again.

Yet again she did not answer.

"Young Mistress!" Dul suddenly said. "I'm going to go out to sea!"

The girl looked at him with surprise.

"What about your tambourine? Have you forgotten about it already?"

"No, but tomorrow or the next day, I'm going to sea. Not much use in me being here if I don't have the nerve to go out to sea."

"I know," she said. "But why now?"

Dul merely laughed in reply.

The girl turned again toward Mardinah. "What about you, Mardinah? Are you willing to marry Dul?"

Mardinah lifted her shoulders as if to say that fate cannot be sought and luck cannot be determined.

"You're not going to be sorry?"

"What's there to be sorry about, Young Mistress?"

"Our fates have turned out so differently. Like you, I, too, was forced to marry and to move to the city while you're forced to be here, in this village."

When Mardinah nodded, the girl continued: "But Dul is a good man and he wants to work."

Mardinah nodded in agreement.

"I just hope that you'll be happy even if he doesn't have anything to give except the love that can be found in each fisherman's heart." The girl suddenly felt her eyes begin to tingle. She looked again at Mardinah and squeezed her hand. "I'm happy that you can accept your fate." Her voice was that of an older woman now: "Just remember that when your husband is out at sea, you'll have to work like the other fishermen's wives, grinding the dried shrimp. At dawn, when he goes out, you'll walk with him to the shore. During the day, if a gale wind blows, you'll leave your house and watch the sea. And if he's late in coming home, you'll stay on the beach, until he and his boat are safely on shore."

"I will do that, Young Mistress," Mardinah promised.

"It won't be like living in a big house in the city," warned the girl. "It will be much better. In the city, you're always locked away inside the house, inside your room. How long was I there without being able to see the ocean, to feel the warmth of the sun outdoors, or to meet with my parents and family? At least here, Mardinah, you can meet people any time you want."

The four then continued their stroll in silence, and soon they were back at the edge of the village, where now, it seemed, the entire populace was waiting for them, ready to escort Dul and Mardinah to the home of the village chief, who would act as the official witness to their marriage vows.

Old and young, men and women, several long lines of people were there, stretched out beneath the row of coconut palms that paralleled the shore. As the four climbed the beach, with Mardinah and Dul now walking ahead, the crowd began to cheer.

Suddenly, from somewhere in the crowd, there came the jangle of Dul's tambourine, causing the tale-singer to stop and look around. He waved his hand, as if summoning the musical instrument, and suddenly, the tambourine came flying through the air toward him, as if drawn to its owner by a mysterious force. Dul caught the tambourine expertly, hugged it to his chest, then put his lips to it. Lovingly, he ran his supple fingers across the tambourine's skin, then put his ear to the instrument's wooden frame.

A low and sorrowful moan emerged from his throat. Then, suddenly, with all his strength, he drummed the tambourine with his fingers, producing a sound that was, in turns, meditative and seductive, and quickly hushed the cheers of the crowd. Dul played his tambourine as he never had before, sometimes shaking it high above him so that only the jangles sounded, sometimes throwing it into the air.

By the time the procession had made its way to the village chief's home, the sheath of the tambourine was torn. The crowd stopped as Dul placed his broken tambourine on the ground. He stared at the instrument, then bowed and picked it up again.

People watched in curious silence when he suddenly broke free from the crowd and began to look around, to the left, to the right, and then began to claw at the ground. When his hand finally found a large stone, with one swift movement he brought the rock down on the frame of the tambourine, smashing it into pieces. Then, like a magician, with his eyes fixed on the crowd of villagers, his audience, he threw the pieces into the air, making the tambourine disappear. Raising his arms, he bowed to enthusiastic cheers.

Going back to Mardinah, Dul took her by her arm and firmly led her up the steps to the veranda of the village chief's home.

Behind the crowd, the girl stopped to watch as Dul and Mardinah disappeared through the doorway of the village chief's house. When they had vanished from view, she could not help but wonder what the future would bring.

PART FOUR

For the Girl from the Coast, life at the Bendoro's mansion in the city became increasingly lonely as time went by. She almost never saw her husband's younger male relatives: They spent most of their days in school and, at night, slept in the prayer house. They hardly ventured into the main house. They seemed utterly disconnected from her life. They were like creatures from a different world and, almost always speaking to one another in Dutch as they did, she rarely understood a word they said.

Her husband's visits to her room were only at night, usually when she was somewhere between consciousness and sleep. As for the kitchen staff, they were strange beings for her, moving about like shadows in twilight and speaking only when spoken to. Such was also the case with the vegetable vendor, who posted himself each morning beneath the overhang outside the kitchen window, and the meat seller, who took up position at the rear entrance, between the kitchen and the back steps; they, too, seemed to be of an altogether different breed.

As for the many beggars who gathered outside the gate to the house on Fridays after noontime prayers, and to whom she distributed the household's tithe, for all she knew about them, they might have suddenly emerged from the ground beneath her feet. They were there for an instant, and then they were gone.

This was her life: no relaxed conversations, no trading of gossip, no smiles of friendship. She had a closer relationship with the furniture in the house than with the other people who lived there. And even the furniture, as beautiful as it was, she now found thoroughly uninviting, as unappealing to her as yesterday's catch of fish on the drying rack. Virtually everything felt strange to her, even the sound of the wind that whipped through the treetops and rustled the roof tiles at night.

Since coming to the Bendoro's house, she had only one constant and faithful companion: the sound of the waves, roaring so clearly in her ears at night, so softly during the day.

Upon her return to the city, the Bendoro had not chastised her for staying away so long. In fact, he had shown her no extraordinary attention at all. His first questions to her when they did finally meet were, "What did your father say? Do they need a prayer house in the village?"

She had answered him, "No, Bendoro, they have one already."

"And a recitation teacher?"

"Yes, they have one, too."

"What do the people think of him? Is he good at his job?"

"They say he's all right."

"Can any of the villagers speak Arabic?"

"I'm sorry, I forgot to ask."

"You must ask next time."

"I will."

"And your father, did he like the sarong you bought for him?"

"Very much so, Bendoro. He was very happy."

After that brief conversation, the Girl from the Coast did not see her husband for three days and three nights.

Now, it seemed, when returning from one of his trips, he almost never brought her a gift—but then she never had expected him to. The large house in which she lived had gradually taught her to grow accustomed to a life without expectations. Her life, made up of her duties and tasks—from supervision of the kitchen to making batik, from shopping for food outside the kitchen door to serving her husband's meals—and those lonely nights, the especially empty Thursday nights, the beginning of all good Muslims' day of rest, when her husband would never come to her room and the other nights of the week when she waited for him as well, stretched out in front and in back of her, like two sections of a silent path on which there were no other passersby. No one else was on it, just she, herself, alone.

The Bendoro never asked her about Mardinah. She was but a speck of ash blown from the hearth and lost in the greater universe. At first, the girl had found his lack of curiosity about Mardinah completely disconcerting. Wasn't she somehow related to him? Wasn't he interested in what had happened to her? As for Mardikun, who had died at sea, no word was mentioned, either.

During the first two weeks after her return to the city, there had been talk floating around about a fishing village that had been attacked by pirates. The source of this story, it appeared, was the two drivers who had been forced to walk all the way back to the city on foot. From what the girl heard, the government authorities had thus far showed no official interest in their tales, but one night, when her husband was lying beside her, in bed, he himself began to inquire what had happened:

"You said your parents were all right, didn't you?" he began.

"Yes, Bendoro, I did."

"So nothing happened when you were home?"

"No, nothing at all."

"People have been talking about a pirate attack. Was there one?"

"No, Bendoro."

"Thank God it was only a rumor."

After that, he asked no further questions.

One day not long afterward, a Chinese man came to the house to see the Bendoro, who received him in the open-air reception hall. There, they sat in rocking chairs, speaking to each other. The girl was in the central room of the house at the time dusting the dishes, and though they spoke in formal high-Javanese, this was now a language she could speak with ease, so she could not help but understand what they were saying.

"I heard that pirates attacked a fishing village," the Chinese man said to her husband.

"Which village was that?" the Bendoro asked.

"If I'm not mistaken, sir, it was your wife's village."

"My wife?" the Bendoro almost screamed. "I don't have a wife!"

"I'm sorry, sir, forgive me, but I was asked by my newspaper in Semarang to make some inquiries. The home office must have made a mistake."

"Leave!" the Bendoro spat at the man. "Leave before I get angry."

"Of course, sir, forgive me," the guest pleaded as he bowed and left the hall.

Suspecting that her husband would now want to question her

further about the event whose existence she had denied, she immediately fled the center room, broom and feather duster in hand, to the safety of her bedroom, where she sat in her chair waiting for her husband to come and the interrogation to begin.

She couldn't tell him the truth, she knew that much. She would have to deny that anything had happened. Hadn't people from the city caused more than enough trouble for her village already? "Dear God, watch over my village," she prayed. "Please keep the military and the police away."

And so she waited, but her husband didn't come to her room. Instead, he called her to him. In a cold and angry voice that reverberated throughout the house, he cried, "Young Mistress, come here!"

The girl's heart jumped; she could feel it pounding inside her chest. She leapt from her chair and rushed out of her room, in the direction of her husband's voice. "I must save my village. I will save it," she vowed silently.

Forgetting her own fear, she quickened her step. In the sitting room, she found her husband seated in a rocker. She raced to him and squatted on the floor before him, bowing her head respectfully.

"You called me, Bendoro."

"What did you tell me, woman—that nothing had happened to your village?"

"Yes, Bendoro, that's what I said. Nothing happened when I was there. God was watching over me, Bendoro, and I was safe."

"Then what am I hearing? What happened there?"

"Nothing out of the ordinary, Bendoro. The men went fishing, the women dried the fish and pounded shrimp."

"Then what's all this talk about a pirate raid?"

"If pirates had attacked, Bendoro, there would be no one left.

They would have killed the men and children and taken the women captive. Thanks to your blessings, Bendoro, I am safe. No pirates come to my village."

"Fine, then," he said dismissively, "but listen to me: Tonight I'm having a visitor, a royal personage from Demak."

The girl's heart skipped a beat. Who was it? she wondered. The Regent? Was she to be forced to see the man whose plans would have wrought disaster for her village? Her mind whirled with the thought. Again she vowed that whatever happened, she would keep her village safe.

"Get everything ready and make sure the house is clean. Take some soap and wash the floor of the center room; I want it spotless. And get the boys to help out; they're growing up to be a lazy bunch."

"Yes, Bendoro."

"And the lavatory off the center room, you must put that in order. After you've straightened the shelves in the cupboards, put some camphor in them, and on the dressing table, set out some powder, eau de cologne, boot black, a brush and comb, and pomade. Make sure you don't forget anything."

"Yes, Bendoro. Will that be all?"

"Yes, now get to work!"

"Yes, Bendoro."

The Bendoro said nothing as the girl raised her hands and pressed her palms and fingertips together to her forehead, then bowed and began to leave the room. After moving backwards a distance, still in squatting position, she stood and retreated to the central part of the house.

After the Bendoro had sent away her former servant, the girl had taken over management of the household, and now the center room, as well as the rooms adjacent to it, were no longer unfamiliar spaces. Inset in one corner of the center room was a triangular-shaped sideboard on which a large book rested. Often, she would open the book to look at the pictures inside, though she didn't know who the people were who were depicted. There were also numerous images of strange and unfamiliar items, the names and uses of which she could only guess. Whenever she was in that central room, with broom and feather duster in hand, she would open the book. Maybe, one day, her own child would be able to read the book, she frequently mused, but that thought always gave rise to the intensely agonizing question of whether her hands would ever hold anything other than brooms, dusters, and washrags. Or wax writers, vegetables, and the dirty dishes from the Bendoro's meals. At times like these, she was sorry that she had never learned to read and write or to properly recite the Koran.

That day, as had happened so many times before, her hands moved swiftly over the furniture, the feather duster first removing the fine layer of dust that had settled on them, her cloth then bringing the teak wood to a shine. After the furniture was clean, she would roll up the rug, take it out to air, and pound it with a heavy wire beater.

But today, everything felt different for the girl. A powerful enemy was coming to call, setting foot in the fortress where she had sheltered her heart. Despite the anxiety that oppressed her, the girl carried out her work as methodically and carefully as she knew how. She dusted each and every piece of furniture and made sure every object in the room was clean—except for her husband's heirloom weapons, that is, a row of ceremonial spears standing upright in their stand that the Bendoro had forbidden her to touch.

In her husband's room, when cleaning the oval mirror on the door of the armoire, she noticed how pale and tired she looked. She had a sickly color. "Am I ill?" she asked herself. Her cheeks looked strange; small veins stood out beneath her tawny-colored skin. She stared into her eyes' reflection; they had lost their former shine. "Am I ill?" she asked again. She found it difficult to pull herself away from her own reflection. "Yes, I am tired," she finally admitted. In the fifteen days since her return from the village, she had not been able to rest properly. Her legs bothered her. They felt heavy and swollen, as if they were two or three times larger than normal. During the day, she constantly found herself breaking into a cold sweat. Often she felt dizzy and had to sit down.

When she heard the Bendoro cough in the center room, she continued her work but found it impossible to stop looking at her image in the mirror. When her husband came into the room, she was still staring at her reflection, her left hand stroking her hair into place. The sudden appearance of her husband's image, beside her own in the mirror, startled her.

"What are you doing?" he asked.

"I'm sorry," she said automatically.

"Are you tired? Why don't you have the servants helping you?"

"I can do it myself," she insisted.

Without turning to observe her husband's movements, she knew that he was changing into his prayer sarong and putting on his pilgrim's cap. Without watching him go, she knew that he was leaving the house, going down the stairway to the sand-covered courtyard at the front of the house, and following the sandy path that would take him to the mosque.

The girl took a deep breath then exhaled. The furniture in the room, all so mammoth in size, now looked flimsy to her eyes. Even though the walls of the Bendoro's house were made of stone, it would never be as strong as the shack her parents in the fishing village called home. She went to the window and looked out at the prayer house. There, her husband's nephews were sitting on its front veranda, with textbooks in hand.

As she was watching, one of the young men happened to look up, but when he saw her at the window, he immediately bowed his head and continued his reading.

Suddenly, she felt as though she didn't exist, as if she'd never been born!

A sharp and sudden pain in her chest, like a knitting needle plunging into her rib cage, caused the girl to catch her breath and to clutch her side with her left hand. What was happening to her? "Am I really sick?" she asked yet again as she tottered to her husband's bed. Resting her right hand on the edge of the bed, she eased herself to the floor. She wanted to lie down on the mattress, but she didn't dare. Helplessly, she waited there for the pain to pass.

When the attack was over, the girl hurried from the bedroom and called two of the women servants to continue the work of scrubbing the floor. While they worked, she sat on a small stool, her eyes misting, her teeth clenched, whenever another attack came to pass. Each time an attack came, she felt, as if in slow motion, a needle pass through her rib cage and bury itself inside her gut. And each time the needle found its target, cold sweat oozed from her pores.

Two hours she sat there, attempting to supervise the women servants as they cleaned the room. Only when the room was dry did she finally rise and leave, locking the door to the room from the outside before fleeing to her bedroom. There, she lay down on her bed, trying to keep down the contents of her stomach as waves of air bubbles rose from her abdomen to her throat. Sometimes, it was only air that issued from her throat, but more often, the eruptions carried with them a foul-smelling and bilious liquid of tamarind-juice color that left in her throat and mouth a terribly bitter aftertaste.

Finally, recognition dawned. "I'm pregnant," she whispered to herself.

She called a servant and told her to fetch a bronze spittoon for her from the godown. After the servant returned, the girl then asked her to give her a neck and shoulder massage.

She lay facedown, across the bed, with her head hanging over the mattress edge and her mouth pointed toward the spittoon below her on the floor.

As the servant was kneading the girl's neck with her hands, she said knowingly, "You're pregnant, Young Mistress."

"Looks like it," the girl replied.

"Praise heaven, Young Mistress. I pray that God will grant you a son."

"Yes, a son," she said wistfully.

"Would you like me to cover you, Young Mistress?"

"Yes, a blanket would be nice for my legs, but fold it to make it thick."

"Yes, Young Mistress."

"And stay here with me, will you?" the girl asked the servant.

"Of course, Young Mistress," was the servant's reply.

But then the girl felt ashamed. What was all this fuss about? No woman in the village was ever pampered in such a way when she was pregnant.

"That's all right," she said with a sudden change of mind. "You can go and clean the back room. The Bendoro has a guest coming tonight."

"Oh, who's that, Young Mistress?" the servant inquired.

"Hush! That's none of your business!" the girl reprimanded.

That evening, as the rest of the household waited for the Bendoro's guest to arrive, the girl lay powerless in her room. Her head felt so heavy she didn't think she would ever be able to lift it upright again. When the Bendoro came in the room to speak to her, she covered her face with her pillow. He lifted the pillow from off her face and put his hand on her forehead.

"You're pregnant," he whispered, and immediately left the room.

As though through cotton-stuffed ears, she listened as her husband called together his young male relatives and delivered to them a host of commands. Several hours later, she heard the sound of another voice, that of a woman, as the Bendoro sat at the dining table with his guest.

As weak as she was, the girl strained to hear their conversation.

The woman had a high voice and spoke with a tone of accustomed authority: "I'm happy to see you don't have a woman living here. But tell me, I haven't seen Mardinah. Where is she these days?"

The Bendoro answered honestly, "I don't know where she is."

"That's odd," the woman said. "I sent her here. Didn't she ever come?"

"I'm sorry," the Bendoro apologized, "but I never deal with servants."

"Spoken like a true nobleman!" his guest declared. "It's no wonder so many have set their hopes on you."

"And what kind of hopes would that be?" he parried.

The woman laughed meaningfully and, for a moment, their conversation ceased.

At that very moment, the girl's eyes misted over again as a wave of air pushed the contents of her stomach upward. She turned on her side and stretched her head over the edge of the bed, but nothing emerged from her throat except a retching sound and a few spoonfuls of thick and bitter-tasting yellow liquid that slid from her mouth into the spittoon below.

When she turned over and placed her head on the mattress, she heard the conversation in the dining room resume.

"Who's that?" the guest asked. "Is that Mardinah?"

The guest must have heard her, the girl thought miserably.

"No," the Bendoro answered.

"I know what's going on," his guest said accusingly, "but why is she here, inside the main house? She should be in the kitchen! Look at me," she then demanded, "look at me straight in the eye and tell me if it's right for that woman, whoever she is, to be under the same roof as me."

The Bendoro's hurried apologies to his guest brought immediate tears to the girl's eyes. She sobbed with the realization that after almost three years in her husband's house, she now knew there was a greater power than that which was held by her husband, and it was in the hands of a woman.

Who is the woman? Who is she? the girl asked herself through her tears. She sobbed again with the premonition that her own fate was to be determined by that woman. The immense size and solidity of the Bendoro's house, which she had called her home for almost three years, now meant nothing at all. There was a force stronger than this stone fortress. Her heart screamed until weariness finally dragged her to sleep.

Early the next morning, the girl woke at dawn to hear her husband praying. "My husband," she voiced. But was he her husband? Apparently not, it seemed. He was her *bendoro,* her master, her lord and king, but not her husband. And she was not his wife. She was nothing but a wretched and humble servant, a girl from the village, a girl from the coast, still nameless after all this time.

And that morning, when her stomach began to churn again, she once more felt ashamed of herself, incredibly ashamed for lying in bed, something no pregnant woman in the village had the freedom to do.

The cacophony of crowing roosters outside made her head ache and caused her stomach to heave faster and more frequently. She tried to think of the rooster her family owned and the welcoming crow it released each morning when her father set off to sea. The crowing of cockerels in the city was strange, sounding like sarcasm to her ear.

At sunrise, when a servant entered the bedroom to tend to her needs, the girl learned from her that the Bendoro's guest of the previous night had already gone. She uttered a silent prayer of thanks; the Bendoro was not going to send his pregnant wife away.

For the next three months of her pregnancy, the girl, as was the custom among the privileged class, remained inside her room, lying in bed, behind closed doors and windows. During that time, she felt as if she were living in a cave. Again and again, she felt ashamed of herself. In the village, a woman, whether pregnant or not, had to rise each morning when her husband went out to sea and had to be waiting for him at the cove upon his return. And between those two daily time posts, she had to clean the house, look for food, chop wood, and prepare meals for her family. Yet here she lay, a village girl herself, alone and without strength.

After her three months of confinement, the girl was finally permitted to resume her daily tasks, but now, she found, her husband was almost never at home. The servants informed her that he was now spending most of his time at the mosque, so that is where his meals were sent. Throughout those months of pregnancy, the girl felt terribly lonely; she longed to sit beside her husband, to spend time with him; but what right did she have to expect that? she asked herself. She was only a servant. At times, she inexplicably found herself crying, for no reason that she could ascertain. It seemed that the life she carried in her womb was not her future child but a prospective enemy.

She wanted to pray to God, to complain of the injustice she felt, but found herself unable; not having kept up with her Koranic studies and lessons in recitation, she didn't know the proper way to pray, the proper prayers to recite. She now regretted this but, as a consequence, was forced to rely on her instincts and to entrust everything else to fate.

No matter what, she sometimes reasoned, her child, the boy or girl she carried in her womb, would have a better fate than that of his mother. He wouldn't be born in a fishing village; he wouldn't be taken away from his village; if it was a girl, she wouldn't be given to some *bendoro* in the city as a practice wife. Her child would be born in a large house so solid that no wind could penetrate its walls. Her child would be born within the realm of his father, the Bendoro. He would share in his father's power and be able to act with authority. And in time, he would sire future *bendoro,* without ever having to go out to sea in search of fish, without ever having to face large waves, to brave the darkness, or to feel saltwater licking his feet.

When attacked by these sudden and incomprehensible feelings of loneliness and melancholy, the girl would automatically stroke the living mound beneath her breasts. "Be safe, my child, be safe," she'd say, "and let your mother find safety with you."

For the Girl from the Coast, the tumultuous period of personal travail had passed, and now there stretched before her, into the future, the sweeter days of motherhood. Soon she would be able to hold a tiny living creature in her arms, a child that would suckle at her breast, a son or daughter for her to nurture and raise, who would some day be big and strong. But first the creature had to be born . . .

And then, one fine day, the creature in her womb did emerge, not beneath the eyes of the Bendoro, who was absent that day, but with the assistance of a renowned midwife.

Breathing heavily and nearly exhausted from the exertion, the girl had delivered the child into the world. And then she had waited to hear its cries. How many minutes had passed? It seemed like hours and still the child hadn't made a sound. Was it dead?

So tired that she could not open her eyes, the girl whispered, "Cry, please cry," as her hand traced the shape of the warm bundle of flesh that was now lying on her stomach. "Cry, cry," she pleaded softly, but still found no reply.

A sudden attack of fear made the girl's heart pound. She wanted to sit up and blow life into her baby's chest. It wasn't moving or making any sound. She wanted to scream, to shake the child awake, but she had no strength in her. When she was finally able to open her heavy eyelids, she saw the midwife lifting her baby into the air by its feet. It was so small and so pale in color. "My baby, that's my baby!" she screamed silently. Why didn't it cry or make a sound?

The midwife was mumbling, some kind of mantra it seemed. The girl wanted to scream at her. What was she doing, lifting her baby like that? Was she trying to kill the thing? But no sound emerged from her mouth, nothing but a tiny whimper that was drowned by the sound of her own breathing.

"Be patient, Young Mistress," the midwife whispered.

"Dear God, save my baby," the girl prayed.

"By God's will, your baby will be safe," the midwife told her.

"Why doesn't it cry?"

The midwife continued to hold the baby by its feet, shaking it gently up and down. "There's too much fluid, Young Mistress."

Suddenly the baby whimpered, then released a weak scream.

"My baby!"

"That's better, isn't it, Young Mistress?" the midwife said.

The girl took a deep breath then let her body relax. With her eyes shut, she drifted toward sleep, hardly aware of the midwife's doings.

A few minutes later, when the girl's eyes opened again, she found a small creature, her newly born child, lying beside her. Her hands searched the baby's body. "Two arms, two legs," she whispered. A wave of relief went through her. Her baby was not crippled. "Two ears, two eyes, a mouth . . ." Everything was fine. And the shape of the baby's nose—it was just like her own.

The baby slept, unaware of its mother's observations.

At the end of the bed, the midwife was sitting on a low chair. The girl smiled at her. "Is it a boy or girl?" the girl whispered, anxious to hear the former for an answer.

"A girl," the midwife answered.

"Has the Bendoro been in to see her?" the girl asked.

"No."

"Has she cried yet?"

"No."

The girl sighed. All she could do now was to wait for her husband's arrival and, as was the custom for women in her village, to then say to him: "This is your child. For nine months, I raised her in my womb. Accept her now as your own child. I was only carrying her for you."

Before the sun had risen that day, the girl's child was bathed and made ready for her father's arrival. It was now nine o'clock in the morning, and still the Bendoro hadn't come. In the fishing village, when a pregnant woman was judged to be within three days of giving birth, her husband, the father of her child, would stay with her until the baby's birth. During that period he would not go out to sea. He would be there, beside the mother, watching over both the mother's and the child's safety. The girl recalled a neighbor man who, before his wife had their first baby, waited outside the door of his house both day and night. When the baby was born and started to cry, the man, too, broke into tears and bolted inside, forgetting to first open the door, and nearly knocking himself unconscious.

Who was she to offer her daughter to, if not to the child's own father? Didn't her husband, the child's father, care about his own daughter? No, that was not possible. He was, after all, the baby's natural father. But why didn't he come, why didn't he peek into the room, if only just to see her?

The midwife got off her chair and stood beside the girl as she wiped the tears from her face.

"The Bendoro will come," she said soothingly.

"But how long has it been?"

"He probably has a lot of work to do."

That evening, the Bendoro opened the door to the girl's bedroom and stepped inside, but came no further than the open doorway.

The girl turned her head toward him. She wanted to say, "Forgive me, Bendoro, this is your child . . ." but fear kept the words in her throat.

"So, that's over now," he said flatly. "I hear it was a girl."

"Yes, Bendoro, that's right."

"A girl," he said again.

The voice of the Girl from the Coast trembled as she spoke, "I'm sorry, Bendoro . . ." But her husband, as if he hadn't heard her, turned around and left the room, closing the door behind him.

She then turned toward her daughter. She embraced the child and smelled her fine hair.

Later, when the girl's daughter could open her eyes, the girl stared at her in silent awe. She saw in her daughter's slanted eyes the same shape as her own. She had the same lips, the same nose, the same slight body, too. She would always be small, just like herself, a wispy thing as light as cotton wool.

The girl's longing for her husband, the Bendoro, was now depleted. How long had she waited for him to come, with a polite and acquiescent look in her eyes? Didn't he want to see his daughter? In her mind, she saw him staring lovingly into his child's eyes. But when would that happen? He never came to see her.

The months passed by. The girl no longer performed her former tasks. No fire burned beneath the wax pot for her batik. She rarely set foot in the kitchen to oversee preparation of the Bendoro's meals. And then one day, completely unexpected, her father appeared at the house. He was alone, without the girl's mother, and after being shown to his daughter, he immediately took his granddaughter from her, kissed the baby, and rocked it in his arms.

"So, how old is she? Three months?" he asked.

"Three and a half," his daughter answered.

"Nobody sent word," he told her.

"But isn't that why you came," the girl asked, "to see your granddaughter?"

"Of course, of course, if I'd known, that is," he stuttered. "And now I'm seeing her!"

The girl rephrased her question: "Then why did you come? To buy line for nets?"

"No," he answered.

"Then what? Resin, needles?"

"No, we're still using the ones that you brought."

"Then how's Ma? Tell me how Ma is."

"Fine, she's fine; everybody's fine."

"And Mardinah?"

"She's pregnant," the father announced.

"That's wonderful. And did Dul start going out to sea?"

"That he did," her father answered. "He goes out on the chief's boat. Everybody likes him; it's too bad he doesn't tell stories anymore."

The girl returned to her earlier line of questioning: "Why did you come here, Papa?"

"The Bendoro called me here."

"Why? To talk about building a mosque?" The girl then hastened to add, "I told him the village already had a mosque and a teacher and that the children were learning to recite the Koran and studying Arabic."

There was a tone of reprimand in her father's voice. "Why didn't you just tell him there's no time for that kind of thing in the village? That even the little boys have to help their fathers fish?"

"I was afraid."

"But it's the truth."

"So, does Ma know that she's a grandmother?"

"Not yet, but she'll be mighty glad. She'll want to have a celebration."

"Will you be staying long, Papa?"

"I hope so, if it means I can see my granddaughter here."

"How did you get here?"

"Yesterday, a driver with a carriage came in from the city. The driver said the Bendoro wanted to see me, so he stayed overnight and we left first thing in the morning."

"The Bendoro isn't home all that much anymore, Papa."

"Well, was I ever home that much?" he asked her.

"You must be hungry," his daughter said. "Have you eaten?"

"Yeah, we ate on the road. Your mother packed some rice for me. I brought you some milkfish," he added. "It's a good time of year for them and I left some for you in the kitchen."

At that moment, a servant interrupted their conversation to inform the girl's father that the Bendoro was now home and was ready to see him.

The girl's father gave his grandchild back to his daughter and went to present himself to the Bendoro.

The girl put her daughter down on the bed, then sat down in her chair. She wasn't able to hear the conversation between her father and her husband, but she was glad to have her father there in the house with her. She was pleased to have been able to give her father a grandchild and knew that her mother would be delighted to hear that she had a grandchild. This made the girl feel all the better. The whole village, in fact, would be happy for her. And proud, too, that a child of one of their own people, the daughter of a *bendoro,* had been born in a big house in the city.

It wasn't long before the girl's father returned from seeing the Bendoro. He went straight to the bed and kissed his granddaughter. The girl could not help but notice the downcast look on his face.

"What's wrong, Papa?"

Her father placed the palm of his hand gently on the baby's stomach.

"What is it, Papa? Why won't you say something?"

"I'm sorry, but you must gather all your clothes."

"What's happening, Papa?"

"Don't ask me," he told her. "Just don't ask. We have to leave."

"Where are we going?"

"Home."

"Home?"

"Yes, home," he said curtly. "What, don't you like your village anymore?"

"No, there's nothing wrong with it. Of course not, Papa. But what's wrong?"

"Just get ready to go home," he snapped. "This isn't your place anymore."

"What are you saying, Papa?"

"What do you think I'm saying? You've been divorced."

The girl's body started to tremble. She was going to swoon. Her father quickly put his arm around her, keeping her on her feet. "Be strong," he told her, "be strong."

"But Papa! But Papa . . ." was all the girl could say.

"What is it?" he asked.

"I haven't even presented my baby to him."

"Then do it now. I'll go with you."

"His own child," she mumbled, "his very own child."

"Come with me, I'll take you," he said again.

With the girl's daughter in her sling and her father walking behind, the girl entered the center room where the Bendoro was seated in a rocking chair. She fell to her knees before him. "I am sorry to disturb you," she said. Thinking only of her child now, she had suddenly forgotten her fear. "I have heard that you divorced me."

"Do you object?" the Bendoro growled.

"No, Bendoro. I'm just a servant, only able to do as you command."

"So? Is that all?"

The girl removed her daughter from the sling. "I haven't presented this child to you, Bendoro. This is your daughter. Nobody else's child but your own."

"Put her in her bed."

The girl's eyes were downcast as she spoke. "This humble servant of yours is the girl's mother, Bendoro. How am I to look after her in the village? As she is the daughter of nobility, I cannot raise her in the village."

The Bendoro glanced at the girl dismissively. "I'm not ordering you to raise my child."

"But my lord, am I to leave without my child?"

He was growing impatient. "What's all this talk? You've never been talkative before."

"I speak for my child. What wouldn't a mother do for her child?"

"As you said, the girl is my child. Now, you can leave this house and you can take your clothes and jewelry, too, everything I ever gave to you. That's what I'm telling you to do. I've given your father compensation," he added, "enough to buy and fit out two boats if he wants. As for you . . ." He held toward her a small cloth bag, heavy with coins. "This is for you. Find yourself a good husband and forget you've ever been here, in this house. Do you understand what I'm telling you? You are to forget you've ever known me!"

"Yes, Bendoro."

The girl began to look around the room as if unsure of where she was.

"Take care to make good use of this money and don't ever set foot in this city again. Be damned if you ever disobey me. Do you understand?"

The girl's father spoke up in protest: "Where is she supposed to go?"

"Anywhere, as long as it's not this town."

"Yes, Bendoro."

The Bendoro stared at the father and then at the girl: "Well, what else do you want me to say? The carriage is waiting for you."

"But my baby, my lord. What will happen to my baby?" the girl whimpered miserably.

"What about her? Stop thinking about her. There are lots of people here to take care of her. Put her out of your mind."

"You're asking me to leave without my daughter? To never see her again?"

"I'm telling you to forget her. Pretend you never had her."

The girl began to sob. "I know I must go, Bendoro, but how can I go without my daughter?"

"Didn't you hear me?" he yelled. "You don't have a daughter! You've never had a daughter."

"But, Bendoro."

"Leave!" he barked.

"This money, this jewelry, they don't mean anything, not without my daughter, Bendoro."

"Then you can give them to her."

The girl and her father were at a loss for words as the Bendoro rocked back and forth in his chair.

The girl began to leave, retreating from the room, backward, on her knees, and was followed by her father. On reaching her bedroom, she clasped her daughter tightly to her breast.

Her father tried to console her: "Forgive me, forgive me. I never thought it would end like this."

"What did I do wrong, Papa?" she asked weakly.

The girl's daughter opened her eyes and began to cry.

"We must go now," her father said.

"I know, Papa, but I want her to drink from my breast one last time."

"Yes," he agreed. "Let her drink this one last time."

The girl unhooked her camisole and gave her breast to her daughter. "Drink up," she whispered, "drink up."

With her daughter cradled in one arm as she sucked at the nipple of her breast, the girl used her other hand to stroke the baby's hair. "What wouldn't I give to you?" she whispered. "What wouldn't I sacrifice for you?" It was difficult to fight the tears that were welling in her eyes. "Even my right to be your mother, I now give up for you . . ."

Her father, standing beside the girl as his granddaughter fed, could only shake his head. "I'm so sorry," he mumbled. "I never thought it would turn out like this."

The girl looked up into his eyes. "You're a good man, Papa. You didn't do anything wrong."

"But you're crying."

"And you are, too."

"What else can I do? What kind of father doesn't love his children?"

"My first child, Papa . . ." the girl intoned.

"I was stupid, such a fool. Can you forgive me?" he asked his daughter again.

"There's only one thing I will never forgive . . ."

Her father nodded in understanding. "You're wise for your age. And you're right, too. No mother should ever have to give up her rights to her child. It's not right!" he stated emphatically. "But there is one thing," he added. "This granddaughter of mine will be a noble, not like one of us."

"The life of the nobility is awful, Papa," the girl told him knowingly. She then looked at her daughter. "Oh, my baby, why don't you want to drink?"

"We can't stay here much longer," her father told her. "We don't have the right to be here anymore."

The girl drew herself more erect. "Listen to me, Papa. This baby is my daughter. I gave birth to her. I suffered for her. Look at her nose, Papa. It's my nose. She is my baby girl. Didn't I lose enough of my blood to call her my own?" She rocked the baby and nuzzled her. "Oh, you're such a pretty girl, such a sweet thing." She looked at her father. "And you are her grandfather, Papa. Won't you say something?"

"What can I say? Don't you think it's been hard on me to see you, my own daughter, suffer this way?" He stared sadly at his granddaughter—"And now what will become of her?"—and then at the ceiling. "Will there be no end?"

"This is my baby, my daughter," the girl said again. "What am I supposed to say?"

Though neither father nor daughter could voice the answer to that question, their hearts raged.

"This house is like a graveyard," the girl said lifelessly.

"No heart," her father affirmed, "cold and hard as stone."

A bitter smile passed over the girl's lips. "Maybe that's why he wanted us to build a prayer house."

"We have to go," her father told her.

"What about my baby?" the girl pleaded.

A voice called to them from outside the door: "The carriage is waiting out front, Young Mistress."

The girl broke down in sobs.

"Your clothes," the father said. "I'll take care of them for you."

"Leave them, Papa." She looked at her daughter through her tears. "Maybe the more things of mine that are left here, the more she'll think of her mother someday."

"What will you wear in the village?"

"The same as everyone else."

"Oh, my child . . ."

Again, they heard someone calling, "Your carriage is waiting, Young Mistress."

The father stared at his daughter, still prone on the bed embracing her child.

"What do you want me to do?" he asked helplessly.

"She's just a baby, Papa. Let her finish feeding. I want her to be full. This might be the last time she feeds from me."

"But this isn't your house anymore. Let's take the baby outside. You can nurse her beneath the tree outside, by the city square."

"I can't do that. Think of the wind, Papa. She's not even had her first haircut, not even touched her feet on the ground. The wind would make her ill."

"I know, I know," he said, "but we can't stay here any longer. The carriage is waiting; you heard it yourself."

The girl had managed to gather some of her former strength. "No matter what, Papa, the Bendoro was my husband. Until a few minutes ago, he was my husband. Could he be that cruel to the mother of his own child?"

"There's no telling the ways of the nobility, my girl."

"Maybe not, Papa, but this baby is mine."

"At least you'll know that she won't grow up poor. Here,

she'll be taught how to rule. Someday, she could even be giving orders to you."

"She's my baby, Papa. I'd let her do that. I'd be willing to have her tell me what to do."

"It's not being told what to do that hurts, but I guess you know that. I'm just sorry that I didn't know until after it had happened."

"She is my baby, Papa. I gave birth to her. Let me stay a little while longer with her. If that means offending the Bendoro, then so be it; she needs her mother's breast. Tomorrow, I won't be here to feed her. You understand, don't you, Papa?"

The girl's father said nothing as he paced the room nervously. Finally, the girl got off the bed and went to him. "Let me speak to the Bendoro one more time, Papa. You go outside and wait for me under the trees by the mosque in the city square." He looked at her uncertainly. "Don't worry, Papa. Wait for me outside."

Acquiescing to her request, the girl's father left the room, her eyes following him until he had disappeared from view. She then took a broad sash, fashioned it into a sling, and put her daughter inside. Over and over, she kissed the girl's cheeks, her forehead, and her small white fingers.

Suddenly, she began to feel weak again. "My baby, my baby," she whispered, "whatever will happen to you?" She walked slowly toward the door and through the house to the center room where the Bendoro was still seated in his rocking chair. An open copy of Koranic interpretations was in his hand. Without speaking, she took a place on the floor behind the Bendoro's chair.

"I'm sorry to disturb you, but I've come to hand over this child of mine to you. She is your child and no other's. Please take her from me."

"Put her on the bed!" was all he would say.

"I can't do that, sir."

"Didn't you hear my orders?"

"I am this baby's mother. If her father won't even hold her or take care of her, then I will take her home to the village."

The Bendoro jumped to his feet, causing his chair to rock wildly back and forth. He stood in front of the girl, towering over her as he stared down his nose at her.

"You can be angry with me," the girl told him, "but a child is not a piece of jewelry—a ring, a necklace, or whatever—that you can give to just anyone."

"What are you saying?" the Bendoro demanded. "That you intend to kidnap this child?"

The girl raised her head and looked straight into the Bendoro's eyes. She then slowly rose to her feet and stood erect before him, her daughter in the child's sling.

"Even a hen will protect its chicks, sir. And you are talking to me, a human being—even if I can't recite scripture at the mosque!"

"Get out of here!"

The Girl from the Coast turned away from the Bendoro and headed toward the back entrance of the house, the baby still in her sling.

"Leave that child here!" the Bendoro screamed, but the girl had already left the room.

The Bendoro placed his book on the small side table next to him, grabbed his walking stick, and ran after the girl, finally catching up with her just as she was going down the back stairs to the kitchen. The entire household staff had gathered there, watching the scene with fear in their eyes.

"Stop her!" the Bendoro screamed at them as he waved his cane.

Like a platoon of soldiers, the servants, both men and women, immediately surrounded the girl.

"I'm not a thief!" the girl screamed defiantly. "Everything I own is in the bedroom. Take it if you want. The only thing I'm taking is my child."

She kicked at the servants, trying to hold them back, but other servants came running until the girl was completely surrounded.

"You *are* a thief!" the Bendoro barked. "Now put that baby down! Do you want me to call the police? Or the military?"

"This is my baby! Mine!" she yelled back at him. "I had her and she's mine, even if her father is a monster, a devil." The servants struggled to free the baby from her arms. "Let me go," she screamed at them.

Suddenly, the girl was blinded by pain. She had been struck in the mouth by something hard; the Bendoro had hit her with his cane. Bleeding and stunned by the blow, the girl felt her child yanked from her protective embrace, leaving her with nothing but an empty sling hanging from her shoulders to her womb.

"That's my baby!" she shouted at the crowd.

"Throw her outside!" the Bendoro ordered.

The servants herded the girl to the central courtyard, even as she struggled and screamed. Looking up, the girl saw in an open window of the second floor of the building next door a woman staring down, vacantly, at her. As if this woman might be a savior, the girl called out to her: "Help me! They've taken my baby. Her father is the devil, but she's still my baby!"

The woman in the window wiped her eyes, then turned away and closed the window.

"Why is he stealing my baby?" she screamed at the crowd of servants. "He could make a dozen in a week if he wanted to. He's just torturing me. Yes, him, the Bendoro, your master! He's torturing my baby. Where is she? Give her to me!"

By this time, the girl had been pushed through the gateway opposite the central courtyard.

"My baby, my baby! Give me my baby!"

She struggled to remain steady on her feet, but then someone pushed her roughly and she fell to the sandy ground. Before she could rise again to her feet, she saw, out of the corner of her eyes, the gate to the central courtyard being slammed shut. Then she heard a voice telling her, "Forgive us, Young Mistress."

"I want in. Can't I come in?" she pleaded.

"I'm sorry, Young Mistress, but you can't. I'm sorry we had to treat you this way."

Lying in the sand, the girl started to sob.

"Trust us, Young Mistress," one of the female servants consoled. "We'll take care of your girl."

"I'll hold her and take her for walks in the evening," one said.

"I'll watch over her at night," another offered.

"Thank you, thank you," was all the girl could say.

"I'll help you to your carriage, Young Mistress," someone said.

The girl didn't resist as one of the servants lifted her to her feet. As a group, the servants then helped her to walk away. She placed her weight on the same people who had once waited on her. They led her out of the front courtyard, across the road, and to the edge of the city square, where the girl's father was waiting beneath a bay tree.

Seeing his daughter, the girl's father jumped to his feet and raced to put his arm around her. He then helped her into the carriage.

After the carriage began to pull away, he said consolingly, "That's what happens to people like us. As mean as the sea might be, it's more generous than a nobleman will ever be."

The girl leaned her head against his chest. "Where are we going, Papa?"

"To the place where you were born," he answered, "to the place your ancestors are buried."

She embraced him tightly. "I couldn't fight them anymore, Papa."

"There's no place more generous than your own village, my girl."

The carriage made its way through the city and out to the Postal Road that Governor General Daendels had built, its wheels turning on the hardened surface. For the passengers of that carriage, the row of pines that flanked the road held no interest. The alternating patches of teak forest and mangrove swamps along the coast seemed to them like clouds passing meaninglessly across the darkened sky.

"What will I say to Ma?" the girl asked her father.

"You don't have to say anything," he said. "A mother knows what her child's gone through, even if she didn't see it herself."

"I know what my baby needs, Papa."

"Hush now, get some rest. Sleep . . ."

The girl's lips trembled as she thought of the many times she had struggled to stay awake at night while waiting for the Bendoro to come to her room. Now, her father was telling her to sleep and she was not able to. The rhythmic pounding of the horse's hooves on the road's hard surface, each clip and clop, was another pounding of a hammerhead on the walls of her heart.

This was the kind of carriage that took me away from my parents and village, the girl thought. *And now it's the same kind of carriage taking me away from my marriage and my daughter.*

The girl's eyelids felt so incredibly heavy. *What will I do in* the village? she asked herself. To whom would she offer her labor? she wondered.

"Papa?"

"Yes?"

But the girl could say nothing more. She was thinking of the villagers who had followed her with torches the last time she had been home and how they had called her "Mrs. Bendoro." She thought of Mardinah, too, but then her thoughts turned back to her daughter.

Was she crying now, her little darling? The girl put her hand to her breast. Her blouse was wet with milk. What use were these breasts now? "No, no, I mustn't think that way," she chastised herself.

And then she thought of the Bendoro—so tall and thin, not muscular at all, but, oh, what power he wielded, though he had never gone out to sea. What would he teach his daughter? To look down on her own mother? "My God," she thought, her girl might one day grow up to be just like her father.

"Maybe it's all for the best . . ."

"What did you say?" her father asked.

"When my baby grows up, and when she finds out her mother was nobody, just a girl from a fishing village, maybe she'll be embarrassed to have a mother like me."

"Why do you say that? You shouldn't say such things."

"But maybe it's for the best. Yes, maybe it's for the best, even though it feels so very hard right now. It will be better for her not to know her mother. She can become like her father. She can learn how to command. She'll live in a big house and won't ever have to look at the sea. That's what I have to give to her, Papa. That's what I have to give."

The sun overhead had passed its zenith and stray dark clouds occasionally blotted the sun, causing dark shadows to fall on the fields beside the road.

The girl's eyes followed the fleeting shadows. "It feels so hot and stuffy, you just know it's going to rain."

She thought of the Bendoro's home. It was so nice to be in such a big house when it rained. She never got wet there. No raindrop ever touched her body.

As the clouds gathered and the sky grew darker, the sound of thunder mingled with the roar of the sea. When the cooling rain began to fall, the draft horse, wheezing from its exertion, gained a second wind and began to trot faster. By the time the rain had stopped, the carriage had come to that branch in the road that carriages could not pass. The girl stepped out of the carriage and looked around her. The trees were the same, only darker and more green now, as they were wet from the rain.

She heard something, a baby's cry, and her breasts suddenly felt so swollen they throbbed from the milk inside. She stepped onto the path that led to the village and walked slowly, somnambulantly, forward. Not wearing the sandals that had covered her feet the past few years, she could feel the fine and dampened sand caress her soles. She looked down at the sand and then stopped, staring in wonder at the distance between her footprints, now so much greater than it had been when she left the village four years ago. Her breasts throbbed once more and she felt a shiver run through her. Again, she heard a baby cry. It was her daughter, calling to her, of that she was sure.

"She is my daughter," the girl said to herself, "but she will be a noblewoman and live in a big house. She will learn how to rule . . . No, no," she suddenly cried, "I hate the noble class and those hellish places, those buildings of stone they call their homes. From inside, no cries are ever heard."

And when her daughter was grown, she, too, would not be able to hear her mother's complaints. As it had been since time eternal, her daughter, as a noblewoman, would rule, and she, her own mother, would be treated like a villager. Her daughter would treat her just as the Bendoro had treated his wife during her time with him. "Dear God, use your power to keep her from ever recognizing me. And keep me from ever seeing her again. But protect her, this child of mine, who will never know her mother, though she did once taste her mother's milk." This was the girl's prayer.

Her eyes studied the ground again and her enlarged footprints in the sand. When she looked up, she saw her father standing in front of her.

"You'll be treated as you once were when you were born," he told her. "The whole village will come out to greet you and give their blessings."

She was the flower of the fishing village, the Girl from the Coast. Yes, everyone would welcome her back. But then she remembered her own child and how she had come into the world with no one to welcome her except for her mother and an old midwife because her own father had shown no concern.

"It's going to be hard in the village, you know, especially since you've been living in the city," her father warned.

The girl took another two steps but then suddenly stopped and turned around and called to the driver: "Wait, don't go!"

Her father was startled. "What are you doing?"

"I can't go back, Papa. I'm going to go away." She fell to the ground, kissing her father's feet. Her batik wrap was covered with sand. "Forgive me, Papa, but I won't be able to look into Ma's eyes, or the eyes of anyone in the village. Forgive me, Papa, but I must go away, by myself."

Her father didn't know what to say but finally asked, "Didn't you promise not to go back to the city?"

"I am going back there, but not to stay. Tomorrow, I'll go south."

"Where to?"

"To Blora, Papa."

"Who's there?"

"I once had a servant who was thrown out of the house by the Bendoro. Maybe I'll find her there."

"You should stay here, in your own village," he told her. "You don't know any other place."

"Forgive me, Papa, but you go home alone. Buy yourself a new boat in Lasem. That can be your replacement for me. And tell Ma and the rest of the family and the other villagers I'm sorry. Just pretend I don't exist. Your boat will be a much more cheerful child than I could ever be again."

The girl stood and embraced her father, who stood dumbfounded. She put her hand into his pocket and took out a few silver coins. "I'm sorry, Papa, for taking these, but I will need a few to get by."

With a final hug, she then turned away and walked decisively back to the carriage. Once in her seat, she looked at the driver and ordered him to leave.

The driver looked at the girl and then back at her father. "What am I supposed to do?" he shouted, but the girl's father just shook his head.

Taking the driver's whip in her hand, the girl flicked the horse on its underbelly, causing the horse to jump and begin to trot away. The wheels of the carriage spun through the sand, rolling toward the Postal Road. The girl did not look back but kept her eyes focused on the road, straight ahead.

People say that in the month after the Girl from the Coast was driven from the Bendoro's home, a carriage often stopped outside the front gate of his residence, and that each time that happened, a face would appear at the carriage window, peering at the mansion from behind the window's curtain. After that month, the carriage never returned again, and no one could ever say for sure who it was that had been staring at the mansion from behind the carriage curtain.

EPILOGUE

In the month that followed her divorce and eviction from the Bendoro's house, the Girl from the Coast went to his manor almost daily, hoping to glimpse just one more time the daughter she had left behind. But good fortune was not on the girl's side, and finally, with her purse nearly empty and her heart numb from hopelessness, she left Rembang, going south toward the central part of the island. She would never return to that city, she decided; the pain

---

The Girl from the Coast was originally intended as the first volume in a trilogy of novels on the growth of the nationalist movement in Indonesia, with the story line based loosely on the life history of the author's family. Because the other two novels in the trilogy were destroyed by the Indonesian military, this epilogue, which was not part of the original novel, was prepared by the author and translator specifically for the publication of this English-language edition in order to provide readers a greater sense of closure to the tale.

of the memories would be too great. Nor would she ever return to the fishing village where she was born. Far better for her to live on in her family and friends' memories as the Girl from the Coast, a fellow villager who had been able to escape from the cycle of poverty there, than to live out the rest of her days with their eyes of pity on her. Perhaps, if she were lucky, she thought, she would, on her journey south, be able to locate the kindly servant who had once helped her face down the Bendoro's nephews. And so she left Rembang, never to be heard of again by anyone who knew her . . .

Although the Bendoro's servants had helped to chase their former mistress, the Girl from the Coast, from their master's home, they had done so from fear and not from ill will. Each vowed silently that they would keep their promise to look after and care for the daughter their Young Mistress had been forced to leave behind.

In time, the Bendoro did marry his social equal, the noblewoman from Demak, and though initially she had been highly disconcerted to find so many young children at her husband's home—the bastard children (as she saw them) from her husband's "practice marriages"—she could not simply banish them from the house. They were, after all, the Bendoro's responsibility. Care for the children, their feeding and clothing, was relegated to the household staff. Nonetheless, in these days of growing liberalness, where the children of nobility were expected to speak Dutch with ease and to be practiced in Western etiquette, she did see to it that they were given an education, even the daughter of the Girl from the Coast, who had come to be given the name Sa'idah.

Raised in luxury with a wealth of opportunities available to very few of the children of her day, Sa'idah grew up to be a clever and comely lass. She was well read, fine-mannered, and spoke Dutch and Javanese with equal ease. As a teenager, she was one of the star pupils of HIS, the Hoogere Inlandsch School, the Dutch-language school for children of the nobility that had opened directly across the city square from her father's urban estate.

The headmaster of the school and one of Sa'idah's teachers was a man who had given himself the family name "Toer." After moving to Rembang to take over the administration of HIS, he had immediately called on the Bendoro and had secured rental of one of the houses within the Bendoro's estate, a two-story dwelling that faced the city square and also HIS.

Mas Toer, as he was called, was a man of many talents—educator, composer, and writer, among others—and his steely discipline was a fine example for his students to follow, but what set him most apart from his colleagues was his deep-rooted sense of nationalism. Though his views frequently brought him into conflict with Dutch government authorities, it was this free-spirited nature of his that first attracted the young Sa'idah to him. She recognized in him a love for both the country and the people—especially the common people by whose hands she herself had been raised—and a need for greater independence than was allowed by either the Dutch government or the constraints of the Javanese nobility. Though Mas Toer was not a young man—he was thirty-one and still a bachelor for having had to support his many younger parentless siblings—Sa'idah was not so young, either. In fact, at the age of eighteen she was virtually on the edge of spinsterhood.

The Bendoro's wife was not unhappy to see the growing attachment between Mas Toer and her stepdaughter Sa'idah. With children of her own, whose bloodlines were not tainted by non-royal blood, she encouraged the girl's relationship, and when her husband died suddenly, she gave Sa'idah a choice: to move and find employment of her own or to marry Mas Toer; she simply could no longer be responsible for the girl's welfare.

And so it was that Sa'idah, daughter of the Girl from the Coast, came to marry Mas Toer, the nationalist headmaster of her school. But his future was far more unsettled than it at first appeared. He had another falling out with the Dutch authorities for the nationalist content of his school lessons. Fortunately for him, however, the administrators of the nationalist-oriented Budi Utomo school system came to be aware of his skills and recruited him to establish a new Budi Utomo school in Blora. So it was that he and Sa'idah packed their belongings and headed toward Blora to begin a new life of their own.

One day, shortly after the Toers had settled in Blora, when Mas Toer was at the school teaching and Sa'idah was in the house trying to arrange the place to her liking, an older woman appeared at the door. Carrying a large woven basket on her back, she asked Sa'idah for any cast-off items that she might have for her to resell at the secondhand market in town. Something about the woman's appearance, something about the woman's air—her apparent spirit of independence, perhaps—attracted Sa'idah to her, and though the young woman was truly weary at that moment, instead of summarily dismissing the older woman as yet another beggar looking for a handout, she invited her to sit down with her on the front veranda for a rest and a cup of tea.

Despite the woman's obvious lack of formal education, Sa'idah soon found that the woman could easily keep up her end of the conversation and was not at all averse to airing her own point of view, an oddity given the vast social distance between them.

When asked by Sa'idah where she had obtained her independent streak, the woman answered that life had given it to her. Though fate had taken her from the village where she was born and had torn the one child she had borne from her arms, fate had also given her the strength to get by in life and to make it on her own. The only regret she had, she said, aside from losing her daughter, was never having been given the chance to raise another. Her second marriage had produced no heirs.

"But when you left the village, where did you go? Where were you taken?" Sa'idah asked her.

"I was given in marriage to a nobleman in Rembang. I lived in a big house there, full of servants, until my daughter was born and I was chased away."

Sa'idah looked at the woman with growing apprehension on her face. "And who was your husband?" she asked.

"I called him 'Bendoro,' of course, but he was assistant to the Regent of Rembang."

"But that's my father!" Sa'idah exclaimed.

In that instant, the two women knew they shared a common bond, and in the hurried conversation that ensued, they learned the truth of their relationship. And finally, after almost two decades, the Girl from the Coast was reunited with the child that had been torn from her arms.

In the days and months that followed, Sa'idah spent every free moment she could with her mother. As the years passed and Sa'idah came to bear nine children of her own, she frequentl[y] begged her mother to move in with her. Despite her hard life the woman always refused; she cherished her independence to[o] much. Nonetheless, she visited the house as often as she could an[d] came to play a very influential role in the upbringing of the cou ple's children, especially that of her first grandchild, a boy by the name of Pramoedya, who, when his father was banned from teaching and his mother died of tuberculosis, came to be the breadwinner in the family home.

Such was the love of this grandson for his grandmother that two years after the death of his mother, when she herself fell gravely ill, he vowed to her that someday he would try to tell the world her life story.

"But why?" she asked humbly. "I'm no one, just a girl from the coast."

"But you are everyone, Grandma," the young Pramoedya told her. "You are all the people who have ever had to fight to make this life their own."

ABOUT THE AUTHOR

PRAMOEDYA ANANTA TOER was born in the town of Blora in Central Java in 1925, and during his lengthy career as a writer, he has spent more than seventeen years imprisoned by both colonial and independent governments. Many of his major works, including his tetrology, *This Earth of Mankind*, and his autobiographical collection of writings, *The Mute's Soliloquy*, were written while he was being held without trial as a political prisoner from 1965 to 1979, mostly in a forced labor camp on eastern Indonesia's Buru Island.

Pramoedya is the author of more than thirty works of fiction and nonfiction that have been translated into over thirty languages. In addition to his own books, he has also translated into Indonesian novels by Steinbeck, Tolstoy, and Gorki, among others.

The recipient of numerous major international literary and freedom-of-speech awards, the writer now lives with his wife in the small town of Bojong Gedé, south of the city of Jakarta.

CPSIA infor
Printed in th
BVOW07s2

377031